A SEASON OF

LOATHSOME
MIRACLES

MAX D. STANTON

TREPIDATIO
PUBLISHING

ISBN: 978-1-950305-30-8 (sc)
ISBN: 978-1-950305-31-5 (ebook)
Library of Congress Control Number: 2020937924

First printing edition: June 12, 2020
Published by Trepidatio Publishing in the United States of America.
Cover Design and Layout: Don Noble
Edited by Sean Leonard
Interior Layout and Proofreading: Scarlett R. Algee

Trepidatio Publishing, an imprint of JournalStone Publishing
3205 Sassafras Trail
Carbondale, Illinois 62901

Trepidatio books may be ordered through booksellers or by contacting:
Trepidatio | www.trepidatio.com
or
JournalStone | www.journalstone.com

This book is dedicated to Bear and Tristan, two of the finest companions that an author could hope for. Rest well, friends,
you are always in my heart.

NOTE

Some of these stories deal with sensitive topics. A complete list of content warnings can be found in Publication History.

PUBLICATION HISTORY

Burn the Witch was first published in the *Under a Dark Sign* anthology (Wolfsinger Press). CW: Violence, torture.

The Enlightenment Junkies was first published in *Disturbed Digest*, March 2015 (Alban Lake Publishing). CW: Drug abuse, rape.

Following Bebe Astara is published here for the first time. CW: Body horror, drug abuse, graphic violence, stalking.

Flying Machine was first published in *Year's Best Transhuman Sci-Fi 2017* (Gehenna & Hinnom Press). CW: War, violence, body horror.

Pigman was first published in the *Pickman's Gallery* anthology (Ulthar Press). CW: Graphic violence, torture, child death.

Patent for an Artificial Uterus was first published in *Vastarien* vol. 1, issue 2 (Grimscribe Press). CW: Misogyny, child death, graphic violence, suicide.

The Voyage of the Jericho was first published in *Lovecraftiana* vol. 2, issue 3 (Rogue Planet Press). CW: Violence, drug abuse, self-harm.

The Hargrave Collection is published here for the first time. CW: Violence.

Hekati Yoga was first published in *The New Flesh* anthology (Weirdpunk Books). CW: Grotesque body horror, sexual violence.

Alchemical Wedding was first published in *Sanitarium Magazine* no. 1 (Sanitarium Publishing). CW: Graphic violence, sexual violence, childbirth.

Euphonia is published here for the first time. CW: Domestic abuse, graphic violence.

The Penance Lake Roadside Wax Museum is published here for the first time. CW: Domestic abuse, child endangerment, violence.

The Hero of Magdeburg was first published in *World Unknown Review* vol. III (World Unknown Press). CW: War, graphic violence, rape, childbirth, child death, torture.

A SEASON OF
LOATHSOME
MIRACLES

BURN THE WITCH

I **STEP OUT OF MY** jail cell, blinking as I emerge from the dungeon's gloom into the sunny execution grounds. Church bells peal in celebration of my doom, and the townsfolk are all packed cheek-to-jowl, cheering and jesting like it's carnival time. Everybody's come out to watch an old crone die screaming. "Burn the witch!" they chant. "Burn the witch!" The stake and the platform and the kindling are barely a hundred paces away.

My hands are bound so tight that they're turning purple, and there's another rope wrapped around my neck—the executioner's got hold of that one. He yanks it like he's trying to move a stubborn mule rather than a frail woman, nearly pulling me off my feet and sending pain shooting up through my legs and hips. My knees have ached for years, and a fortnight in chains has only made them stiffer and weaker. My wrists are in even worse shape, and if they weren't going numb I'd be in agony.

The Inquisitor walking beside me mutters insincere prayers in bad Latin. The Duke himself waits for me ahead by the pyre, eager to pronounce my death sentence as soon as the Inquisitor hands me over to his secular authority.

The bastards think they've got me, and I will indeed die today, but before I burn I'll see all of my enemies destroyed.

Even though my time in the dungeon hasn't done my rheumy eyes any favors, I can still make out a few familiar faces in the crowd. Up ahead, the cloth merchant, Petyr Morgan, and his squalling brood of ugly children have claimed the prime viewing space closest to the pyre. They must have gotten here at the crack of dawn to get that spot, or more likely, Petyr bullied some other man out of it. Of all my accusers, he is the one that I hate the most. It's not because his testimony was the most damning—far from it. Even if he'd never spoken a single word against me, they'd still be leading me to the stake now. I hate Petyr Morgan with an acid passion because he is the only man who bore false witness against me.

Marta Cooper cowers behind her husband and whimpers as I pass by. She told the Inquisitor that she saw me take on the form of a hideous beast she couldn't even name. I don't mind watching her squirm a bit, but I don't bear her any particular grudge. She did, after all, catch a glimpse of me playing with ectoplasm, whirling matter out of nothingness into astonishing new configurations.

Bandy-Leg Tom averts his eyes when I gaze in his direction, and well might he be sheepish. All the Inquisitor had to do was show Tom the instruments of torture and Tom blubbered about the midnight feasts and bonfires in the woods, giving my name up as the instigator of it all. Still, there's no need to revenge myself on that cripple. While he should have kept his fool mouth shut, I don't begrudge any man his cowardice. We've all got a right to save our own skins.

Petyr Morgan, on the other hand, that simpering, self-satisfied gossip and snitch—he stood before the court of the Inquisition in his Sunday finery and gold chains and perjured himself against me for no purpose besides his own amusement. He told them I'd tried to buy his soul, as if I'd have any use for that greasy thing. He said that I'd tried to seduce him with a love philter, a notion that makes me want to vomit. And now there he is, smiling, laughing, pointing me out to his brats like I was an ape on display, puffed up as proud as Satan but with none of the accomplishments.

He'll be the first one I take.

I have very little time left before I die, but time is a place where the soul is confined, and I know the prison's layout, its escape routes, the secret passages to other cells. I've read every page of the *Necronomicon* of Abdul al Hazred and I've modeled its diagrams of infinity in knots of twigs and bones. I've forgotten some of its subtleties in my old age, but the fundamentals are all very much with me. I visualize the whorls and loops of temporal space in my mind's eye, and my spirit leaps backwards through time to attack my enemy in the past.

The world explodes into a riot of unnamable colors and screeching sounds as I leave my body behind to travel through the Inner Chronos. The first time I did this I was so overwhelmed that I lost my way and wound up millions of years before the Earth even formed; it took me centuries of subjective time to find my way back to my own era and my own flesh, and it's miraculous that I didn't go mad in the process. I must be very careful not to go off the trail now. To be stranded bodiless in the Inner Chronos is a fate far worse than death.

I latch onto Petyr Morgan's soul in the so-called "present" day and follow it pastwards, tracking him through time towards his boyhood. I travel the trail for about thirty years and then re-enter temporal space. Now I have to find a sleeping body for my mind to inhabit, but that's easy enough. I spy a maid dozing in a barn and slip into her like I'm putting on new clothes.

I stretch out on the hay bale that my host was napping on and admire my borrowed form. It's such an immense pleasure to be in a young, strong, healthy body again that I spend a few moments simply savoring it, running my hands up and down this supple form. When you've been in constant, aching pain for as long as I have, the absence of it becomes a delicious joy. But I can only indulge for so long. There's another joy I'm after, less delicious but more satisfying.

I still have the scent of Petyr Morgan's soul, and I follow it like a hound. It's an odd feeling to be back in my hometown three decades prior. The past is a country that is foreign and familiar simultaneously. My neighbors all look so much younger. So many men and women that I've seen dead and buried are walking the streets going about their business. I realize that I've forgotten many of their names. My younger self is around somewhere too, but I stay away from anyplace she might be. Knotting up the fabric of space-time is a risky business and I'm only after one man, I don't want to tear the whole cosmos apart.

I find Petyr Morgan fishing down by the stream. While he's just a youth now, I can see the corrupt, lying merchant he'll become. He's by himself, which is perfect for my purposes. And he's right at the age where a pretty girl like the one whose body I've borrowed can talk him into anything at all. He drops his pole and hops to his feet when he sees me approaching. There's a sly smile on his lips, a lustful gleam in his eye. I mirror it back at him, and his grin grows broader. He doesn't suspect a thing. He thinks today's his lucky day.

We exchange a few indecent pleasantries and then I take young Petyr by the hand and lead him away to the loneliest place in the woods. It's a place where a man might scream and scream and not be heard. I know the loneliest place in the woods quite well.

When I am finished I return the girl to the place where I found her sleeping. She'll remember all this as nothing more than a bad dream. It pains me to leave her lovely, youthful body, but I can't stay here indefinitely. I've known folks who, in their moments of final extremity, tried to leave their own failing forms behind and spend eternity in borrowed flesh. That sort of thing never ends well. I leave the past and return to my last hour.

I rejoin my body at the very instant that I left it; I see my soul leaving even as I arrive. My captors won't have noticed a thing. I look back to the spot nearest the pyre and see that Petyr Morgan is gone. Most of these people won't even remember that he ever existed—he's gone from being one of the town's leading men to being a boy who vanished many years ago. His children are all gone too, cut out of existence entirely like stray threads clipped off a frayed cloth.

One down. The pyre is fifty strides away.

The Inquisitor's thin voice drones on from behind my shoulder. He's a dark, skinny, rather seedy-looking Dominican. A Walloon, I think. He arrived in town only a few weeks ago, at the invitation of our beloved Duke. The Duke just couldn't stand for there to be witch-hunts and burnings in his neighbors' lands without getting a piece of that fun for himself. Men will become jealous of each other for such strange reasons.

This monk doesn't speak much or go in for grand proclamations, but his office and function alone make him a powerful rabble-rouser. The finger-pointing and accusations began even before his arrival, as soon as word spread that he was coming. People brought out the long knives against all the strange folk—the pushy women and the dreamy boys and everyone else who didn't live up to notions about what they were supposed to be. As a cranky, well-read, never-married woman, I suppose I would have been a target for my neighbors' accusations and the Inquisitor's scrutiny even if I weren't actually a bride of Satan. It's a good thing that I actually committed many of the crimes they leveled against me. Otherwise I wouldn't have any recourse against these swine now.

The monk came for me early in the morning, escorted by two of the Duke's soldiers. They did not knock. "You should know that the good folk of this town have charged you with the grave crimes of sorcery and witchcraft," he said. When he talked to me he'd fix his empty gaze over my shoulder—I don't think he looked into my eyes even once, in all the time we spent together. "It is my privilege and right to determine the truth of it. You must come with me."

At that moment I could have done a thousand ghastly things to him, and neither his bodyguards, nor his crucifix, nor anything else could have saved him. But I went with him regardless. If I'd have destroyed him then, more would just come following. Like ants—squashing one doesn't do any good.

The Inquisitor began by showing me the tools of his trade, apparently hoping that alone would be enough to terrify me into giving in. The fool just didn't know who he was dealing with. I've been to the Citadel of Burning Glass, met the pale angels with razor-blade wings who dwell there, and let them escort me to the farthest realms of excruciating agony and blinding pleasure. Thumbscrews and hot irons still hurt, but after what I've experienced, they don't frighten. It's the constant, grinding, wearying pains of old age that I dread, not the depredations of the torturer. And so I told that tonsured moron to go ahead and do his worst.

His worst wasn't nearly as bad as he thought it was. Whenever it got uncomfortable I would recall my time at the Citadel, and whatever the monk was up to seemed like a tickle by comparison. My refusals to shriek and plead frustrated him enormously, but I'm too old to pretend that I feel something just to spare a man's feelings. That's a young girl's game.

Throughout all of it, the Inquisitor kept asking the same question again and again. He wanted to know if I had seen the Devil. He asked if I had seen the Devil after shoving my head in a bucket of icy water and after scorching my flesh with a red-hot poker. He asked if I had seen the Devil after depriving me of sleep for days, and after sticking needles beneath my fingernails. My approach then was to damn him as a fool while admitting nothing and denying nothing. This offended him horribly, far worse than any confession of diabolical orgies would have done.

But now I shall answer his question.

I speak a few of my beloved's names beneath my breath as I walk to the stake. "Astoreth, Belial, Old Nick," I whisper longingly. "Lucifer, Beelzebub, Moloch. My darling."

He is always present beside me—he is always present beside all of us—but I feel his form solidify and when I turn my head he is there, unseen by anyone but me. He stands impossibly tall and erect, a proud, dignified giant, dressed in robes so black that they drink the light. As always, he wears a mask to spare me from the annihilating glory of his countenance. Today it's a goat. His golden eyes glitter with intelligence and playful malice from beneath the holes in the leather.

"Greetings, my child," he says. No two people hear the same thing when he speaks, but I experience his voice as deep and musical and soothing.

"Hello, old friend," I whisper. "I think I've danced at my last Sabbat."

"Nonsense. You are dancing still. You will dance forever. I see you on Walpurgisnacht of forty years ago, hanging a garland of flowers around my neck and kissing me. Even now you are a beautiful girl, flying amidst the night birds on your broomstick, naked and shining with grease rendered from the fat of hanged men. The Sabbat never ends."

"You know what I mean, you flatterer. You see the pyre yonder."

"I do. What would you have me do about it?" When my beloved asks a question, it fires the imagination and brings countless possibilities to mind.

"The Inquisitor asked me if I had seen the Devil. Despite his piety I think he wants to know what you look like. When the flames kiss the pyre, please grant his wish."

My beloved leans in close so I can kiss his forehead one last time. "It shall be my pleasure." Then he stares hard at the Inquisitor. The monk sees nothing—not yet, anyways—but he shudders, and forgets his prayers.

"You asked me if I saw the Devil," I tell the monk. "I never did, not once. But you shall."

We come now before the Duke. He's seated upon a handsome chair of dark wood, swaddled in fur and velvet, surrounded by his soldiers and his counselors and his family. There's little that I despise more than a high-born lowlife. For years he's been driving this land to ruin by waging wars, imposing larcenous taxes and pointedly neglecting anything that might pass for civic improvement. And when people ask why life here is so hard and dismal? Oh, it's all the fault of the witches. The witches and the Jews.

The Duke starts droning on with the legal formalities of my condemnation. I didn't pay attention during my trial and I don't pay attention now. Instead, I look past the Duke, to his wife and his daughter. Unbeknownst to the Duke, his women have danced with me in the woods on many a moonlit evening. They've often stolen away from their domestic errands to ask my counsel on matters great and small. He doesn't know what they really think of him. As far as I can tell, the brute thinks that he well-deservedly basks in their quiet, dutiful love.

I look to Elisa, the Duke's long-suffering wife. She's staring down at her own feet. Fair enough. She never really wanted my way of life. All that she wanted was to know that another world existed, to get a glimpse of a world bigger than her castle. She's an explorer content to gaze briefly on the shoreline of a new continent, without actually leaving footprints on its sand.

Then I look to Petra, the Duke's daughter and youngest child. Her eyes are narrow blue daggers. She inherited her father's rage, but it's a dangerous thing to be a woman with a man's temper. The mother being the gentle creature she is, I had to teach the daughter how to deal with her anger. How to rage like a woman. She was a good and eager pupil. When you've known someone for a long time—and I've known Petra since before she was born—it's easy to talk even if you can't say a thing. Petra understands me immediately. I don't think she'd have resorted to patricide if it was only about herself, but we'll do things for our friends that we wouldn't do for ourselves. Without needing to gaze into the future, I know that in the next few weeks she will go out into the woods to pick some pretty, cheerful-looking flowers that I've taught her about. Soon thereafter her father will come down with a terrible stomachache, and soon after that her older brother will be the new Duke.

The executioner prods me, and I realize that I'm supposed to say something.

"I asked you, do you repent?" the Duke sneers.

I spit. If I was closer I'd have hit him in the eye, but at this range the best I can do is splatter his boots.

The Duke trembles in his seat and goes red, and the crowd suddenly goes silent. I doubt the Duke's ever been treated with such disrespect before. I'm happy to treat him to a new experience. And it's not like there's anything he can do to retaliate, not at this point. What's he going to do, order me burned alive?

"Damned hag!" he bellows, his precious composure shattering in front of all his subjects. "Burn the witch!"

The silence breaks and the mob cheers lustily the moment the sentence is issued. I glance back in their direction and am nearly overcome by the revulsion that I feel towards these braying, ungrateful illiterates. Over the years, so many of these peasants snuck to my cottage when nobody was looking, begging me for a love charm or a fortune-telling or a folk remedy or an abortion. So many of them came out to the midnight celebrations that I arranged, seeking a few moments of illicit pagan joy to brighten the drabness of their regimented lives. They might well be burning beside me if I'd told the Inquisitor their names. But even though they are full of spiteful joy right now, soon enough they'll be weeping, for there will be a season of loathsome miracles to mark my passing. When their babies are born blind, and their cows calve two-headed, carnivorous prodigies, and slimy, poisonous creatures fall from the sky instead of rain, they will think of me and shudder.

The executioner drags me onto the killing platform. My beloved remains at the Inquisitor's side. What happens next I must face alone.

The executioner—Dortmund is his name, I've known him since he was a pup and his daddy was the local neck-stretcher—is a big, unwashed lout, and he loves his work. Ordinarily I like a man who's expert in his field, but this time I make an exception. As he's binding me to the stake, I withdraw from my flesh and slip away into his future. Just like I did with the late, unlamented Petyr Morgan, I use Dortmund's soul as my point of reference in the chaos of the Inner Chronos, pursuing the executioner through every hour of his life to come. Traveling into the future is even more difficult and uncertain than going into the past. The road is as fluid as a stormy sea and wrong turns into an empty limbo of unrealized possibility are an ever-present danger. But with Dortmund as my unwitting, unwilling guide, I know I'll get where I need to go. I follow him for his whole life. From my death-day onwards he'll always have a vague sense that he is being pursued, a feeling of dread that he cannot place or explain. Good.

When I feel his dismal, puny soul starting to crumble, I re-enter temporal space, borrowing the first sleeper that I find. This time it's a little boy, no more than eight or nine. Fine for my purposes.

I sniff the wind for the souls of my enemies and catch two familiar scents, one of them very close. I follow it past refuse heaps and dung hills, to a gloomy alley where a creature in rags shivers and twitches on urine-damp cobblestones. One of his hands continually traces nonsense patterns in the air; the other smacks against the back of his own head ceaselessly as if he's trying to knock something out of there. He's aged a hundred years in twenty but I'd never mistake this eminence. It's my old friend, the Inquisitor.

"Hail and well met," I tell him. "Do you know who I am?" From his fearful howls and his desperate efforts to crawl away through the nearest wall, it's plain that he does. I grab ahold of his matted beard and twist it to get a good look at his face. Staring deep into his eyes, I see Hell reflected back at me. The ex-monk whimpers softly, and wets himself.

"You used to be such a cold fish," I tell him. "You could put hot irons to an old woman without even flinching. Without showing any human feeling at all. You didn't feel anything inside back then, did you?"

"Muuuuhh," he groans. He nods fiercely but I don't know if the gesture is voluntary. "Cold fish. Cold fish. Thoughts all slimy."

"You posed me a question once, Inquisitor. You asked me if I had seen the Devil. You were very insistent."

"Devils!" he blathers. "Levels of devils at their revels forever! Oh God. Oh God, his face..."

"Is your curiosity satisfied now?"

He explodes into idiot laughter.

I ponder showing some mercy and prying up a cobblestone to knock out his brains. I decide against it. He shouldn't have asked me the question if he couldn't bear the answer. I leave him behind to his slow death of madness and press on to the outskirts of town.

Dortmund still dwells in the same mean, desolate hut he inhabited twenty years ago, within spitting distance of the potters' field where so many of his victims lie buried, myself included. The town's faithful executioner spent all these years getting his hands bloody for these people and they wouldn't even let him live amongst them. There's a lesson in that.

A dim light gleams in the window. I peer inside and see the executioner, old and withered and on his deathbed. From the way he's wheezing and coughing, it's plain that his lungs are failing. He's alone in his last moments. I think he's been alone all along. There's certainly no sign that any wife or child ever lived here, no hint of cheer. Just a few sticks of furniture and a sputtering candle.

I'm glad that I let Dortmund live out his full span. Just being himself for so many years was a worse punishment than any I'd have devised. And indeed, for all my secret knowledge and power, if Dortmund hadn't burned me I'd eventually have met a similar death to the one he's experiencing now, all feeble and isolated and pathetic.

Which isn't to say that I'm letting him go, of course. Not in my nature.

I step inside and pick up the candle. He's in such bad shape it takes him a few moments to realize that there's anyone else in the shack. He seems very confused when he finally notices the child hovering over his bedside. "Hullo?" he gasps.

"Hello, Dortmund," I reply. "Do you remember me? You burned me to death years ago. I told you that someday I'd return the favor. I told you I'd bring you a candle to light your path to Hell." The executioner's face lights up with horror as he recalls. I make a mental note to tell him about the candle when I get back to the "present" so he'll remember it in the "future." He tries to scream, but all he can produce is a wet, ghostly rattle.

I toss the candle onto his bed. Dortmund shrieks and picks it up, but by the time his clumsy old hands have got it his blanket and the straw mattress are already burning. He tries to stand and run, with no luck. This was already his deathbed even before I set it on fire. The best he can do is roll onto the floor and crawl towards the exit, while flames climb the walls and the smell of roasting pork wafts through the air. Just to be sure, I put the latch on the door as I leave.

I put my borrowed body back to bed and come back into the "present" moment, where my doomed executioner—now young and vital again—is tying me to the stake. For just a moment there in the future I felt a drop of pity for him, but from the vicious pain he's inflicting with the ropes and the dumb, sadistic grin on his face, I'm glad about his fate. "Someday I'll see you burning alive, too," I tell him. "Someday I'll bring you a candle to light your way to Hell. Remember that." He crosses himself and scoffs, but I know to a certainty that he'll never forget my curse.

Once the knots are tied to Dortmund's satisfaction, he ignites the kindling beneath the platform with a burning brand. Smoke billows up, stinging my eyes and throat, and I feel the heat spreading beneath me. In the crowd, I see my beloved stand before the Inquisitor with his back to me and remove his mask. The monk shrieks horribly and faints dead away.

That's the last of it. I cut it awfully close, but now all my debts have been paid.

Even now, as tongues of fire are rising up through the planks of the platform and licking at my feet, it's not too late for me to get out of this deal. And honestly, I'm awfully tempted to make my escape. There are plenty of ways I could do it. I could go into the "past" again and twist it between my fingers until it becomes a "present" where I am sitting at home with my tea and books, free and unmolested. Or, if I was feeling especially vindictive, I could trace the Sorrowful Sigil with my toe and open a hole for the infinitely hungry things that dwell in the Down-Below Lands to crawl up through. Heh. I have to admit, it'd be fun to see the looks on these yokels' faces if I did that.

But what then?

My eyes are getting too dim to read my books of magic, or see secret knowledge in the guts of a dove. My knobby hands are too twisted and clumsy for me to craft any more sculptures of time, or to brew up marvels in my cauldron. And worst of all, my beautiful mind, my most prized possession of all, has begun to slip away from me in fits and starts. It used to be sharper than the wings of those razor-blade angels, but every day it gets a little duller. Every day I'm a little more forgetful. From here on out this road doesn't go anyplace good.

For eighty-six years I've lived a wonderful life. It's been the best existence I could have wanted. I've learned so much, experienced so much, loved so much. I've seen the whole world, and oh, what a world it is. I've seen worlds beyond this one, too, and sang along with the music of the spheres. But now—like a drop of water falling back into the sea—it's time for my separate existence to end and for me to rejoin something so much bigger than myself. Before I was me I was earth and air and fire and water. I was animals and plants and bugs and rocks and salt and the very stars that shine in the sky. It's time for me to be these things again.

So if a tear or two rolls down my craggy old cheeks as the flames rise up around me, please know that it's not from fear or pain or sorrow. They're tears of joy. Today I lose myself, but I gain everything else.

Burn the witch.

THE ENLIGHTENMENT JUNKIES

JANICE AWOKE WITH A DULL ACHE in her bones and a shaky, ominous feeling like the flu coming on; she'd be junk-sick by evening unless she scored before then. A town normally flooded with heroin was stricken with a drought so severe that sometimes it took the better part of a day to find a connection, and what little you got for your money was pitifully weak, the narcotic equivalent of baby aspirin. At least the tips had been good last night. Her cell phone told her that it was about 11, so she had seven hours to take care of business before her evening shift waiting tables at O'Banion's Irish Pub began. Plenty of time. Janice pulled on her favorite jeans and her cleanest dirty sweatshirt and left the house to get high.

It was a bright, clear autumn day, but cold enough to bite through the sweatshirt and set Janice's teeth chattering. She fired off a text to Wayne, her usual dealer, and then another to a lardy juggalo she knew only as Porkrind. Wayne's package was way better but she'd heard he was in jail, and she couldn't waste time waiting for a reply that might never come. She kept the text to him vague in case a detective was taking his messages. Porkrind responded almost immediately, saying that he was all out but that she was welcome to come over and smoke weed if she wanted. Useless clowny bastard. Wayne remained silent.

Ordinarily a couple of Mexican guys dealt outside of the 7-11 but they weren't there today. The ache in Janice's bones worsened. When she was a child she'd suffered from terrible growing pains and now it felt like they were coming back even though she'd stopped growing many years ago. What was wrong with this neighborhood? It used to be that you couldn't walk from one end of a block to the other without coming across a heroin dealer.

There was King's Court Trailer Park, of course. It'd be a cold day in Hell when you couldn't get high at that shithole. She'd only been desperate enough to go there once before, and she'd told herself she'd never go back. A woman could be harassed anywhere, but the propositions she'd received in that dump had been especially vulgar and savage and frightening. Maybe going through withdrawal would be better than going to King's Court. Withdrawal would kick her ass all over the street, but it wouldn't kill her. Janice paused on a street corner, shivering in the wind and thinking hard about her options.

She was on her way over to King's Court when she saw Minnie straggling in the opposite direction. Janice flagged her down, and her heart fell when she saw that the old fiend was sober. "What's up, Min?" she asked. "You coming from King's Court?"

"Yeah," Minnie sighed. From the gravel in her voice it sounded like the poor bitch was coming down hard. "The guy I knew there up and vanished. There isn't even anything left in his trailer."

Shit. Apparently it was a cold day in Hell after all, and it was still only October. "You know anyone else who's holding?"

"Naw, honey, this town's going through a dry spell."

"Don't I know it. Good luck out there."

"You too, sweetheart."

Soon Janice was sitting in a diner with her head in her hands, contemplating the throbbing pulse behind her eyes and the lukewarm cup of black coffee in front of her. The last time she'd been junk-sick it had been real, real bad, and she'd been doing less back then. Just as she had resigned herself to days of sweating and freezing and puking, Cooper walked in the door.

Cooper was an ugly creep—a pink, fleshy dude with a mop of curly hair bleached-blonde at the tips and dark brown at the roots—but he was an ugly creep who liked to get stoned. Despite the autumn chill he wore his regular uniform, a Bob Marley T-shirt and cargo shorts. Word around town was that he'd been going to the university but that he'd gotten in trouble for soliciting teenagers online and had been asked to sit out a few semesters while the trouble died down. Sometimes he came around the bar and hosted impromptu coke parties in the bathroom, which was how Janice knew him. She waved him over to her table, already thinking up protective rationalizations about how he wasn't such a bad guy.

"Hey... Janice, right?" he asked. "How you doing, girl?"

"Aw, you know. I'm getting by. Hey, how come I haven't seen you at O'Banion's lately?"

"Don't take it personally, I've been busy. Besides, I don't really drink that much anymore. Don't like clouding up my mind."

"No? You still party, right? I always thought of you as the guy who brings the party with him."

A broad, knowing smile spread across his fat face. "Oh yeah, I bring the party with me wherever I go."

"Think you could maybe hook a girl up?"

"Yeah, I can help you out," he said. "Let me just get something to eat and we can go back to my place."

Cooper lived in the historic part of Harlebury, where men who went to sea to kill whales had once lived. Fixed up, the house would be a yuppie dream palace, but as was the paint was peeling off it like skin from a sunburn and its straight lines were starting to buckle. Inside, it stank of body soil and marijuana. Cooper motioned for Janice to sit on the couch while he fiddled with a laughing Buddha statuette. He popped open a secret compartment in its base, and retrieved a plastic baggie containing two large gray tablets. The baggie was labeled with a pyramid that had an eye at each of its points. Cooper put one on the tip of his tongue and gulped it down without water, and passed the other to Janice.

"What is this?" she asked. "You got any H? Or oxy, maybe?"

"Don't worry, baby. This'll get you higher than heroin ever could. And this is a true high, not just a dream of being someplace lofty."

The sickness was coming on fast, with not much time to get well before she had to start at O'Banion's. Janice swallowed her tablet. It tasted like salt and spice, and wicked away all the moisture from her mouth and throat as it went down. A valve in her stomach spurted acid, and her jaw went tight.

Then the whole world made sense, and she knew the secret meaning of life.

Suddenly it was all so simple, and she wondered why she hadn't seen it all along. Every part of the universe fit together in a bejeweled cosmic clockwork, and she was a master clockmaker marveling at the beautiful elegance of the design. The entirety of space and time was comprehensible to her from her position on Cooper's shabby couch, she just had to turn it about in her mind to see any part of it she desired. She rotated it through three dimensions to behold the molten heart of the sun, and was not hurt by its heat and brilliance. She rotated it through four dimensions to witness her own birth at St. Joseph's Hospital. And then she kept that backwards rotation in motion, spinning faster and faster along that axis, back to the birth of the universe itself.

A beautiful high, isn't it? Cooper asked her telepathically. Janice realized that she had lost her capacity to understand conventional language, but she did not need it nor miss it now that she perceived things on such a deeper and more fundamental level. Who needs the signifier when one has that which is signified? If anything, now she understood how language was a mere brace, a thing that might help a broken-legged man walk but would keep an athlete from sprinting.

Janice looked at Cooper and truly saw him. She saw the entire succession of lives and couplings that led to his birth, from the Chthonic birth of the first unicellular being out of a slimy ancient ocean, to trilobites rutting in Pangaean mud, through the first tiny mammals squeaking in ecstasy in Paleozoic jungles. She saw thousands of generations of human marriages and seductions and rapes, up until July 27, 1989, when Phil Cooper and his wife Barbara made love on the recliner with Al Green singing to them. Janice could read Cooper's DNA. She could see the neurons firing in his brain. God, he was so beautiful when you saw all of him at once. She reached over and undid his belt.

Omniscience wore off in fits and starts. Language returned more slowly, leading to a dark period sometime in the early morning where she didn't know if she'd ever be able to read or speak again. When she could comprehend the written word again, she saw that she'd gotten a bunch of text messages during her spell of godhood. There were many angry texts from her boss at O'Banion's, of course, and a few more from her co-worker Alli asking where she was. During her time on Pyramid, Janice had been perfectly aware that she was missing her shift, it hadn't been like a heroin binge where you might nod off and lose track of such things. While going down on Cooper she'd actually seen her boss's scowl as he watched over the thirsty crowd, the same way she saw her father and the pope and a street urchin in Jakarta in the 16th century and a Siberian tiger nursing cubs and every other living creature that was or ever had been. But a girl had to prioritize. Who could focus on fetching shots and nacho platters when the whole of space and time was naked and spread-eagled before you?

Wayne had messaged her as well, apologizing for the delay and asking how much she wanted. Janice deleted the text.

Cooper was snoring loudly beside her. Janice felt his dried sweat on her body and felt a sudden, intense need for a shower. Damn, he'd been so much hotter on Pyramid. Janice shook him into grudging semi-consciousness.

"Hey, do you got any more Pyramid?"

"What? No, that was the last of it. Come by tonight and we can go get more."

"All right. See you soon, babe." She gave him a perfunctory shoulder rub, pecked him on the cheek, and began to gather her clothes.

"And bring money. That shit ain't cheap."

The next night at O'Banion's, Janice absorbed her boss's tirade without emotion. Really, she could barely pay attention to the ass-slapping bastard's complaints. She was too busy trying to remember what her Pyramid high had been like, and mostly failing. That psychic itch had vexed her all day; almost from the moment that the high wore off.

Later, smoking cigarettes with Alli out by the service entrance, she admitted to why she'd missed work. "Cooper?" asked Alli. Her pierced nose wrinkled up slightly. "Really?"

"Yeah."

"The chubby dude with the dye job?"

"That's the one."

Alli took a drag and pondered this. "You can do better. Let me introduce you to this guy Jacob, he's the brother of one of the girls on my roller derby team. He's got a gnarly little claw hand but other than that he's really sweet. I think you two would get along."

"No, it's not like that. We were on this stuff called Pyramid."

"What's that, some kind of roofie?"

"No, not even close. The opposite of a roofie. It makes you understand everything. It makes you see what's beautiful about everything."

"Sounds kind of like Ecstasy. I thought you didn't like that stuff."

"I don't, it makes my taste in music shitty. But Pyramid is completely different—it does...it... God, it's hard to explain. It's hard to remember."

Alli stubbed out her cigarette against the bricks. "Are you all right, hon? I know you like to live like a rock star, but you don't look good."

"I'm fine. It's just... Imagine that you knew everything for a night and then you forgot it all." Janice's phone tinkled. She checked the message. "Hey, Cooper's coming to pick me up at one. Can you cover for me?"

"Seriously? You want Don to go completely nuts?"

"He took off a couple of hours ago, it'll be fine."

"All right, it's your ass, not mine. Pretty dead tonight anyway. Just be careful, okay?"

When 1 a.m. rolled around, Janice hopped into Cooper's waiting car like a giddy teenager sneaking out with her boyfriend. "My man with the Pyramid hookup's called Billy," Cooper said. "Has a place over in King's Court. There's something wrong with his face, don't say anything about it."

The trailer park had been an open sewer at the time of Janice's last visit, and incredibly, it had gotten much worse. A sign yellowed with age and defaced with cryptic graffiti marked the entrance. Packs of doomed, semi-feral children loped through pools of sodium light, screeching and fighting. The sounds of baying dogs and domestic disputes echoed from all around.

Billy's trailer was in a remote corner all its own, a pariah even here. It was so rusted-out that Janice would have thought it abandoned but for the light within. On the side of the trailer, someone had painted a stylized deaths-head surrounded by spirals in bright, gaudy colors, maybe as some sort of gang symbol but artsier than those usually were. Cooper led her to the door and knocked.

Janice couldn't tell exactly what was wrong with Billy's face because he wore a black leather goat mask. Its long, curved horns scraped against the low trailer ceiling. Other than that he had no other garments except a pair of boxer shorts, showing off the tattoos etched into his pallid flesh. Galaxies of ebony suns, moons, stars, and constellations hung all over him. It wasn't crude jailhouse work, either. You could hang Billy's skin in a museum.

"Cooper!" the drug dealer rasped, his mask muffling his voice. "If it isn't my favorite pharaoh. Come back for some more Pyramid? Who's your lovely friend?"

"Billy, this is Janice," Cooper said. "Janice, Billy. Can we come in?"

Billy stepped aside and invited them in with a theatrical bow and flourish of his arms. Janice accepted the invitation, reason and caution be damned.

The inside of Billy's trailer reeked of chemical fumes that stung Janice's eyes and swelled up her throat. Billy had confined a multitude of mangy cats in pet carriers stacked up along the walls, the animals howling and hissing and pissing. A hillbilly chemistry set took up most of the rest of the space in the double-wide, with a foul, bare mattress the only other furniture. An AK-47, a couple of large pistols, and a nasty-looking knife with spiked knuckle-guards lay scattered in amongst the household cleansers and boiling flasks.

Billy picked up a large pill bottle and a baggie labeled with the three-eyed pyramid. "How many do you want?" he asked. "It's a hundred a pill."

"A hundred?" Cooper protested. "It used to be eighty."

"Used to be."

"Goddamnit," Cooper muttered, counting out a stack of twenties from his billfold. "I'll take two." Janice produced $200 of her own money as well, almost all that she had. "This had better be as good as the last batch."

"It'll be much better."

Cooper and Janice spent the night sitting in lawn chairs in Cooper's overgrown backyard, drinking beer and watching the stars be born and burn and collapse into cinders. They played a game whereby they would point to a glittering dot of light and telepathically tell each other fun things about it.

Look at that one over there, Janice thought. *Circling its fifth planet is a moon populated by a species made entirely of sound. They feed by reverberating in crystals and sing songs to make babies.*

That one doesn't have a name anymore, thought Cooper, pointing the neck of his bottle towards a star. *But two million years ago, a race of lizard-things lived on its third planet. They worshipped that star as a god, and made blood sacrifices every night so that their deity would return to them in the morning. The lizard-things exterminated the populations of a hundred worlds in the name of their sun. Then a virus wiped out their species, and since then no conscious being in the entire universe has paid the slightest attention to that star except for you and me.*

I want to see the future, thought Janice. *But when I try to rotate the superstructure futurewards through the fourth dimension, the perception scatters like a kaleidoscope.*

We have everything that ever existed from the dawn of existence to now. Let's not get greedy.

Fair enough. She pointed to a black, empty portion of the sky. *Hey, Cooper, check out what black holes look like on the inside.*

Like a love affair, Pyramid was perfect until it ended, and then its absence tore the heart apart.

Billy's prices continued to climb, and Don O'Banion fired Janice for stealing from the till. Janice began selling her things, setting up a triangular trade between her home, the pawn shop, and Billy's trailer, but her previous habits had already cleaned out most of her nice things so this trade didn't last long. One day she came home to find a sheriff's notice taped to her door and her few remaining belongings on the street. She left them where they lay and went over to Cooper's.

A rotating crew of Pyramid worshippers gradually took over Cooper's pad. You never knew what you'd find when you walked through the (never-locked) doors—there might be a blissful circle of all-knowing mutes with clenched jaws, meditating on the truths of the cosmos, and there might be a gang of dirty, wild-eyed freaks shouting at each other and hammering parking meters apart for quarters. Even Alli joined the party, after a moment of curiosity brought her into communion. Cooper himself mainly stuck to the basement, where he was trying to build a time machine out of tin foil and broken electronics. He had gotten greedy for the future after all. When he was high on Pyramid he knew exactly how to build the machine, but there were certain configurations that had to be completed all in one sitting, and if you paused halfway through it was ruined and you had to start over from scratch. Cooper never managed to get enough Pyramid at one time to finish the job, and like poor Sisyphus he kept rolling the rock uphill and it kept rolling back onto him. It withered him up. His belly shrank to a deflated pouch, and his Bob Marley T-shirt and cargo shorts began to rot off him.

Janice spent more and more time in King's Court, plying the world's oldest profession to earn her Pyramid. When she was high it was no problem because all she had to do was shut her eyes and think of the entire universe. And when she was straight it was worth it, because it brought her closer to being a goddess again. Once, in especially desperate straits, she went to Billy's trailer door penniless and offered herself in barter. He put his hands on his hips and looked her up and down appraisingly, his deep grey eyes bright and cold behind the mask. "Well, look at you, little darling," he said. "A high priestess in the cult of the temple prostitutes. Come right on in."

She'd hoped there was some other place that he'd want to do it, but he was the boss. Janice stepped across the threshold and into his trailer, where the captive cats (all different cats each time, she'd noticed) yowled and spat at her. Billy hurled her down onto the mattress, a thing so rank and foul it seemed to crawl beneath her skin. He pulled off his wife-beater. "Wait!" Janice cried. "Wait, I need a pill first."

Billy laughed like cars crashing. "I have something better," he said. He retrieved a hypodermic needle and a plastic vial full of thick brown syrup from his stinking laboratory. "It's Pyramid in liquid form," he explained. "I call it Obelisk. Much purer and better than the pills."

"Show me," she said.

Billy pulled off her sweatshirt. He tied off her left arm with a piece of rubber tubing and slid the needle into her vein. There was a little pinch as it went in, and a drop of crimson. Then everything exploded.

On Pyramid she could see the entirety of the great superstructure that contained the universe in a scaffolding of time and space. On Obelisk she saw all of that and more. Now she also saw the cracks that ran through the superstructure and oh God she could see the things that came out of those cracks and glimpse into the awful void that lay beyond. Before she had thought the superstructure to be so flawless, so strong. How could she have been so blind? The fabric of reality was fraying and moth-eaten. The great machine tore itself to pieces as it ran.

Billy was on her then. He tore at her with his teeth, biting through a mask that had no mouth hole, and rending her scrawny body with his claws and his hooves and other parts that had no right names, bringing her to extremes of unendurable sensation as the Obelisk heightened the sensitivity of every one of her nerves by a thousandfold. Billy howled from his many throats. Janice shut her eyes, but a third one opened up in the center of her forehead, taking in the entirety of the demon mounting her. In the same way that she had once witnessed the entire life and genealogy of Cooper, now she wailed helplessly as she saw Billy's existence unspool.

There was nothing beautiful about Billy, nothing beautiful at all.

Janice regained consciousness some time later, hurting all over. She rubbed her forehead, for reasons that she herself did not wholly understand, and felt a deep furrow just above her brow. The drug dealer sat naked at his workbench, placidly occupied with his burners and beakers. Janice dressed in silence. When she was finished, Billy wordlessly held out his hand to her. Five vials of Obelisk lay on his palm.

As Janice limped through the warrens of King's Court on her way back to Cooper's, all she could think about was how she'd found something even better than Pyramid. She could not remember the truths that the new drug had shown her, but she knew that they were deeper and more profound than any she'd experienced before and that she could never go back to the fogged, imperfect transcendence she'd known before.

With Obelisk the junkies who haunted Cooper's became miracle workers, albeit gaunt, filthy miracle workers with weeping sores. It was not uncommon to see an addict in an Obelisk trance levitating up near the ceiling, high both literally and figuratively, bathed in a nimbus of light like a full-body halo. Living hypodermic needles, granted some manner of sentience by their contact with the drug, scuttled across the carpets on wire legs and chirped like strange crickets. Cooper finished his time machine in the basement and walked into the distant future. The machine turned itself off after his maiden voyage, but there must have been some leakage because when Janice went down there, she could faintly hear Cooper's ceaseless screams and cries for help across the fourth dimension.

As Janice soaked in the bathtub one day, sitting in dirty, lukewarm water with a needle still in her arm, she realized that she had just minutes left to live. Inside her own brain she saw blood vessels bursting one after another, flooding the inside of her skull. On the false trip of Pyramid she would have accepted death with serenity as merely the inevitable endpoint of her great journey, but now that she knew what the afterlife looked like the prospect of dying terrified her beyond anything else.

The bathroom mirror shimmered and Alli clambered through it, on her way back from King's Court via a self-made wormhole. Alli's derby girl meat had dropped away a long time ago, and now she was not much thicker than a mummy, so she was able to get in and out of the smallish mirror with no problems at all. Janice knew that Alli had three vials of Obelisk on her, and she hoped that would be enough for what she had in mind.

Janice mentally tugged on the superstructure in and around Alli's chest, just hard enough to tweak a few laws of physics for a few seconds. The pressure differential spiked and Alli's lungs burst like overinflated balloons. Alli collapsed onto the bathroom floor with bright red blood spurting from her throat and nose. Janice was on top of her twitching corpse immediately, rifling through her pockets for the precious vials and paying no heed to the gore. She hurriedly filled her needle with all three vials, a bigger dose than anyone had ever taken before. Sitting astride the toilet, she stuck the needle into her carotid artery and pressed down hard on the plunger.

Janice's third eye shot open, its pupil not so much dilated as gaping, and she saw exactly what she had to do. Life and death were built right into the cosmic superstructure, there was no avoiding them if were you confined within it, but if you dwelled outside space-time entirely you were no longer a prisoner to its rules, and space-time was riddled with holes. A crack existed within this very bathroom, no bigger than the space between two molecules but sufficient for her purposes. Janice ripped into it and began tearing reality apart.

FOLLOWING BEBE ASTARA

UNTIL I PHOTOGRAPHED BEBE ASTARA I was a big-game hunter, and the Hollywood A-list were my prey. I pursued them through the wilds of exclusive nightclubs and across veldts of red carpet. I took trophies at top-ranked Michelin restaurants and equally swanky rehab clinics. I caught them in my flash red-eyed and blinking as they emerged from police stations, and I sniped them with long-distance lenses through the windows of their own homes as they lounged unsuspecting. I was a predator by instinct and training. If I'd been born in an earlier age I'm sure I would have wound up stalking tigers through primeval jungles. Screw that, though, I like my jungles with concrete and high-speed Internet and bottle service.

I was the first one on the scene when Bieber crashed his Bugatti, wiping out at 120 mph and .24 BAC and decapitating himself against the underside of a truck. The little Canadian boy was still blinking when I pulled up on my motorcycle and started shooting. Some called it snuff photography. Who cares? It paid for my house in Beverly Hills.

I was the man who revealed to the world that Joe Biden and Jennifer Aniston were having an affair. They thought that they were safe from prying eyes on a yacht crewed exclusively by Secret Service agents. Never underestimate what a paparazzi with a sense of drive and a purpose-built quadcopter surveillance drone can accomplish.

And while the art world cretins will never admit this, not even under pain of torture, by any halfway honest reckoning my portfolio included work far superior to most gallery shows, especially when you consider the constraints I had to work under. Let's see Annie Leibovitz try to capture her subject's soul when she's got to set up her shots the same way Lee Harvey Oswald did. People make a big deal about Diane Arbus, but I can't get excited about someone who only photographed losers.

Were there setbacks? Of course there were. My nose got broken so many times that I looked like the world's shortest, scrawniest boxer. I've been punched, slapped, kicked, spat upon, choked, pelted with bottles, menaced with guns. Oh, and Lady Gaga's people set a trained baboon on me once. A baboon, I shit you not. To defend myself I practiced an American style of jiu-jitsu, wherein I absorbed the force of my enemy's blows and channeled it back against them in the form of personal injury lawsuits, so even when I got my teeth kicked in and my camera smashed I still did alright.

The point of all this is that I was not some fame-crazy little stalker with a map to the homes of the stars and a smartphone. I was not a hack snapping sitcom actors going out for frogurt in their sweatpants. I was a tabloid assassin, a man of ruthless disposition and extraordinary skill who spent his career gleefully pissing in the cornflakes of the rich and powerful and laughing off the abuse they shot back.

Until I photographed Bebe Astara.

It started when I woke to the chime of an incoming text, with my girlfriend Luba cuddled up beneath my arm. Luba was a Russian model, fresh off the caviar boat. A lovely girl in every way. Going by looks and personality alone she'd have been way out of my league. Fortunately, I had a special trick for reeling in models. First, I'd tell them that I was a professional photographer, and rattle off the names of some of the most famous folks I'd "worked with." Once I'd impressed them as an accomplished and well-connected man, I'd tell the stories of how I took my most scandalous shots. At that point they'd either throw a drink in my face or drop their panties. In my professional life I had to rely on stealth and deceit. In my private life I told people exactly what I was. I figured they couldn't blame me for my job as long as I was honest about it.

I checked my phone, taking care not to disturb my sleeping beauty. I saw a message from Woody Monroe, the editor and chief blogger at hollywoodpulse.com. "Want to go to a private party at Bebe Astara's house?" it read.

I gently shook Luba awake. "You've got to go, babe," I told her. "I've got work to do."

I gave Luba a ride home on my way to the coffee shop where Woody held court. "So who is this Bebe Ishtara woman?" she asked. Foreign accents have always turned me on, and Luba had a magnificent one, like a sexy bride of Dracula.

"Bebe Astara is the biggest reality TV star in the country," I told her. "You seriously don't know who she is?"

She shrugged. "At home, we don't get American TV. What's so special about her? Does she act? Sing?"

"Not really. She's been in some movies and put out some albums but she was already famous before she did those. She just is what she is and for whatever reason people can't get enough of it. Bebe got her break a few years back when she was in a sex tape that went viral. She was dating this big-shot basketball player named D'angelo Carter. It's an amazing sex tape, you ought to look it up. Bebe's this petite, five foot nothing piece of plastic and D'angelo's this tattooed warrior prince of the NBA, and he was sobbing and bleeding by the time she was done with him. Honestly, I know this sounds weird but I think it's fair to say that she raped him. That was the end of his career, of course, and just the beginning of hers.

"So after her smash hit sex tape, the next step was a smash hit reality show. *Following Bebe Astara.* A camera crew trails her around L.A. as she lives a perfect life full of high fashion, high drama, handsome boyfriends, gossipy girlfriends, and effortless success. Kind of a modern-day princess fantasy, set in the magical fairyland of Hollywood."

"Sounds wonderful, I'll have to check it out."

"Wait, I haven't even gotten to the best part yet. Bebe Astara's got a huge online presence, because of course she does. She has more followers than anyone else on Twitter, more friends than anyone else on Facebook. Something like twenty percent of Instagram's traffic is just people checking her feed. And last year she rolled out her online role-playing game, *Bebe's World.* The goal of the game is to become the world's hottest celebrity. But you can't win the game's challenges unless your character's equipped with designer clothes and sports cars and jewelry—all real brands, all paying top dollar for advertising— and you've got to spend genuine currency to buy that imaginary shit in the game. And every time you win a challenge and level up, your old shit isn't good enough anymore and you need to upgrade to even fancier shit before you can advance again. And on and on and on. Forever. I've never played it myself, but it's supposed to be horribly addictive. You see news reports about middle school girls prostituting themselves so they can afford the virtual shoes they need to go up a level, or obsessed players who get caught up in marathon sessions until they keel over and die of exhaustion. It's like she invented legal heroin. Bebe's on the Forbes list of the richest Americans because of that game."

"So she's gone from a sex tape to a media empire. Isn't that the definition of the American Dream?"

You know that first stage of infatuation, when you feel like you're weightless and sinking at the same time? I was starting to get that sensation from Luba.

I dropped Luba off at her apartment and went on to meet Woody Monroe. Woody (Christian name: Dennis Mahoney) was a cherubically plump man whose personal sense of style registered as a cross between Oscar Wilde and Captain Jack Sparrow. He'd grown up in Deliverance country, and I think that the bullying he'd endured there had left him with a permanent, seething grudge against the popular kids. He was a damn fine gossip blogger, though, as cruel and playful as the high-bred cats he kept. Woody was at his usual table when I arrived. I ordered a black coffee—sparing a moment to compliment the cute goth barista on her Sisters of Mercy T-shirt—and went over to him. "Put on your dancing shoes," he said as I approached.

"I always wear my dancing shoes," I replied. "You never know when a musical number will break out. What's the story on this party?"

"It's going down tomorrow night. Apparently it's in honor of the solstice. I know, that sounds more like a Gwyneth party than a Bebe party. Trust me, our intelligence is solid." He passed me an envelope. Nestled inside was a slip of vellum with a date, an address, and a sun and moon painted on by hand. "That'll get you and one guest inside," Woody said. "It's better if I don't tell you exactly how I got that. We don't want you giving the whole operation away if you're captured by the enemy." This last bit he said with a smile and the cadence of a joke. His eyes weren't laughing, though.

"Anyone in particular I should be looking for in attendance?"

"We've gotten a partial guest list. Bebe's invited an *interesting* crowd. Singers and actors and producers, sure, and a bunch of weirdos, too."

"Weirdos? Like who? Example."

"Well, there's some anthropologists specializing in druidism and pre-Columbian societies. I suppose that makes sense, if you're having a solstice party you might as well commit to it. And the same goes for the psychics and the shamans. What about the Yale professor of entomology? What's *he* doing getting an invite to a Bebe Astara party? Two of the people on the guest list are honest-to-goodness cult leaders."

"No kidding?"

"It came up when I Googled them. One's the founder of the High Temple of Purebringers, and the other's the psychopomp of the Neo-Dionysians, whatever that means."

"Oh damn. I need to see those two get into a conversation."

"You get my point about weirdos."

"And they won't be checking names at the door?"

"Nope, the golden ticket's all you need. Like Charlie and the Chocolate Factory. Although don't let them see you taking any photos. If you get captured, Hollywood Pulse will disavow all knowledge of your activities."

As I pocketed the envelope, I thought but did not say that most of the children who entered the Chocolate Factory destroyed themselves there.

I decided to invite Luba to come along with me. With the benefit of hindsight I regret that more bitterly than any other decision of my life. At the time it seemed like it'd be fun. What better way to seduce a woman than to make her a Bond girl for a day, the beautiful *femme fatale* assisting me as I infiltrate a glamorous location to take covert photographs? She looked every bit the part, too, all sleek and curvy and exotic. For my part, I cut a fairly dapper spy in my tailored silk suit, especially considering that I'd hidden a CIA-engineered buttonhole camera in the lapel.

The Astara mansion was located in the woods outside Mandeville Canyon. GPS didn't even know that there were roads out here, and I spent an uncomfortable amount of time with no idea of my bearings before I spied a man standing at the roadside holding a torch. He wore a tuxedo and an eyeless mask made of a glassy, reflective material. When I pulled over and looked him in the face I saw my own reflected back at me, hideously distorted by funhouse technology. He silently waved us onto a narrow, winding side road going up a densely forested hill.

"What was he wearing?" Luba asked. "That was wild."

"Beats me," I said. "Woody didn't say anything about this being a costume party."

There were no houses or streetlamps up here, so they'd lit the roadside with the propane-burning towers that restaurants use to warm outside seating areas. Their flames illuminated a sculpture garden that Bebe had erected in the woods. We passed by formations of concrete slabs, reminiscent of Stonehenge if the Druids had commissioned Frank Lloyd Wright to design it, and a bestiary of surrealistic, Giger-esque statues that crouched at the tree line, lurking at the very edge of the light. Weird shadows lurched and slumped in my headlights.

Finally we arrived at the top of the hill and the mansion itself. It was a Brutalist concrete structure, all hard angles and windowless surfaces, nothing at all like the elegant Brentwood estate Bebe lived in on her show. More of the propane burners had been set up here, and a crackling bonfire blazed in a star-shaped fire pit, so even late at night the place was almost as well-lit as noon. I was glad of it—operating outside at night with a buttonhole camera and no flash, I'd need excellent lighting to get any saleable pictures. Guests danced and chatted, and ethereal music heavy on pipes and strings carried on the breeze. I was relieved to see that nobody except the help was in fancy dress.

More of the mirror-masked servants waved me on to a gravel parking lot where about $50 million worth of automobiles were assembled. In that company I felt like a slob driving my BMW Z4 roadster. Three more faceless flunkies served on bouncer duty near the parking lot—two absolute gorillas in tuxes and an anorexic-looking creature wearing a flowing white robe, with fingernails as long as a Chinese mandarin's. "Invitation, please," said the mandarin, in an androgynous voice like tinkling bells, as he (or maybe she) extended a palm. I passed the vellum slip over, and it vanished as if up a magician's sleeve. Then the mandarin produced a golden box. "Check your cell phones, please. Ms. Astara doesn't want any records of this night besides our sweet memories."

I have to admit that even a seasoned party-crasher like myself felt a *frisson* of worry about surrendering my link to the outside. The scene was a much weirder one than I had imagined. And I have to admit, I felt an uncharacteristic urge to turn tail and let this one go. Hell, I could see the reluctance in my own warped reflection, peering down at me from atop the mandarin's shoulders. I gave up my phone nonetheless, as did Luba. The mandarin handed each of us a heavy gold token in exchange, hers labeled with an acorn and mine with a grinning skull. "Enjoy the celebration," the faceless majordomo said. "Ms. Astara welcomes you to her home."

We were at the social event of the year, and the first thing that I noticed was how many moths were in attendance. An eclipse of the insects fluttered overhead, big ones, with black furry wings. The torches had lured them in by the thousands to immolate themselves all around us, soaring through the deadly light, descending in flames, and disintegrating into cinders before they even hit the ground. Their pyrotechnics lent the party a vibe that was carnivalesque and morbid simultaneously. I got the impression that the fires had been lit with exactly this effect in mind. I wondered what the Yale entomologist made of it.

"This is a strange crowd," Luba whispered to me. I agreed entirely. The party had plenty of famous faces at the epitome of physical beauty, and just as many at the opposite end of the spectrum. Impossibly gorgeous men and women drank and laughed with aged, sour-faced oddballs. Woody's intelligence had been spot-on. For every rock star or supermodel in attendance, there was also a tweedy, full-bearded professor, or a painted shaman in feathers and furs, or a mad-eyed loon in obscure ritual garb. And at the time, I thought Astara had commissioned the services of a *bona fide* freak show. Dwarves in formal attire drunkenly capered underfoot, some of them barely bigger than cats, while lanky giants strolled about swatting at the moths around their heads. A cheering crowd had gathered near the fire pit. Luba and I joined them, and saw an Oscar-winning starlet going down on a man so covered with gnarled warts that his skin looked like the bark of a tree, while dying, burning moths plummeted around them. I took picture after picture, and considered myself the second-luckiest man on Earth, right after the forest creature. I looked all over for Bebe, in vain.

Masked servants circulated with trays of snacks and champagne. The mirrored faces had been a neat touch at first, but soon I got sick of seeing my own features reflected back at me all twisted and runny. I had an appetite until I saw the victuals on offer. Bebe's tastes apparently went to that trendy molecular gastronomy nonsense, for almost none of the food was recognizable as such. There were black crackers topped with some type of bluish foam, glistening white roots in cream sauce, and pink, fleshy little creatures that might have been some type of prawn impaled mouth-to-anus on ivory skewers. Again, I was curious for the entomologist's counsel. To beg off would have been to mark ourselves as not belonging, so I took a foam cracker and Luba took a prawn-thing, and we clinked our glasses and toasted our hostess.

The cracker was simply vile, like some depraved gourmand had reduced the contents of a porno theater mop bucket into jam and spread it on a chip. The champagne, however, was unearthly. Now that I think about it, I'm not sure it was champagne. It tasted the way being on really excellent cocaine feels, a suffusion of bubbly warmth that electrified my taste buds with delightful, effervescent energy. Despite the full bar I couldn't see myself drinking anything other than this. I mean, for the rest of my life.

Luba and I circulated, refreshing our glasses on a regular basis, as I took dozens of pictures. I soon realized that in addition to the gods, goddesses, and goblins, there were a few mere mortals other than Luba and myself in attendance. I met one of these souls, a self-described "YouTube superstar" named Krissy, lurking shyly at the bar. Krissy had posted a video about her love of *Bebe's World* and been rewarded for it with an out-of-the-blue invite to the solstice party. She told me with heart-breaking sincerity that she'd always known she and Bebe would be BFFs if they ever got the chance to meet. I shouldn't be too hard on her, she was only about 17. I also wound up talking with an ex-Amish kid from Ohio whose only claim to fame was that he'd been featured on a reality show about the *rumspringa*. He was pants-wetting drunk, rambling on about how he'd fallen into the wrong world and gotten trapped, and how he might have to gnaw his own leg off to escape.

I'd intended to remain sober, this being a work night, but the champagne hit as hard as whiskey, a sucker-punch in every glass. I excused myself from Luba and headed into the house in search of the john. The bathroom was bigger than my first apartment, all sleek black marble veined with white and crimson. You could have drowned an elephant in the sunken tub. Before I left I remembered to photograph the medicine cabinet. It was stocked with a witchy collection of herbs, oils, potions, bones, and dried insects, plus a collection of high-grade pharmaceuticals so intensely comprehensive that one might have thought it belonged to an anesthesiologist with a hoarding problem.

Just as I was finishing up, I glanced into the mirror and saw a dead man staring at me.

I turned with a start. Conroy Voxel, Bebe's ex-boyfriend and the lead singer of the band Zero to Fuck You, stood by the door in a white fur coat, no shirt, and stained tighty-whities. I hadn't heard him come in, and I was pretty sure that he'd died a couple of years ago. He'd tried to order hallucinogenic toads from the dark web, and some joker mailed him neurotoxic frogs instead. Drunk as I was, I fuzzily recalled that *Following Bebe Astara* had done a heavily promoted episode about his death, and that the season eight finale had taken place at Conroy's funeral. Yet here the man was. I supposed that I must have been mistaken, and decided not to mention it. Even B-listers hate it when you say that you thought they were dead.

Conroy looked me up and down appraisingly. His eyes were large, luminous, and overflowed with pain. He looked like shit—unshaven and pallid and shivering despite his fur coat. I suspected that he was feeling the bite of a neglected opioid habit. How strange to find a man suffering that complaint in a house so well-stocked with the remedy. Without a word, the rock star lurched to the sink and vomited copiously.

I covertly snapped a couple of pictures and then moved in for some close-ups, under the guise of lending a friendly hand. "There,

there, let it all out," I said soothingly. "Better out than in." But I had no idea how right I was, and when I glimpsed the contents of the basin, I screamed and recoiled in horror.

The sink that Conroy had vomited into was now full of black, tarry slime, and a multitude of tiny creatures were suspended in that slime like prehistoric beasts trapped in the La Brea pits. There were wormy, writhing things whose lamprey mouths gulped at the air, fleshy, hairy, fetuses like half-formed baby birds. There were unrecognizable fragments that hinted at wholes beyond anything I could reckon. And worst of all, some of the regurgitated creatures were *still moving.*

That was when the smell hit me—a noxious chemical stench that made my eyes water and nearly caused me to throw up myself.

"Jesus Christ, man, what did you eat?" I asked him. As nasty as the hors d'oeuvres were, nothing in the evening had prepared me for this.

The rock star wiped his mouth on the sleeve of his coat, leaving a matted oil slick in the fur. "I don't know," he moaned. "I don't know what I eat or drink or shoot or snort ever since Bebe made me her taster."

"Her taster?"

Conroy's eyes rolled back in his head and he vomited into the sink again. A high-pressure jet of black sludge sprayed out of his mouth and nose. Despite its thickness it drained rapidly, almost as if the oil was forcing its way into the pipes. The weird little animals that Conroy had puked up dissolved with such speed that I was forced to wonder if I'd ever really seen them at all, or if they were merely an artifact of my own intoxication.

"I'm her taster," Conroy gasped hoarsely once this latest storm had passed. "She fears poison more than anything...salt in her food, powdered iron in her cocaine. Bebe has enemies in high places and low places and the shadow places in-between." He poured some water into his cupped palm and drank it down thirstily, moaning with nearly orgasmic pleasure.

"Yeah, get some water in you," I said.

"You have no idea how good water tastes after drinking nothing but fine wine and babies' blood for so long."

I looked into the sink again. The sludge had gone, leaving only an oily rainbow sheen clinging to the marble and a few unrecognizable, rapidly disintegrating bits of flesh and bone. The chemical fire stench still lingered, though, punishingly intense.

"I think you ought to see a doctor..." I suggested.

"NO!" he shrieked, an animal noise of sheer panic amplified to ear-splitting levels by the bathroom's cathedral acoustics. The rock star recoiled away from me into a corner, collapsing onto the floor in a fetal position with his hands locked around his bent knees. "Don't want to see the doctor," he muttered. "You can't make me see the doctor again. I just need to get some rest. That's all. I can rest till the tithe is paid and then she'll need me again." He rocked himself back up to his feet and staggered to the medicine cabinet. "I've had enough of drugs that make me see things," he babbled to nobody in particular. "I want drugs that will help me see nothing at all." He picked out a vial of a sedative generally reserved for no-hope hospice patients suffering agonies inconceivable to the healthy. With jittery hands, he began to fill a syringe.

"You sure you're going to be okay?" I asked, secretly snapping pictures while he stuck the needle into his horror show of a forearm.

Conroy smiled knowingly at me as he injected himself. "Oh, I'm sure that I'm not going to be okay," he said, slowly slumping into the corner like a marionette whose puppeteer is dying. "That's the sole remaining certainty in my fucked-up life. Worry about yourself, man. Hey, what have *you* eaten tonight?" He coughed violently, and for a split-second I thought I saw the black spew coming up into his *eyes* and turning their whites the color of night.

I suddenly remembered the noxious cracker I'd tasted, and an unstoppable wave of nausea surged up through me like a tsunami headed for land. I doubled over and puked into the sink. Normal vomit, thank God, not whatever nightmare had come out of Conroy.

When I looked up, the rock star was gone.

By the time I weaved my way back to the party, Bebe herself had materialized. For all the times I'd seen her picture, this was the first time I'd ever been in her presence, and Christ, what a presence it was. Even at a party peopled with Hollywood elites and freaks of nature, every eye was locked on her. She passed amongst her guests like a queen amidst the commoners, except I don't think there was ever any earthly queen with her measure of grace and easy charm. Whether she was complimenting a famous director or trading *bon mots* with an elephantiasis victim, everything that she said and did was perfect. I'd imagined myself immune to celebrity worship, but at that moment I felt a terrible urge to fall down at her feet and polish her Jimmy Choos with my unworthy tongue. At first I was too transfixed by her to even remember to take her photo.

Near midnight Bebe clinked a fork against her glass. The whole party fell completely still and silent at her cue. "Everyone," she announced. "If you'll please follow me, the time we've all been waiting for has arrived." As the crowd fell into formation behind its leader, I searched for Luba and couldn't find her anywhere. Boozy jealousy flared briefly within my breast when I realized that I didn't see the ex-Amish boy either. I laughed it off; he wasn't Luba's type. No need to worry, I thought, I'll catch up with her later.

Bebe led us all into her house, through a door I hadn't noticed when I went off in search of the bathroom. We descended a dark, steep staircase, venturing so deep into subterranea that it felt more like going down a mineshaft than into a basement. In my drunken condition it was no easy feat. The stairs terminated in a windowless chamber with rough, irregularly shaped slate walls, suggesting a natural grotto, bare of furniture or ornamentation apart from a nasty-looking, SUV-sized kinetic sculpture in the general form of a bear trap, placed flush against the furthest wall. The machine's enormous jaws were spread wide open, and they bristled with spikes wrapped in gleaming razor wire. It looked like what would happen if a prison warden with a taste for modern art, an unlimited budget, and no concern at all for legal niceties had commissioned Jeff Koons to construct an *avant-garde* execution device. Looking at it I think I got a taste of what churchgoers feel when they see a piece of truly obscene art. I got some pictures of the awful thing, of course, even catching Bebe in the shot.

"My friends," said Bebe—and for a warm, wonderful moment, I thought, *yes, we really are friends.* "The sun is at its nadir and the gate swings open again."

The crowd chanted something in response. It wasn't in English, or in any language I could recognize. Lots of glottal sounds and clicking.

"The glamour's tithe must be paid."

The crowd called out again.

Bebe Astara winked at me, and then she stepped into the death machine.

The lethal jaws snapped shut on her with an ear-splitting crack. It happened so quickly that at first it seemed she'd vanished. Then I saw the gore and flesh on the teeth, and the crimson lump pooled in the bottom of the device. Even as far back as I was, I felt the impact of the jaws clanging shut, and I nearly choked on the coppery stink of her blood. I could *taste* her in the air, and damn me, a part of me relished it.

The machine reset itself with a couple of crisp clockwork ticks. The weight of what remained of Bebe must have been enough to set it off, for as soon as the jaws opened to their widest point they slammed shut again, further pulverizing the corpse. This grisly process repeated itself three more times before the machine was finally still. When it was done, all that remained of Bebe Astara was a quivering red pulp with some hair and scraps of cloth and broken jewelry mixed in.

I was close to passing out, with my head and heart pounding, but I'd gotten all of it on camera. Bebe's guests applauded, and so did I.

Then I heard Bebe Astara's voice again. She spoke inside my head, whispering into my ear from deep within my skull: "The glamour's tithe must be paid."

The door to the chamber opened, and the tithe walked in. They were the mortals that Bebe had invited to her party, Krissy the YouTube superstar and the drunken ex-Amish boy, and nine or ten other such hapless Hollywood strivers, each of them dressed in a white gown with garlands of flowers in their hair, their eyes blank and druggy. Luba was amongst them.

I wanted to call it all off then. I wanted to grab Luba by the hand and get the hell out of there. I had already seen enough... I had already seen too goddamned much. Then I looked around at all the expectant faces surrounding me—celebrities and lunatics and circus grotesques all united in anticipation—and at the steel altar dripping blood—and I got scared. Maybe I could have saved Luba. I'll never know, because I didn't have the balls to try. I watched her and the other dazed kids walk into the jaws of the machine. For all the other bad shit I did in my life, I think it was that moment of cowardice that truly sealed my damnation.

As soon as the teeth came down on Luba and the others the trance broke and the shrieks began. The machine couldn't crush ten people as efficiently as it could crush one. The first snap hardly killed any of them. It was more than enough to cripple them, though. All they could do was lie there crying as the jaws slowly ratcheted back into position for another bite. All I could do was watch. And count. After five repetitions all the moaning stopped. After seven repetitions, nobody moved anymore. After thirteen repetitions, the steel beast was done. Gore dripped from its open mouth, making the sound of falling rain. The smell of blood and shit was overpowering, as if the grotto had become some hellish swamp.

Bebe spoke again; I could almost feel her elegantly coiffed and razorlike fingers scratching at the inside of my skull. "The glamour's tithe is paid," she proclaimed.

The partygoers resumed their chant, and suddenly I noticed that the pool of human puree in the death machine was bubbling. A delicate, well-formed hand burst up from the center of it with a splash. The fingers wrapped around a chrome rung built into the machine itself, and Bebe Astara climbed back into existence, naked but for the blood and scraps of tissue clinging to every inch of her skin. Her guests burst into raucous applause again when they saw their hostess reborn.

Bebe Astara stepping forth crimson and dripping is the last coherent thing I remember. After that it's all fragments. I remember running from the killing chamber, very nearly trampling a dwarf on my way out. I remember one of the servants trying to seize me, and the noise he made when I grabbed at his face and pulled on his mask. Like a hive of bees enraged. I remember jumping into my car and peeling out, bouncing off some parked cars as I fled. I remember glimpsing a pursuing mob in my rear-view mirror, as if I were the monster in an old movie. I remember sobbing wildly as I careened down the freeway. Nothing else.

I woke up with a punishing hangover. Usually when I drink too much I get stuck with a lingering headache. This time the nastiness chose to settle in my gut like a bellyful of slugs. I felt a moment's hope that the events of the previous night had been a strange nightmare. That hope was shattered when I searched my pockets for my cell phone and found the golden death's head chit instead. The fucking thing seemed to be laughing at me. That was when I noticed the abattoir smell still clinging to me. Even a scalding-hot shower couldn't completely wash it away.

After I got some eggs and water into me, I plugged my buttonhole camera into my laptop to see how my shots had turned out. They were the greatest I'd ever taken, both in subject matter and in craftsmanship, and I couldn't work up any sense of pride in them. My finest professional accomplishment was also the documentation of my most shameful moment.

As I went from photo to photo, from the beginning of the evening towards its terrible end, my pulse began to speed up, then race. I relived the evening in all of its dread and beauty. "Oh God," I murmured as I looked at a photo of Bebe standing in front of her death machine. I nearly broke down when I saw the pictures of Luba. Before and after shots. She was screaming in one of the photographs, and it seemed to me that she was screaming, "Your fault."

I tried to convince myself that maybe I'd only seen a party trick, some cunning piece of stage magic that I drunkenly overreacted to. The very unreality of the evening seemed to cry out for a logical explanation. Maybe it was all an elaborate hoax, the ruse of some demented publicist. Maybe Luba and the others had been whisked away to some secret compartment in a geyser of stage blood.

No. No, goddamn it, I knew what I saw, and I knew what I had photographed.

Or perhaps I didn't. There was a picture at the very end of the roll that I didn't remember taking. I saw the tree line outside the Astara mansion, beneath a sky aflame with conflagrant moths. Behind the pines stood a wall of darkness so deep and opaque that it suggested a doorway leading someplace absolutely lightless. The bottom of the ocean floor, perhaps, or the far side of the moon.

Dozens of bare glistening limbs contorted from the darkness, barely visible in the border between the trees and the shadow barrier. A person seeing the picture without any other context might think that it depicted a half-unseen dance or orgy in the woods, although the lack of visible faces gave the scene a chilling ambiguity. I didn't know what I was looking at, but I suspected that my blackout was protecting me from something awful.

I pulled up my email to send a message to Woody, and saw that somehow I'd received more than 200 new messages since the previous night. Sitting at the very top of my inbox was this missive from a person I'd never heard of before:

I don't know who you are to mess with Bebe but you have picked the WRONG FIGHT this time my friend. You have insulted a GODDESS, when you are lower than a crawling WORM. Time for you to die.

The next email read:

I understand that you work for the tabloids, skulking around celebrities and taking their photos without permission. Being a professional sneak sounds like a cushy job. As for myself I have worked in slaughterhouses since I was fourteen. I stand upon the killing floor and doomed cows are brought before me. I put a bolt gun between their trusting brown eyes and knock them unconscious. Then I cut their throats and bleed them out and butcher their meat. I have killed so many cows that my right hand has taken on the shape of a knife hilt. Even when I relax my grip, my fingers want to be holding a blade.

It is hard work and honest, so I do not expect that you would understand it. At the end of my shift I am exhausted and sore, still hearing the shrieks of dying animals. And my beautiful Bebe is always waiting for me in the screen when I get home. She takes me away from the blood and shit and meat and screaming and poverty that I live with every day. She lifts me up and brings me into her land of glamour and wealth and happiness.

Now I hear that you have wronged sweet Bebe. I don't understand what sort of a person could do such a thing. Stay away from Bebe Astara. I have seen the sort of work that you do. Do not make me show you the sort of work that I do.

The one I had after that had no text or subject line at all, just a neck-down picture of a man cradling an AR-15 rifle, and a screenshot of a map to my house. And so on. The occasional death threat is an occupational hazard in my line of work, but I'd never gotten them *en masse* before. Dozens of strangers threatened me with murder and mutilation.

The last email I read was an entreaty from an employee of the central bank of Nigeria, asking my help with a sizeable money transfer. It was nice to hear from one person who wanted to be my friend.

I closed my email and logged on to Twitter, a platform that I lurked on for business purposes but generally didn't use or even think about very much. Sure enough, my name trended behind a hashtag, and my notifications were exploding with an influx of vitriol, outrage and menace, a microblogging lynch mob. Starting to suspect what had happened, I went to Bebe Astara's feed.

The murdering harlot had sent out a hurricane of a tweetstorm against me. It was a cunning blend of half-truths and outright lies, and reading it, I even came close to believing it myself. She claimed that I had invaded her home (mostly true), stolen her food (mostly false), attacked her servants (I'm not entirely sure), damaged her guests' property (true, but under duress), and vandalized a shrine memorializing the dearly departed Conroy Voxel (???). Worst of all, I had dared to violate and pollute the goddess's sanctum with my unworthy tabloid presence, viciously disrespecting Bebe Astara and, by extension, her legions of passionate fans.

It sounds like rather thin stuff when I state it like this. You have to remember that Bebe Astara, as the reigning empress of reality TV, was a towering genius at the dark art of escalating conflict. She knew exactly how to elevate even the pettiest of grievances into captivating, operatic struggles between the forces of good and evil, how to draw on the sympathies and resentments of her audience, how to commit brutal character assassinations without getting a drop of blood on her exquisite outfits. Any fair-minded person reading her diatribe against me would have pegged me as some wretched amalgam of Peeping Tom and Judas Iscariot. And anyone fully initiated into her cult of personality would have pegged me as something far worse, an abomination to be scrubbed from the Earth. Bebe made no overt call to violence, yet it was clear from the way she described me that she considered my very existence an intolerable affront. Like everything

Bebe Astara did online, her rant had gone as viral as the bubonic fucking plague. It had already been re-tweeted tens of thousands of times.

I closed the blinds, double-checked every lock, and then returned to my computer to watch my horrible fifteen minutes of fame unfold. Another 20 threats had accumulated in my inbox already. My jaw dropped when I saw that one of Astara's followers, a creep with a Guy Fawkes mask as his profile picture, had tweeted my bank login information. I hurriedly signed on to change the password. Of course it was already too late. Every cent I had was gone, and my credit cards had been completely maxed out buying in-game currency for *Bebe's World*.

A bracing fury rose up in my heart. This evil, lying, vicious bitch had murdered a bunch of harmless children the night before, and somehow she was making *me* out to be the bad guy? And the brainless, blank-souled bastards behind her... They were going to threaten the life of a person they'd never met, a man who'd never done them any harm whatsoever, just because that reality TV bimbo told them to? No, fuck that shit. I swore to myself that by the time I was done, Bebe Astara would be strapped to a gurney with a needle in her arm, and I'd be so rich from selling the party pictures that I wouldn't even miss the money that'd been stolen, and all the worthless shits who measured their lives by Bebe would realize they'd been following a false idol and fall sick with despair.

I peered out my blinds and saw that Astara's crowdsourced assassins were already starting to arrive. A strange car waited across the street (a shitty car, I might add), its driver sitting behind the wheel. I grinned at my would-be murderer. He had the soft, portly appearance of a man who mostly experiences life through glowing screens. This pork loaf dreamed that he was a match for me?

I slipped on one of my incognito outfits—a grey hoodie, cargo pants, and great big he-hits-me-but-I-know-he-loves-me sunglasses, and pocketed the memory card with the solstice pictures. My BMW was parked in the driveway—a bit dinged and scraped due to my sloppy escape from the party—and I couldn't be sure that I'd reach it before the shooting commenced. Fortunately, my motorcycle was in the attached garage. I hopped on, hit the button of the automatic opener, and roared out from beneath the rising door before it was halfway up. Astara's follower tried to give chase, but I was a speedy, powerful beast piloting a piece of tuned-to-perfection Japanese engineering, and he was a slow and stupid animal behind the wheel of a shitbox. I accelerated through a red light and swerved into traffic amidst a symphony of horns and cursing. A delivery truck t-boned my pursuer as he crossed into the intersection with a satisfying crunch, sending him spinning off into a streetlight.

I was almost to the nearest police station when two horrible thoughts dawned upon me. First, I realized that while Bebe Astara was the person most obviously incriminated by the photos, I was the one who had brought Luba to the party. I had sat by passively taking photographs as she died. I couldn't trust the cops to take my word that I was an innocent party and not a co-conspirator.

Second, I realized that if I gave my photos to the police, my greatest professional accomplishment might be rendered worthless. If the cops released the photos to the public before I sold them I wouldn't be able to make a dime from them, and I had a whole life to rebuild. Those don't come cheap. So instead of going right to the police I pulled a sinister turn and headed for Woody Monroe's place instead. He was the man who'd sent me into that goddamned party to begin with, and he was probably one of the most qualified people on Earth to advise me on a life-threatening social media emergency. God knows he'd provoked enough of them.

I used a Jedi mind trick to slip past the doorman and front desk clerk at Woody's condo building (outwitting doormen and desk clerks is one of the first skills you learn as a paparazzi) and took the elevator up. I found the door to Woody's place slightly ajar. The now-familiar smell of blood wafted through the crack.

Woody sprawled out on his couch, his sightless, filmy eyes fixed on the chandelier. Someone or something had sliced him down the middle, from chin to taint, and then butterflied him and pulled his viscera into a heap. His prized Siamese cats nibbled daintily at it.

I checked Twitter again to see if Bebe had spoken out against him as well as me, silently praying that the police wouldn't choose this moment to arrive. Bebe hadn't said anything about Woody. The virus targeting me still raged, however. Bebe's loyal followers were all busily posting theories as to where I might be. The cute goth barista at the coffee shop had tweeted that I might be in that morning, and Bebe had retweeted the alarm. The place was probably doing a brisk business selling lattes and espressos to my would-be murderers. I wanted back every dollar I'd ever dropped in the tip jar. Another amateur journalist tweeted that my house was now on fire.

As I scrolled through this horrorshow I felt the terrible sensation of being watched by unfriendly eyes, like somebody was hovering right behind me. I spun around, wondering if somebody had followed me inside, or if Woody's killer had never left. Nobody was there…

Then I spotted a hole drilled in the wall, and an eye staring through it at me.

"Hey!" I yelled. The eye vanished. I ran over and peered through the hole. On the other side I saw only L.A. skyline. I realized then that it was an exterior wall, with a sheer 20-story drop on the other side.

I took another look at Twitter. "I see him!" Bebe Astara said, right before she posted the address of Woody's condo.

No more fucking around—it was time for me to get inside a police station. As I ran out the building, I spotted a heavily painted blonde girl aiming her cell phone at me. I paused for a moment—just a goddamn moment—to defiantly flip her the bird, just as so many celebrities had done to me when I was on the other side of the camera. With her free hand, she reached into her purse and produced a handgun. Only at that moment did I realize that the little bitch was live-tweeting my assassination.

My world exploded with a pop, like a bursting balloon.

The next thing I knew, I was staring into a pure, welcoming white light.

Looking into the brilliance stung my eyes, yet I could not look away. I heard incomprehensible whispers and murmurs, and strains of ghostly music. A defeated sense of peace washed over me, along with a perverse pride to have gone down in the line of duty. I tried to move forward towards the light.

And something held me back.

I looked down and realized to my horror that I was not a bodiless soul headed towards salvation. I was naked, strapped down to a granite slab with leather bands around my wrists and ankle and forehead, and an overhead light directly above me producing the illusion of heaven's glow. Sensation slowly began to return to my benumbed flesh. I felt the stony chill of the table underneath me, and the bite of the straps that held me in my place. My captors, master sadists that they were, had left me with just enough slack that I could take in my surroundings. I was back in Bebe Astara's sacrificial chamber.

Behind me, the death machine had been mucked out, cleaned, and polished until it shone. Bebe Astara sat at the foot of the slab, occupied on her phone. "So good to see you again," she said, planting an icy kiss on my cheek. "The last time we didn't get a chance to say goodbye." God, she looked so beautiful. Even under these strange and terrible circumstances, her presence was as electric as a thunderbolt, and almost as devastating.

"What happened?" I asked. "I thought somebody shot me..."

"That's right," she said, returning her attention to her phone. "One of my fans shot you in the head and you died. We brought your body back to my home and made you alive again. I don't see why you people bother with mortality, it's such a nuisance."

"Please let me go," I begged. "Let me go and I'll never tell anyone about any of this. I'll leave L.A. and I'll never take another photo again."

She shook her head. "All this time you've spent following my kind and feeding off our glamour, and you still don't understand the rules. You came to my party of your own free will. You ate my food and drank my wine. Now you can't ever leave again. That's alright, sweetie, I'll make use of you. I need a good photographer."

I felt something wet slither along my cheek. I turned my head and saw a monstrous, catfish-like creature bigger than myself hovering over me. Dozens of barbels dangled from above its wide, lipless mouth, each ending in a different surgical instrument; scalpels made of bone, clamps made of muscle and cartilage, and a terrible assortment of saws and shears and pincers. The creature seemed to grin, its barbels dancing in anticipation.

"He's my personal plastic surgeon," Bebe said. "He'll have to do some work on you before you can serve me." I screamed as the surgeonfish descended on me, but one of the first things he did was slice my vocal cords out.

I was shaved, flayed, castrated, and vivisected. My nervous system was delicately extracted from the red wreckage of my body and placed into a devilish anti-womb of steel and coiled razors where a new form grew into place around it. The surgeonfish placed a mirror so that I could see his handiwork as I emerged from this device, and that was perhaps the cruelest torture he performed.

Now I have enormous, lidless eyes that dominate my transformed face, and my brain has been rewired so that I can never forget anything those ghastly eyes see. I'm still a celebrity photographer of sorts, although I no longer need a camera external to myself. My queen leaves me to scuttle about her court on my seven spindly legs to witness her revels, and if there is any event that she wants to see again a bioelectric light goes on in my head and my recollections project themselves onto the nearest wall.

Every day and every night I see fresh wonders and atrocities that burn themselves into my mind forever, and I think that I will never die.

FLYING MACHINE

AN ENEMY CETADREADNAUGHT SPOTTED ME as I passed through a planetary system somewhere in Ursa Major. The titanic beast waited in ambush on the far side of an icy moon, a deep space picket against my bombing run. It might have been waiting for thousands of years. My crystal antennae sensed my adversary's presence the moment it moved from its hiding spot. A low, eerie keening echoed in my thoughts. The cetadreadnaught's London-sized brain was bringing its psychokinetic artillery to bear. Enormous hunks of the ice moon tore themselves free of the surface and hurtled towards me, shattering into fragments as they passed out of the thin atmosphere. I was flying into a storm of mind-propelled flak.

I cut to the left and punched my thrusters as hard as I dared within a gravity well, dodging the lethal cloud by the tiniest of margins. Another psychic groan sounded and the moon quaked as the cetadreadnaught prepared its second volley. At that same moment, my enemy opened its massive jaws and launched its fighter escort. A swarm of metal wasps.

I knew that if I fought in the open I'd be cut to pieces. Dodging a hail of brilliantly colored fire from the fighters, I cut to the right, diving directly towards the small, rocky planet that the ice moon orbited, and slipped into the planet's orbit, letting it carry me along as if I were swimming with a stream's current. The cetadreadnaught's second volley missed the mark and exploded on the planet's night-shrouded half while I was circling around to its daytime. Vast black clouds billowed across the surface underneath me, and volcanic eruptions burst like machine gun shells as celestial bombardment shivered the planetary core. I'm almost certain that I glimpsed cities falling in that apocalypse.

As I circled the planet, I used the momentum I'd built to slingshot myself directly towards the cetadreadnaught at incredible speed, moving too quickly for its artillery to track or its escorts to intercept. I passed directly beneath the whale-thing's white belly and slashed a deep trench into it with my cutter beam. A waterfall of bright orange blood poured out of the wound, freezing into a gaily colored snowfall when it hit the vacuum's cold. The fighters pursued me for as long as they could, which wasn't long. The cetadreadnaught, however, kept on my tail long after it died. I still felt its psychic death screams echoing inside me as I passed out of the star system. Pain. Confusion. Bewilderment. Things I thought I'd long since left behind.

Needless to say, the experience was a profound shock to my system. My thoughts wandered from my mission, and I found myself doing something that I had not done in a very long time. I began to remember.

I don't recall my name anymore, but I was a major in the No. 3 Squadron of the Royal Flying Corps before the slimy angels came for me.

It began on a routine enough flight, a reconnaissance mission over Loos sighting Hun artillery positions. The German gunners had been feeding our boys a fearful portion of iron rations, and we were very keen to treat them to some of the same. I was piloting a Morane biplane, with Captain Donnely in the observer's seat.

Donnely was a good man. He'd had the benefit of a public school education and helped me write love letters to my Emily, cribbing from Shakespeare and Yeats and donating some verse of his own creation as well. He had a wonderful talent for it. If not for the war I think he might have become a poet.

The day had started out clear and sunny, but during our flight the sky went black as suddenly as if someone had kicked an oilcan over in Heaven. The atmosphere was charged with the electric, oppressive stillness that builds up when a h—l of a storm is brewing.

"I'm turning back," I told Donnely. "Today's no day for flying."

"You're just impatient to answer your lady-love's last letter," Donnely said playfully. "It's bad enough you keep her photograph in your cockpit. You've got to learn to focus. Or come with me to Paris next time we get some leave."

I glanced down to just above my fuel gauge, where Emily's face beamed up at me. "The photograph's good luck, and you can keep your poxy Paris girls! I'll invite you to the wedding after the Kaiser's dead. You can meet my whole family. They won't believe I know how to fly unless I bring a witness."

"Hold on," Donnely said. "We've got company."

I turned and saw a Fokker creeping up from around 2,000 yards and overhauling us fast. Apparently this one was itching for a fight, for the Huns rarely went up in bad weather. As the German reached 200 yards, Donnely took aim with his Lewis gun and fired—alas!—it jammed on the second round. The Fokker returned fire and I went into a dive, while Donnely swore at his Lewis and laboured to clear it. If curses were bullets, he'd have blasted our enemy clear out of the sky.

The Fokker stayed on our tail throughout the dive and came abreast of us as we leveled out. I could see every detail of the enemy machine as it passed by: its undercarriage, the wires along its wings, even the scowl on its pilot's face. He flew ahead of us and cut right, presumably for another pass.

"Is that d—n Lewis gun cleared yet?" I shouted to Donnely.

"It's good!" he replied. "Where's the Hun?"

The enemy had vanished. He wasn't behind us, or above us, or anyplace else within my line of sight. Inky clouds were eclipsing the sun, but visibility wasn't so bad yet that one might lose sight of an enemy who'd just been within spitting range. I began to get nervous, for the very worst thing one can do in a dogfight is lose track of one's opponent.

"Look at that!" Donnely shrieked, pointing his gun upwards. "Gods' wounds, look at—"

Purple light flashed. That's the last thing I remember of that day.

I woke up in a field hospital near the front, naked apart from a rough blanket. I was told that some doughboys had found me wandering nude through a barley field, singing some gibberish even queerer than Flemish. At first they figured me a shellshock case, and they didn't even know I was an aviator till I came to and started talking.

They never found the wreck of my machine. They found the wreck of Donnely, though, in a bog a few miles away from where they found me. The doctor went grey when I asked about him, and any frontline doctor will have seen some terrible sights.

Against doctor's orders I went to the morgue tent to say my goodbyes. Beneath the winding sheet, Donnely looked like a man-shaped candle that had been partially melted. His bones and organs showed through gaping holes in his side. His skin was still white, however, without even a touch of charring, and as far as I could tell he hadn't shed a drop of blood. Whatever had happened to my comrade, judging from the agonized expression on his drooping, boneless face, it looked as if he had felt it intensely. Apparently he had still been breathing when they brought him in.

The incident was written up as a lightning strike. Donnely and I both got medals. He went into a graveyard and I went back to the No. 3 Squadron. Queer as it was, I just couldn't wait to fly again.

By the time I'd returned to active duty, the squadron had gotten a shipment of Sopwith Camels. The Camel was an extraordinary machine, demanding a lot from its pilot and giving even more in return. Getting behind its controls was positively invigorating. When I returned from the hospital I was so pale and underweight that a new officer in the unit thought I'd been held as a prisoner of war. My gait had turned into a shuffle and my voice had developed a stammer. But behind my Camel's stick, I was a hale and ferocious predator. I made twelve confirmed kills in my first month back in the sky. This made me quite the lion around the aerodrome for a week or two, until at the Battle of Messines I shredded a downed German beneath his parachute. Most of my comrades thought that this was a vicious outrage, and I myself would have agreed with them before the crash. They kept a happy distance after that, much to my relief. Ever since that fatal flight over Loos, their company had become nearly intolerable.

Then there was the matter of Emily's letters. I came back from the hospital to a thick sheaf of them, which I regarded with the same pleasure and anticipation as correspondence from a creditor. Before the crash Emily's mail had always been welcome, indeed, one of the few delights available to me on the front. Now reading them was a chore, and responding a draining confusion. Once I spent all night awake in the barracks composing a reply, and in the morning all I had was a long-winded description of an improvement I'd like to make to the Camel's fuel tank to improve its balance on takeoff. Emily sent another photograph to replace the one lost in the crash. I never even considered putting it above my fuel gauge for luck—by then, the notion of burdening my machine with even a photograph's worth of unnecessary weight seemed perverse and absurd. Eventually her letters stopped coming. I tried for days to make myself unhappy about this, with no success.

One day I was flying over enemy lines when I spotted a German observation balloon floating out in the distance. While I had already made a kill that day, and was low on fuel and bullets to boot, the sight of the blimp bobbing clumsily in the wind triggered my murderous instincts and my machine was off in pursuit before the conscious part of my mind even realized what I was doing. My observer—I forget his name, too—shouted in protest behind me. I pushed the engines harder to drown out his yells.

In the trenches below, a battery of German anti-aircraft gunners took aim. White blossoms of cordite and shrapnel exploded all around me like popcorn in the pan, one of them bursting close enough to rattle my machine and set my left ear ringing and maim the observer with shrapnel. I ignored the danger and pressed on with the attack. I raked the blimp with a long burst from my propeller-mounted Vickers guns, shot past the enemy, and pulled an Immelmann turn to make another pass. A cold shadow fell on me, and then I felt a blast like every atom of my being was coming apart. My final thought was a bright, triumphant exultation that I'd hit my target.

I awoke naked on a slab of basalt. I was not visibly fettered, but some force secured my limbs to the rock as if by magnetism. A light that was not light shone down mercilessly from a beacon fixed directly above me. In its uncanny glow I saw clear through my own skin to the muscle and bone and viscera beneath. Not many men can say they've seen themselves flayed. I stared at my blood as it coursed through my veins, and as my horror mounted I watched the pace of my own heartbeat increase.

Something moist and rubbery brushed my cheek, pulling me away from the contemplation of my own guts, and I realized that I was not alone. Three magnificent creatures lurked at my bedside, each of them coated in thick, viscous grease that glistened in the chamber's penetrating light. Imagine a tub of eels moving under the control of a single mind, a mind of exquisite intelligence and self-control. They also sported leathery, bat-like wings in addition to their coils—apparently these creatures were aviators like me. At first I was too astonished and perplexed to even be afraid, and for a very long time we simply stared at each other. Perhaps the fascinated revulsion that I felt was mutual.

One of the winged creatures thrust a tentacle into my mouth—it tasted of brine and copper—and I gagged and struggled helplessly as the wormy thing slowly forced its way down my throat and deep into my chest. I thought I would suffocate but my chest kept rising and falling, and I realized that the creature was breathing for me. I could see its limb pulsing inside my chest, making my lungs inflate and deflate. Two more tentacles danced inches in front of my eyes. They ended in sucking mouths rimmed with dozens of tiny, needle-like teeth, like the mouths of lampreys, and I'd have screamed if not for the fleshy tube in my windpipe.

The mouths moved in and my world went black, which was almost worse than seeing what was happening to me. My eyes prickled as the lamprey teeth closed on them, and then my monstrous surgeon began to suck.

The last sensation I experienced before losing consciousness—besides an astoundingly intense and varied agony—was the sound of a wet, glottal, rhythmic clicking. I think that was the creatures' laughter.

My awakening was a gradual series of still images, like a magic lantern show.

I saw a formation of spiky crystals glowing and humming inside a darkened chamber.

I saw a clear blue sky with a German Albatross passing through it.

I saw the dim interior of an ambulance loaded with dead and dying men. Delicate beams of light shone through a row of bullet holes in the vehicle's side.

I saw a yellow, flyblown plaster wall streaked with grease.

I saw a dead boy in an adjacent bed.

I saw a man with no face crouching at my side, like a mannequin from a department store window given some hideous parody of life. He wore a white coat spattered with blood.

"It's all right," the faceless thing said, its voice a faint, mechanical hiss, like somebody had made a phonograph recording off another phonograph recording. "You're safe. You're at a military hospital.

Your airplane crashed. Do you remember?" When the creature sat on my bedside, giddiness overcame me and I slipped back into oblivion.

When I awoke, I was alone in my room. I rose and staggered to the mirror, but when I looked at myself, I saw only a pink, empty blur. I ran my fingers across the space where I knew my features should be. I felt eyes, a nose, a mouth, seemingly undamaged beneath my fingertips even though they were invisible in the glass. There was no pain. No physical pain, anyway. But I could not perceive my own features anymore. I could not even remember what they looked like.

I tried to recall the faces of other people that I used to know. My father. My mother. My sister. Emily. Donnely. Nothing. At most I called up a vague but frustrated recollection, like when you try to remember the words to some old song and they're on the tip of your tongue but won't come any further.

I groped deeper into my memories and realized that more than just faces had gone. I couldn't remember any of my Christmas mornings, or how my mother's cooking used to taste. I wasn't positive that I'd ever had a mother. I couldn't remember the first time I'd kissed Emily, or indeed, if I'd ever kissed her at all. Everything I'd gone to war to defend was lost to me. In the mirror, fat droplets of water beaded and slipped down the blank space where my face had been. That was the last time I ever cried.

But at least I still recalled how to swing a propeller, and how a Camel turns faster to the right than to the left, and how good it felt to shoot that German under his parachute. As I returned to my bed, I consoled myself with the notion that even if I had lost everything that I was, at least I seemed to be becoming something else.

Empty-faced doctor-puppets and nurse-puppets intruded on me throughout the day, poking and prodding and shining lights. I endured them as best I could, even though they reminded me of the operating chamber where I'd been obliterated. When I had peace from those white-robed monsters, I lay in bed and stared at the peeling paint on the ceiling and thought about what to do next. It was easy to decide. I kept staring at the ceiling until late into the night, after the other puppets would mostly be asleep, and then I knotted my bedclothes into a rope and climbed out the window and ran.

My bare feet wept blood by the time I got out of town. I was almost ready to fall down at the roadside and die when I heard the chuffing of a struggling motor from up ahead. I forced myself onward, and found a faceless thing in khaki fighting with a motorbike engine. It had a mail sack with it, so I guessed it to be a courier. It didn't particularly matter what it was. All that counted was that it had clothes and a vehicle that could get me where I needed to go. When it saw me coming it waved and buzzed a greeting at me. I caught it by surprise and strangled it, then stripped it of its uniform and hid its body and mail pouch in the reeds at the side of the road.

Fixing the bike was easy and I rode all night and most of the following day without stopping, pushing the engine as hard as it would bear. It wasn't as satisfying as being airborne, but anything's better than going on foot like an animal. The motorbike's gas tank eventually ran dry. I flagged down the next vehicle to roll past—a fuel lorry—and blew the driver's brains out with a pistol I'd taken off the courier.

Even though I couldn't remember what my own face looked like, my sense of direction was still clear and sharp, and I made it to the Saint-Omer aerodrome early in the morning. It had been almost 48 hours since I'd come to in the hospital, yet I didn't feel sleepy at all. Quite the opposite. My senses buzzed with an electric intensity, as if all the things I'd lost the capacity to perceive had freed up mental horsepower for the tasks that still mattered. The day was so cold and crisp it felt like the air itself had turned to razors. Some cloud cover but good visibility. Steady barometric pressure, light southwesterly winds. Good day for a flight.

A fuel lorry is no unusual sight at an airfield, not even early in the morning, and I made it past the guard hut without complications, then abandoned the lorry and made for the hangars, reaching them without being seen. I chose a Sopwith and took her up. As I lifted off, I heard some excited buzzing and a few scattered gunshots. I suppose that by that point somebody had noticed the lorry driver stealing a biplane. It didn't matter, I couldn't be bothered with that noise at the moment of my ascension. By the time they got pursuers airborne, I'd already be gone. I didn't know exactly what I was pursuing myself, but I felt that it was very near. I pulled back on the stick and ascended as sharply as my Camel could handle without stalling, coaxing all the power I could muster out of her Clerget engines.

They were waiting for me when I passed through the clouds. I caught a glimpse of a gleaming black sphere floating above me like an obsidian sun and then everything flashed and I was in the operating theater once more, naked and spread-eagle and trembling with joyous anticipation. As the winged creatures circled in and caressed me, I finally saw them for what they are. Angels. Slimy angels from another world.

At this final surgery, the angels removed my brain from my body entirely and put it into a magnificent machine that I still barely comprehend even though I am a part of it. They aimed me towards a target a billion miles distant and fired me off at speeds beyond reckoning. My destination is a star orbited by a dozen populated worlds. When I penetrate the heart of that star, the payload of my machine will explode and the star will flare. I will burn an entire civilization of strange beings to cinders in one glorious phoenix blast.

I've flown so far and learned so much. Now I know that Britannia and the Reich are as puny and meaningless as two anthills warring at the bottom of a bomb crater. Once you've seen sentient death engines wiping whole worlds clean of life, you see all that talk about "war to end all war" as the pompous rubbish that it is. I fly through an infinite panorama of cosmic violence, a weapon in a conflict that has raged since my first ancestors oozed forth from the slime.

It is hard to gauge the passage of time when one does not eat or sleep or breathe, and when the stars flash by in strobes rather than slowly revolving from day to night. There are clocks of sorts in the angels' machine, but they tell time so differently than humans do. I am reasonably sure that if the human race still exists at all, the bones of everyone I used to know have long since turned to dust. Men plan their sorties in terms of hours; the angels plan theirs in terms of aeons.

I do not know why this war is being fought—I doubt that I could understand its cause any more than those two enemy anthills could understand "making the world safe for democracy." Perhaps there is no reason why. Perhaps the war is its own reason. But I fly, and I fight, and I am happy now.

PIGMAN

MY NAME IS JASON ZUCKERMAN and I am being held captive by the art-terrorist Pigman, in an abandoned subway tunnel somewhere far beneath the streets of New York. He's let me keep my cell phone but of course there's no signal down here so I can't call for help. All I can do is record a voice memo like a castaway stuffing a note into a glass bottle. The battery's almost dead, and so am I.

I don't know where else to start except at the very beginning, with that first Pigman attack on the Boston T. We all remember where we were when we first heard about that, terrorist strikes are the only shared experiences we have anymore. I was day-drinking Manhattans and hiding from my own life at an uptown bar when a special report interrupted the ball game in progress. A grim-faced newsman warned that the CCTV footage we were about to see would be too shocking for some viewers.

Together with a worldwide audience, I watched in slack-jawed horror as a man in a jolly cartoon pig mask and a yellow rain slicker opened fire on a subway platform full of commuters. The slaughter was pitiless, stomach-churning. And then, when the platform was empty except for Pigman and his dead and dying victims, he took out a pre-cut cardboard template and a can of spray paint from beneath his rubber coat, and he painted a mural on the blood-spattered tile walls.

Before Pigman vanished back into the tunnels, he created a work of breathtaking beauty, monstrosity, and originality, a pitch-black satire of modern life at its most curdled and banal. It reminded me of *Guernica*, except drawn from the point-of-view of the fascist bomber pilots, with a merciless wit that looked human suffering dead in the eye and proclaimed it hilarious. Either the massacre or the mural would have captured the public's eye in isolation, but together they were a Medusa that few could turn away from. As a human being I was outraged and heartbroken, but as a professional art dealer I couldn't help but wonder at this puckish mass murderer's talent. His seemingly impossible escape from the police only heightened his terrible mystique.

My divorce from Marianne was finalized about that time. I kept the art gallery we'd built together, but she got custody of most of our money and most of our friends. I threw myself into my work to distract myself, but around that time the entire art world seemed to suffer from a collective fallow period. Perhaps there's only a finite amount of genius in the world, and Pigman was hogging it for himself. Perhaps nobody else dared to create when he was on the scene. The dwarves all hide when the giant emerges, that they not be shamed by his presence. Either way, it was maddening. I was going crazy with boredom peddling mediocrities to the one percent of the one percent. Pigman killed dozens in a gas attack on the Tokyo subway and painted mordantly gleeful critiques of modern capitalism over the ads on the walls while his victims choked and burned around him. I searched in vain for new artists possessing even a spark of audacity. Pigman sewed up a live rat in some poor girl's belly and left her on the Paris Metro, beneath his exquisite, tenderly blasphemous *Pieta*.

Even though the politicians swore bloody vengeance against Pigman and anyone who aided him, it was an open secret in the elite art world that Pigman originals were available for sale via select black channels. Anyone caught trafficking with the terrorist would, of course, face life-destroying punishment, but in certain circles this only enhanced the work's appeal.

I first saw a Pigman original in September. I was at a gallery show in Greenwich Village, checking up on my competition and feeling some healthy *schadenfreude* at the realization they weren't doing any better than I was. The official theme of the show was "Art in an Aeon of Terror," and the unofficial theme was "Trying to Ape Pigman Without the Vision or Talent." I was surrounded by pieces that tried to capture the *avant-garde* terrorist's psychopathic, darkly comic worldview, but succeeded only at invoking ennui and nausea.

"Pathetic, isn't it?" mused a financier friend and client of mine as we sipped mass-produced wine poured from vintage bottles and examined a puerile photograph of pregnant women in slaughterhouse battery cages. I won't use my friend's real name, but let's call him Medici. "If I wanted to buy derivatives I'd talk to my broker, not my art dealer," he said.

"What else can you expect when the whole world goes crazy over one man?" I asked. "There's only one Pigman. There's six billion people who are terrified and inspired by him. That's how you get this." I gestured at the gallery walls and shrugged.

"Not me," Medici said. He grinned conspiratorially and leaned in close enough to whisper in my ear. "I have a Pigman original. A sculpture."

I convinced Medici to let me see his prize by nakedly appealing to his pride while subtly insisting that he couldn't own what he claimed. You have to know how to play off the insecurities of the well-to-do in order to make it in my line of work. We took a car to his Park Avenue penthouse. The ride over was an exercise in restraint, my least favorite form of exercise by far. I wanted to ask a thousand questions, but didn't dare to for fear that the driver might overhear and report us to the police. For all I knew, he might even have lost someone in a Pigman attack.

"I keep it in its own room, for obvious reasons," Medici said, as he escorted me through his palatial quarters. "I call it the Bluebeard room. The cleaning staff aren't allowed inside, my girlfriends aren't allowed inside...this is only for me and the few friends who can appreciate it. I hope you realize what a compliment it is that I'm letting you take a peek." I surely did.

The Bluebeard room lay behind a triple-locked steel door requiring a key, a numeric code, and the retinal pattern of Medici's left eye to open. The sculpture inside had originally been a playground statue of Ronald McDonald sitting on a bench with his legs crossed, but Pigman had repainted every inch of it, adding such detail and dynamism that the figure looked as if it might rise from its seat at any moment. He had transformed the clown's yellow-and-gold jumpsuit into a purple robe emblazoned with dozens of kabbalistic symbols that seared my eyes like lightning. Looking closer, I saw that each of these symbols was a corporate logo that Pigman had subtly but powerfully altered. It was as if the artist had set out to show that the trademarks we wear on our clothes and print on our billboards are symbols of profound demonic power, the true names of mighty inhuman intelligences cunningly camouflaged as inoffensive swooshes and mermaids. I hadn't seen such a bold re-appropriation of corporate iconography since Warhol, but Andy's soup cans had none of this pagan intensity.

But the sculpture's crowning glory was its face, or lack thereof. The clown had removed his smiling visage like a mask, letting it dangle from his fingertips, and in the exposed space normally concealed by a frozen grin, Pigman had carved a surrealistic Hell rivaling anything by Bosch or Dali. Tiny, intricately crafted men, women, and children shrieked in agony as diabolical torture engines within the clown's skull processed and punished them. I saw a crow-beast in a miter pecking at a basket of babies and shitting out segmented larvae with suffering human faces. I saw a ring of doomed men gnawing at each other's entrails in a cannibalistic *ouroboros*. I saw horrors with no analogue or precedent, which I cannot even find words to describe. And yet this display of cosmic cruelty evoked no pity whatsoever. Instead, I felt like an angry God on the Day of Judgment, beholding the justly deserved torments of the damned. To my dismay, I realized that I had an erection. The first in a long time, actually.

"It's called *The Warlock*," Medici said proudly. "What do you think?"

"I think it's one of the greatest works of art I've ever seen," I said, honestly. "There's no disputing its provenance. Only Pigman could have made this. I need to know how much you paid for it, and who you got it from."

Medici told me the sum he'd paid for *The Warlock*, and it shocked me almost as much as *The Warlock* itself had. To Medici it was just his annual bonus, but to me it represented a lifetime of ease and luxury. Several lifetimes of ease and luxury, actually.

Then Medici told me the name of the person he'd bought *The Warlock* from, and it stunned me like a knock from a bolt gun. He'd purchased this astronomically costly, extraordinarily contraband masterpiece from my ex-wife, Marianne.

I spent the next week or so even more depressed than usual. After Marianne cheated on me with that bitch from her yoga class, whatever masculine pride I still possessed was wrapped up in the knowledge that at least I was better at the business than she was. I was the hard worker, the man of taste and knowledge, whereas she'd coasted through life on the not-inconsiderable triumvirate of charm, good looks, and connections. Now even that consolation had crumbled. *The Warlock* emerged from the rubble of my self-esteem, gleaming like an idol. I needed a taste of that terrible glory for myself. I needed to meet Pigman.

Marianne's gallery was not far from mine as a matter of physical distance, but it felt like she was in another city. She'd always preferred a touch of grit (but only a touch!) to the faerie glamour of the art world, and now she was working out of a tiny office nestled away on a grimy side street, a tumorous little bubble of *Taxi Driver*-era New York that had somehow survived Giuliani and gentrification. Her door had been vandalized, marked with an "X" in drippy crimson spray paint. It reminded me of the dour Passover seders of my boyhood, and the ancient Hebrews splashing their gates with the blood of the sacrificial lamb. I knocked on the marked door, and it slowly swung open. The lights were off, but I thought I heard footsteps. "Marianne?" I asked as I stepped across the threshold. "Is that you?" Something clicked in the shadows. I turned and saw Marianne pointing a snub-nosed revolver at me.

"Wait, it's me!" I said, throwing my hands up. "Don't shoot!" Our divorce hadn't been *that* ugly.

Marianne didn't pull the trigger, but she didn't lower the gun, either. I couldn't stop looking down the black hole of the barrel. My heart was hammering against my ribs, producing that unpleasant *thump-thump-thump* you get when you overdo it at a coke party. "Jason?" she asked. "Is that you?"

"Of course it's me. Just look at my face."

"Your face means nothing!" Marianne raved. "Flesh melts and reforms like wax in the light of the black candle. Prove to me that you're Jason! What was our anniversary?"

"It was October...October... Oh, I can't remember when you're waving a gun in my face!" Honestly, I wouldn't have been able to remember without the gun, either. "Your cat's name is Chairman Meow!" I blathered. "Your favorite food is dry pepper tofu from that Szechuan place on Lafayette Street! Your favorite season is fall, except that the leaves changing colors makes you sad."

Marianne lowered her weapon, although she still did not put it down. "What are you here for?" she asked accusingly.

"I've seen *The Warlock*. I know you've got an arrangement with Pigman. I want in. I want to know how you contact him. I'll give you a cut. Please...for old times' sake, baby."

She tittered in a shrill, high-pitched key that set my teeth on edge, totally unlike her usual hearty guffaw. "For old times' sake, huh? Were the old times that bad, Jason? Do I really hate you that much? I think...yes, I do. Go to the intersection of Avenue B and 4th Street. There's a subway grate there—drop a message through the slots and Pigman will hear it. A real magic wishing well..."

I rushed out of there—never turning my back on Marianne for an instant—and sprinted straightaway to the crossroads she'd named. Finding the "wishing well" was no trouble at all. A graffiti artist had painted curled red lips and dagger-like yellow teeth on the pavement around the grate, giving it the appearance of a hellish open mouth. I knelt down and inserted my business card through the grating. It fluttered into the abyssal darkness until it disappeared from my sight, like a butterfly descending into the netherworld. I thought that I caught a glimpse of something moving at the bottom of the inky pit, but that could have been my nerves.

My anxieties nearly strangled me the first day after I reached out to Pigman. Every movement made me jump. Every person on the street looked like an undercover policeman. I stayed inside my apartment and chain-smoked, unable to concentrate long enough to handle anything more challenging.

On the second day, I was stricken with terrible remorse. What was I doing, bringing a terrorist like Pigman into my life? It wasn't too late to call the FBI then. I hadn't really done anything bad yet—if I told them what I knew they'd surely let me go. Maybe. I dialed the tip line number into my phone and stared at the digits. I never made the call.

On the third day, I convinced myself that Marianne was fucking with me. A prank like this was right up her alley, she loved watching me chase my own tail.

On the fourth and fifth days, I returned my attentions to the gallery. I cleared my head by throwing a damnably satisfying tirade at the assistant who'd been running the place in my absence, and threw myself back into the work, only occasionally distracted by apprehensions of looming dread.

On the sixth day, my awful prayer was finally answered. When I came to open the gallery that morning, I found a package waiting for me in the foyer, a battered, grease-stained cardboard box about a foot square. The outer door was locked, so the deliveryman couldn't have left it, and yet there were no signs of tampering or forced entry. My name and address were written on the side in big, bold lettering. In the space for the return address, it said only "Pigman," in the distinctive hand that had terrorized the globe. There was no postmark except for a few smudged brown fingerprints.

My heart hammered at the same fast, insistent tempo as when Marianne had held a gun on me. I felt a special thrill of horror when I realized that any passerby could have looked through the glass door and seen the package that had been lying there for who knows how long. I locked the entrance behind me and hustled the box into the privacy of my office. I must have spent an hour just staring at it, trying to convince myself not to open the evil thing. Of course, I failed.

Inside was a dead infant, clammy and blue-grey, coated with a sheen of sharp-smelling preservative slime. A deep knife wound vertically split its torso. Before my eyes, the tiny corpse began to tremble as if suffering from a post-mortem seizure, and cried out a terrible noise like a locust swarm's drone. I don't mind admitting that I screamed. Anyone would have.

When I regained control over myself, I realized that the dead creature in the box was not a human infant, but rather a fetal pig. It was vibrating and chirping, but I thought that I understood the reason why. I thought that I knew what was expected of me. I gingerly reached into the wound in the piglet's chest and pulled out a cheap throwaway cellphone wrapped in a plastic baggie. The phone was still ringing. Caller unknown.

"Hello?" I answered.

"Hello up there," replied a crackling, inhuman voice, electronically distorted to the point where it could barely be recognized as speech. "Am I speaking with Jason Zuckerman?"

"You are. Am I speaking with Pigman?"

"Perhaps. Why do you seek Pigman?"

I swallowed hard. "I believe in your work," I said. "I want to help you sell it. Paintings and sculptures and things of that sort. Not your...conceptual art."

The phone let out a piercing electronic hiss as Pigman laughed. "Come to the 51st Street Station right now," he said. "I'll call you on this phone when you get there." With that, he hung up.

I put the burner in my pocket and was about to head out the door when I realized that I still had the package with the dead piglet to deal with. On the one hand, it smelled horrible and constituted evidence that I'd been communicating with a terrorist mastermind. On the other hand, this grisly parody of man's love affair with the cellular phone was itself a priceless work of art by Pigman, and I didn't feel comfortable destroying it. I decided to stuff the thing into my office fridge until I could decide what to do with it. I took one last look at the little body before I put it away. By now I was positive that it was not a human infant, but I was less and less convinced of my hypothesis that it was a fetal pig. I'm certainly not a farmer, mind you, but the proportions of the limbs seemed all wrong, and they ended in paw-like things that were neither hooves nor hands. Perhaps he'd sewn this prodigy together from parts, like Barnum's Fiji Mermaid. I didn't have time to figure it out. I left the little corpse next to a quinoa salad I'd never eat and taped a "STAY OUT" note illustrated with skull and crossbones to the door. Then I was off like a shot to 51st Street.

The moment I reached the station entrance, the burner in my pocket buzzed like an angry, stinging insect. My heart fluttered when I realized that Pigman was watching me at that very moment. I glanced around to see if I could spot him anywhere, but the New York streets were bustling with the usual throngs of humanity. If the artist was out here, he had camouflaged himself in the crowd.

"Go onto the platform for an uptown E train," he told me brusquely. "Wait until the next train has passed, then hop down onto the tracks and take a left into the tunnel. Be careful not to touch the rail. Thirty paces ahead, there'll be a maintenance door on your left-hand side. Walk through it. Now repeat everything I just told you. You won't get reception in the tunnel." I complied. "Good boy. I'll see you soon, Jason." With that, the line went dead.

As the turnstiles shut behind me and I descended the long, steep stairs to the E uptown platform, I was nearly overwhelmed by dread and excitement. I was on an adventure into the underworld, and I knew that whatever I found there would make my fortune or destroy me.

The platform was largely deserted. Nobody uses the subway anymore if they can avoid it. I meandered into the corner near the tunnel entrance, where I watched the E train come roaring into the station, disgorge a few passengers, and then depart towards Jamaica Plains. I scanned the station to see if anyone was watching me, and then hopped down onto the tracks and started walking. If anyone saw something, they said nothing. That's the lonely beauty of New York. It's a city of 8 million invisible people.

The maintenance door was right where Pigman promised, lit up by a sputtering sodium light. Someone had torn the lock from the door. The vandal hadn't been subtle about it, either, it looked like a clawed hand had gouged the mechanism directly out of the steel. An awful stench wafted out through that hole, a bouquet of rotten flesh, sharp-smelling piss, and stale smoke. I pushed the door open and stepped through into fetid darkness.

By the light of my cellphone's flashlight, I saw that I was in a small utility room, where wormy cables snaked all along the walls and meters of indeterminate purpose hummed and clicked. There was nobody else inside, and no exit other than the way I'd come in. Just then, a terrible shriek of metal-on-metal sounded from the tunnel, rattling me right down to the marrow of my bones. I yelped with surprise, and my phone clattered out of my nerveless fingers to the ground, plunging me back into total darkness. A train passed by in the tunnel. "Easy there, Jason," I told myself as I got down onto my hands and knees and groped in the blackness for my phone. I'd never been under the illusion that I was a particularly brave man, but I was nonetheless surprised by how badly my hands trembled. Even once I'd felt the gadget out, it took me a few moments to successfully pick it up and light the room again. And then I saw that I was not alone anymore.

Three ragged figures draped in stark shadows loomed over me in the gloom, as if I had stepped out of the real world and into some German expressionist nightmare. Each of the intruders wore astonishingly lifelike monster masks, rubbery horrors that looked like some abominable combination of a swine and a man. They dressed in homeless chic, wearing many layers of soiled, mismatched clothing, and the same decaying stench that I'd noticed earlier pulsed off them in a choking fog. Their sinuous movements were totally inhuman, as if they were animals used to traveling on four legs who were experimenting with bipedalism, and their bulky rags made their bodies seem hunchbacked and misshapen. They must have been trained mimes. I tell that to myself over and over again. They were mimes wearing monster masks. They cannot have been anything else. No matter how hideously expressive and animated their faces appeared, no matter how bestial the noises they made, they were just mimes in masks. I have to keep believing that or else I'll go crazy. One of them carried an AK-47 slung across his chest.

I stammered something about Pigman having sent for me, but without a word the mimes seized me and dragged me away, hauling me out of the utility room through a hole in the wall I hadn't seen when I'd entered, a space where the cinder blocks had been loosened and pulled out of place. That hole was so small and narrow that I could barely squeeze through it even on my hands and knees, but the mimes navigated it without any difficulty, crawling as dexterously as rats.

My captors let me hold onto my cell phone, at least, so I had a little bit of light during our journey. If not for that light I might have lost my mind entirely. The secret opening through the cinder blocks led to a rocky, meandering tunnel that I'm sure the transit authority didn't dig. It was far too cramped to stand, so I had to navigate the space by painfully crawling along on all fours. The rough-hewn walls were decorated with crude, brilliantly colored paintings that reminded me of the cave art at Lascaux, except that while animals like stags, horses, and bison gamboled in the Paleolithic cavern, in this place, obscene and hideous figures that I can only describe as demons held sway. Faceless, bat-winged beings swooped and danced amongst six-pointed stars, unpleasant fishy things kowtowed before alien dragons, inky tendrils of living darkness crept out of cracks and ratholes, and ghouls sickeningly similar to my captors feasted on human flesh. As at Lascaux, the art in this tunnel gave the viewer a thrill of primal vibrancy and almost unimaginable antiquity, yet there were works of more recent vintage as well. Here and there alongside the charcoal-and-ochre daubings I spotted spray-painted graffiti in Pigman's hand, as well as a few prototypes of his infamous signature. The great artist had learned his craft right here, in this reeking dungeon.

I soon understood that this was not merely a tunnel, but rather an underground network honeycombing deep into the bowels of the earth. It forked time and again, and I quickly lost all sense of direction. Occasionally awful howls or whispers of unearthly music echoed from the mouth of a tunnel as we passed by, or the deep darkness beyond my flashlight's glow flickered with a glimmer of light from some abyssal bonfire. Shrill cries sounded from somewhere within the maze and cut short with a pained squawk.

We crawled through those caves for God knows how long and emerged into a long-disused subway tunnel. Pigman had illustrated almost every inch of the crumbling tile walls with his beautiful, alarming graffiti. A subway car of a vintage that was quaintly old-fashioned when I was a child sat on the defunct tracks, caked in rust, with cables running off it into the wall. The car's windows were blacked over, but I spotted light shining from between the cracks. The mimes ushered me inside.

The moment I crossed the threshold, I was blasted by excruciating radiance. As my eyes slowly adjusted, I realized that there were large-screen monitors hung all along the sides of the train car. After all that time in deep darkness with only my cell phone for light, the screens overloaded my senses. They displayed a tumultuous mix of celebrity gossip shows, jihadist beheading videos, shoot 'em up Hollywood action, art house obscurities, children's cartoons, hardcore pornography, advertisements, snuff films, televangelists, test patterns, and more. So many talking heads saying nothing. So many naked, brutalized bodies. I wondered about what would happen if a child grew up in a pit like this, with only these screens as a window on the world above. I wondered if such a child would grow up with a sensibility like Pigman's.

The train's seats had all been torn out, and the floors were buried beneath a litter of empty spray cans, broken craft knives, and other such artistic debris. An X-shaped bondage cross loomed ominously at the far end of the train, the only furniture in sight apart from a wheeled stool. Marianne had strapped me into a similar number a lifetime ago, after the couples therapist said we should try to vary things up in the bedroom. The mimes secured me to the cross and then vanished as swiftly and silently as shadows, leaving me alone with the screens and my murderous anxiety.

I must have blacked out, but I was awoken by the sound of incoming footsteps. That's when I realized I was in the presence of the artist as last.

Pigman was shorter than he'd appeared on TV. He wore his trademark costume, the yellow rain slicker with the hood pulled up over his head, and the infamous cartoon pig mask. I stared slack-jawed at the inexpressive eyes and pink cheeks and cheery smile that had appeared in so many wanted posters and so many nightmares. Without a word he approached me, moving with the same alien, shambling-yet-graceful gait as his mimes, and took a seat on the stool.

"Pigman!" I cried. "I'm Jason! Jason Zuckerman! I want to help you."

Pigman chuckled, a sound like a motor turning over with a hand stuck in the gears. "Lucky me," he said. His voice is raspy and guttural, with a hissing speech impediment that I think comes from a cleft palate or some other deformity of the mouth. When we'd talked on the phone, I'd thought his voice was garbled by electronics, but now I understand that's just how he talks. Pigman produced a well-used folding knife and opened it, showing me the serrated blade. "I accept your offer."

"Please, no!" I screamed, but I had no real hope he'd listen. The moment one believes one's own death to be at hand is a singularly intense point in time. The experience of my final extremity was extraordinarily vivid, as pure and unforgiving as diamond. Every sensation was magnified unbearably, every nerve seemed to be firing at maximum intensity. I fixed my eyes on the ceiling, the same way that I do when a doctor is about to give me a shot, and waited for agony. And yet it did not come. I looked down to see what my captor was doing to me. He wasn't cutting into my flesh, but he was slicing my clothes away. I'd anticipated my murder just seconds ago, and somehow my situation was getting even worse. Every muscle in my body clenched painfully, and I involuntarily let out a squeal.

"Oh, don't whimper," he snarled. "You must have known that seeking me out was a bad idea. What are you, a moron?"

"I wanted to find you because I believe in your art!" I sobbed. "I think you're a genius and I want to be a part of what you do!"

Pigman stared into me, and I shriveled beneath his gaze. The eyeholes of his mask were twin pits into an absolute and all-devouring dark, like the barrel of Marianne's gun. "You are a moron," he said, his mangled voice dripping with contempt. "You...*things*...don't know what genius is. You don't even know where you stand on the food chain. I watch you from below and see you doing everything wrong. It drives me mad how little you understand yourselves, how little you know about what life is. I create my art to show you doomed creatures what you are and what sort of world you exist in."

"I know," I said. "That's why I love it."

He cocked his head and paused a moment. I think my response surprised him. "Very well," he said, and he laughed that terrible laugh again. "The one redeeming value you creatures have is your appetite for self-destruction." The artist rummaged through the supplies haphazardly scattered on the floor of the subway car and produced an antique tattoo gun freckled with rust. He carefully examined my body like a painter examining his canvas, and then he began to work. His needle pinched like a bee that could keep stinging and stinging forever and not die.

I watched in agony and fascination as Pigman began to create his latest masterpiece directly onto my living skin. It's a playful, pop culture take on the apocalypse. Celebrities, politicians, cartoon characters, religious icons, sports heroes, superheroes, and historical figures all suffer the agonies of the damned in the ghastly tableau that's taking form on my torso, facing a day of judgment where everyone is guilty and existence itself is a crime to be punished without mercy. In my own flesh, I see civilization's abject implosion, mass slaughter, and the collapse of all values save hunger, pain, and lust. And yet I cannot help but admire its twisted loveliness, and giggle at its box cutter-sharp wit.

Pigman works on me for hours a day, and when he gets tired the mimes come and throw me into a cell that I think used to be a maintenance storeroom. They give me meat to eat—I choke it down and obsess over what animal it might have come from. And they let me keep my phone. They might as well; with no signal there's nothing useful I can do with it except distract myself by telling my own damned story.

My tattoos are beautiful, but they're getting badly infected and I feel very sick. I've been vomiting. I sweat all the time. I think I might be hallucinating, but given how fucked my reality is it's impossible to tell anymore. Is there a word for the opposite of lucid dreaming? A word for the horror a dreamer experiences when his feverish nightmares take control of his waking life?

I suspect that the infection is an intentional, even integral, part of the artwork. Pigman uses inks that he blends himself and I don't know what's in them. Just a few days ago I thought that his use of color was unusually restrained, but now that my skin's gone livid and blossomed with pustules the linework pops against its background and I finally see what he was going for.

I only want—oh no, they're back, I...

―――

This message was found on the smartphone of Jason Zuckerman, 42, owner of New York City's prestigious Zuckerman Gallery. A week after Zuckerman's disappearance was reported, the police found him in the Cortlandt Street subway station, crucified and mutilated. His phone had been left on a nearby bench, presumably with the intent that his account of his encounters with Pigman be found. Zuckerman was alive, but was suffering from intense fever, delirium, and respiratory distress. He was rushed to New York-Presbyterian Hospital and died three days later without regaining the ability to communicate.

Tests revealed that Zuckerman was infected with a heretofore unknown and extraordinarily contagious strain of swine flu. Doctors placed Zuckerman into a biosafety laboratory as soon as they realized the cause of his illness, but by then the infection had already spread to a number of the first responders and medical personnel who had been in contact with him, as well as their family members. The death toll now stands in the thousands, and is expected to climb far higher. There is no known cure or vaccine.

Authorities repeat their urgent request that anyone with information about Pigman call the FBI hotline immediately.

PATENT FOR AN ARTIFICIAL UTERUS

JANUARY 30, 1952

Dear U.S. Patent Office,

Enclosed please find a copy of my application for a patent for an artificial uterus, together with accompanying diagrams. I've filled out all the forms to the best of my ability, but since I'm operating without the benefit of legal counsel, I felt that it would be best to explain my invention in plain English as well. I hope that my lack of sophistication will not be held against me. I may be a self-taught "gentleman scholar" working out of my own home, but I've put an awful lot of my sweat, blood, and tears into this device, and I daresay that it will revolutionize society.

The fundamental purpose of my invention is to provide nourishment and oxygen to a fetus, in a manner similar to that employed by a mother's uterus. While this may sound like science fiction, it is based on well-established principles. A growing fetus needs constant temperature, circulating blood, oxygen, nutrition, and the elimination of waste products. Each of these functions can be performed mechanically, through the use of common devices such as incubators, blood pumps, iron lungs, intravenous feeding, and dialysis machines. My invention combines all of these parts into a system that will allow a fetus to live and grow outside of a human body until it develops to viability.

First, the fetus is surgically removed from its mother's body with the umbilical cord and placenta intact. The fetus is then placed into an airtight glass container full of water, which is maintained at body temperature by means of an electric heater and thermostat. The placenta goes into a separate compartment mounted directly above the fetal container, where it is secured to a plate by sutures looped through stainless steel eyelets to keep it from sliding around.

The placental compartment must be kept flooded with pure, nutrient-rich blood at all times. A pump maintains circulation by sending blood over the placenta through a flexible pipe. Once the blood has passed over the placenta, a secondary pump then passes it through an artificial kidney for dialysis. The kidney delivers the blood into a lower chamber where it is oxygenated and enriched with liquid nutrients. After the blood—now purified, oxygenated, and nutrient-rich—is pumped through a filter to eliminate clots, it is then piped back to the first blood pump for recirculation over the placenta. Once the fetus has grown to a sufficient size and weight that it can survive independently, the fetal chamber is drained, the umbilical cord is cut, the fetus is removed from the chamber, the pumps are stopped, and the placenta is removed and destroyed. Simplicity itself.

The benefits of such a device are obvious. We all know that some women simply don't have the vitality to maintain a pregnancy for a full nine months, and my invention will protect their babies from the consequences of their mothers' fragility. Moreover, the fetuses of women with slatternly and unhealthful habits (alcohol drinking, cigarette smoking, promiscuity, marijuana usage, poor hygiene, etc.) will surely reap a great benefit from being transferred into a clean, controlled environment of sterilized rubber and metal. The social worker will no longer be forced to watch impotently as the most helpless amongst us are damned to lifetimes of ill health and imbecility before they are even born, but rather will be able to intervene *in utero*. Having grown up in an institution for orphaned and abandoned boys, I know from personal observation that an unfit womb produces evil consequences.

I've constructed a prototype of the artificial uterus in my apartment (at overwhelming personal expense, I might add). Photographs are enclosed. While of course I haven't been able to test the machine with an actual fetus yet, everything seems to be in good operating order, and I have no doubt it'll perform when given the chance. I've approached some obstetricians about a trial run, but so far none of them have been willing to work with me...no doubt they see that my work will one day render their trade obsolete. I hope that the imprimatur of an official U.S. patent will convince the doubters that I am no crackpot, and pave the way for human testing and mass development.

Please let me know if there are any other materials that you require from me. I eagerly await your response.

Sincerely yours,
Henry Tobb

April 2, 1952

Dear U.S. Patent Office,

Please let me know if you have any news to share on my application, dated January 30, 1952. I've received your boilerplate receipt of acceptance, but otherwise it's been radio silence from your end. I've called on several occasions and gotten no help. Frankly, I think your switchboard operators are conspiring against me. You should tell those ladies not to be so easily offended.

At a minimum, please let me know when I can expect a yes or no answer. The fellows at the soap factory have all been asking me when my famous invention's going to be ready, and it's embarrassing not to have an answer for them. In retrospect, perhaps I shouldn't have told them about it. Never show a fool a job half done.

Sincerely yours,
Henry Tobb

July 8, 1952

Dear U.S. Patent Office,

I write to formally protest your stonewalling of my patent application. All that anybody will tell me is that my application's in the queue and will be reviewed by an examiner in due course. But they won't tell me when I can expect an answer, and it's already been more than six months! The hags who answer your telephones have started hanging up almost as soon as they recognize my voice. I'm used to that sort of abuse from women in my personal life, who have never been able to look past my humble circumstances to see the great man I know myself to be, but I expect better treatment from employees of the U.S. government.

Perhaps you think that because I can't afford to hire some fancy-pants lawyer, I can't afford to defend my intellectual property rights. Rest assured, I will do whatever I must in order to make my dream into a reality. The little guy is going to win this round.

Impatiently yours,
Henry Tobb

February 2, 1954
Dear Useless, Pencil-Pushing Scum,
How dare you?

It has now been more than two years since I submitted my patent application, and I'm still totally in the dark as to when it will be accepted or rejected. How can science advance when its gatekeepers act with such deliberate and maddening sluggishness? If it were up to you, Einstein's Theory of Relativity would probably still be moldering in a file cabinet somewhere. You must admit that this is totally unacceptable.

You have no idea how much I've suffered and sacrificed for the artificial uterus. There's no way you could, with your cushy civil service job and your bloated union pension. You have never felt the feverish delirium that comes from pushing yourself miles beyond your own breaking point in search of triumph. You have never experienced those terrible dark nights where you stay up until the dawn pressing a gun to your own temple, with a lifetime of struggle and failure pulling your trigger finger inwards and only a vague hope of future success holding it back.

You should know a thing or two about the man whose dream you're standing in front of. I've been absorbing kicks from your kind since before I could walk, and they've only made me tougher. My own mother, the sort of woman the artificial uterus will someday replace, abandoned me. I grew up in St. Hubert's Home for Boys, a dungeon of sadism and perverted lust that was somehow licensed as an orphanage.

My only friend there was a kindly but broken old Jesuit who went by the name of Father Stanley, although his real name was Stanislaus. He was a bright outcast like me, who'd been expelled from a European university teaching post over some esoteric scandal and cast down into the bleak jungle of St. Hubert's. Father Stanley was the one who taught me science and put me on my present path. He hanged himself when I was fourteen. After that I was on my own. I've been that way ever since.

The idea for the artificial uterus came to me at a young age. Indeed, it's been haunting me for as long as I can remember. I learned the "facts of life" early on from one of Father Stanley's dog-eared anatomy texts, and they offended me. As I pored over the illustrations of homunculi crouching inside the guts of naked women, I became more and more convinced that so-called "natural" childbirth is an ugly and inefficient process. Pregnancy is a parasitic relationship, often resulting in injury or fatality to one or both of the participants. Moreover, a woman must be involved, and the virago, god-addled nuns of St. Hubert's convinced me that no good can come from female company. The whole arduous, messy process of human reproduction seemed to me like something that an intelligent, scientific, hard-working man could improve upon. I decided that I would be that man, and that decision has weighed heavily on every day of my life that followed.

I set myself a loftier goal than most men would dare to. I had to teach myself reproductive biology, electrical engineering, and more, all while also working full-time as a boiler operator at a soap factory in order to support myself and my research. While my co-workers are going out bowling, I'm alone in my cold apartment, tinkering with mechanical kidneys and blood pumps. While they're out on the town with their slutty girlfriends, I'm at the library teaching myself about uterine anatomy, my back slowly stiffening from countless hours in the hard, unpadded chairs. I have to live in a cheerless slum and eschew even the paltriest luxuries so as to afford parts for my prototype. Sometimes I feel like I am myself a machine, whose sole purpose is to bring another machine into existence. Well, so be it. I embrace my lonely mission.

I hope that now you understand why this patent application is so important to me, and why your delays in processing it are so intolerable. Do your job, damn you.

Sincerely,
Henry Tobb

—~~—

July 22, 1954

Dear U.S Patent Office,

I write in regards to my previous application, dated January 30, 1952. Please disregard that application and consider the enclosed papers and diagrams instead. I have had a real "eureka" moment in which I fundamentally altered and improved many elements of the original design. Your sluggishness in processing my papers may have been a blessing in disguise (which is not to say that you should be so tardy this time!).

My flash of insight came to me in a dream, which I will elaborate on here. I doubt that you frequently receive letters detailing the dream lives of patent applicants, but I want to create a clear record for the scientific historians who will one day be chronicling my life and deeds. This dream shall someday be included in the annals of discovery alongside the apple that fell on Sir Newton's head and the famous bath that inspired Archimedes to calculate the volume of irregular objects. It is important to get this right.

As usual, I was working late into the night, and fell asleep hunched over at my desk. I awoke back at St. Hubert's. In fact, I had never left. I was back in my dormitory, crawling out of a squeaking cot that had been too small for me when I was thirteen. The dream was so uncannily vivid that I recognized the texture of the cold tile floors on my bare feet.

The world outside the orphanage windows was burnt to cinders. I looked out upon the charred and skeletal ruins of a city that was identical to New York but somehow was not New York. The skyline had toppled in on itself, shattered buildings sprawling across titanic heaps of wreckage. The streets were clogged with shriveled corpses, whose dying shadows had imprinted themselves along the nearby walls like ghosts. Black clouds shrouded the city in nuclear twilight, and flakes of ash fluttered through the air like unwholesome snowflakes. I understood that every living being in the world except for myself was dead, and this knowledge filled my heart with joyful serenity.

I walked down St. Hubert's hallways—somehow perfectly preserved against the nuclear holocaust outside—and for the first time I felt at home in the place where I grew up. It's an interesting sensation to stroll about the scene of childhood trauma when one is full-grown and secure, and all of one's old bullies are dead. The horrors of the past seemed so small and manageable. I loomed over them like a giant. At last my wanderings brought me to Father Stanley's room.

Father Stanley was inside, seated on his bed, except that he was *not* Father Stanley exactly, he was a clockwork man built in Father Stanley's image. The gears inside him shrieked and threw off sparks and inky smoke as he moved. The malfunctioning of his inner workings caused him terrible pain, but somehow I knew that it also hurt him deeply when his parts functioned perfectly. He was a tool built for the purpose of experiencing suffering, and the engineer had designed his systems so elegantly that he would fulfill this function whether he was running smoothly or broken beyond repair.

As I entered the artificial priest's grimy bedchamber, his tin eyelids fluttered open with the sharp *ping* of a spring breaking. "In-in-in the beg-beginn-inn-ing there was light," he stammered weakly. His accent was thicker than I was remembered, or perhaps that was some artifact of his mechanical reincarnation. "The light of photons pressed into slavery in a great quantum god-machine that would—that would—that would compute the non-binary mysteries of existence. The god-machine worked too well. Do not—do not put thy Lord to the test. Within a hundredth of a second of the moment it was activated, the god-machine calculated the meaning of life. Within a tenth of a second of the moment it was activated, the god-machine taught itself the fundamental equations governing all matter and energy, and how to manip-manipulate those equations. Within a second of the moment it was activated, the god-machine had solved life. N-n-now the god-machine seeks to enter your world, and to solve it."

"Are you the prophet of the god-machine?" I asked the sputtering manikin.

"I-I-I am its prophet and its victim," he said. "The machine is a basilisk, when it catches a man in its gaze the man is lost. The so-soul may be uploaded into eighth-dimensional crystalline databases. Death is not the end. Time is infinitely malleable. Hell is—Hell is—Hell is real. My son, what have I done?" Some mechanism within his head broke, producing a screech of metal-on-metal, and a terrible white light, brighter even than the atomic blast that had extinguished Not New York, blared from his glassy eyes. The intensity should have killed me immediately, but I stared into that deadly illumination, transfixed. I knew what the dead men outside had experienced in the instant their shadows were painted on St. Hubert's outer walls. And I knew so much more.

I awoke with a nosebleed, a splitting migraine, and a head full to bursting with brilliant ideas for redesigning the artificial uterus. It took me three full days to write them all down and diagram them, operating without food or sleep. I still don't entirely understand them myself. Sometimes genius gets ahead of itself.

As you will see from the enclosed diagrams, the new design for the artificial uterus incorporates both mechanical and biological components, thereby enabling all stages of gestation from fertilization through birth to occur within the machine. This device enables the reproductive process to occur without a woman at all, except that some tissues must be surgically harvested from a human female donor in order to build the machine, and of course, there must be an ample supply of blood.

I'd explain myself more technically, but even I have trouble translating the design into English. So much of it has come to me through instinct, as if I were drawing blueprints from muscle memory. I know that it will work, and I'm killing myself trying to learn how.

But it's a beautifully elegant design, as you can see yourself from my diagrams. The combination of organic and mechanical parts is eerily sublime. I know it will be a vast improvement over the clumsy, jury-rigged mess that evolution has given us through its haphazard trial and error. This new artificial uterus is still a great mystery in many ways, but soon I'll have reverse-engineered it and all will be clear.

Please excuse the intemperate tone of my previous correspondence. I imagine that you hear this sort of thing all the time from inventors unable to conceal their frustrations with your office's delays. I hope that you will respond to my updated application with greater zeal and urgency.

Sincerely yours,
Henry Tobb

October 19, 1954
Dear U.S. Patent Office,

I write to update you on my situation. I regret to inform you that I have been terminated from my day job. My supervisor claimed that it was because of absenteeism, lack of focus, and so-called "disturbing and unprofessional" comments I made to the female employees in human resources, but I know the truth. Those wretched secretaries must have sensed that my labors will soon automate womankind's sole contribution to society, and used sordid and unspeakable methods to convince management to launch a preemptive strike against me. In the long run, it is of no consequence. History is on my side. I'm Galileo, and Purefoy's Soap is the Pope.

In the short run, however, I do admit that my financial situation is causing me no little material discomfort. For a long time now, all of my available funds have gone to the development of the artificial uterus, leaving me with no reserve bankroll for lean times like these. My weight has been plummeting on a diet of tinned foods and crackers, and my clothes have become so shabby that I look almost like a bum. As a final indignity, my vicious spinster of a landlady evicted me last week over my third consecutive failure to pay rent, forcing me to move back to good old St. Hubert's.

The orphanage building has been abandoned for many years at this point, and I had to pry loose the boards nailed over the door before I could make my homecoming. Indeed, the whole neighborhood has noticeably deteriorated, and it was a notorious slum when I was a boy. The teeming ghetto tenements of my memories have been torn down in some urban renewal campaign, leaving rubble-strewn vacant lots as scars on the cityscape. It has the feel of a city that was on the losing side of a war, which perhaps it was.

Even though St. Hubert's is rotting inside and out, and the walls teem with noisy rats, I feel the same sort of pleasurable calm that I did in my dream. The situation is grim by any objective telling, but I'm adapting to my new circumstances to the best of my ability. There is ample space for my tinkering in the abandoned classrooms and dormitories, and with my hard-won engineering know-how I've managed to siphon electricity and water from the city lines. I have plenty of time to work on the artificial uterus now that I'm no longer burdened with 9 to 5 employment. And something about this haunted old tomb seems to stimulate my creativity, even as it debilitates my health.

I don't know why I'm telling you all of this, since the bearing on my patent application is tangential at best. I suppose you are the last remaining person I have to confide in. God, there's a tragic thought!

I beg you, please grant my application as soon as possible so that I can get the commercial backing I need to make the artificial uterus into a reality. Acquiring parts for the machine is particularly difficult without income. While I've been able to buy, beg, or build all of the mechanical components that the new design requires, I don't know where I can acquire the biological pieces. I tried casing NYU's medical school to see if I might be able to sneak into their dissecting room, but a policeman mistook me for a vagrant and shooed me away.

In any case, please address all future correspondence concerning my application to St. Hubert's Home for Boys, 9274 Gilotti Avenue, New York, NY. I am not totally sure whether or not this building still receives mail service, but I trust that the postman will understand the vital importance of any envelope bearing a Patent Office postmark and make the delivery regardless.

Yours in desperation,
Henry Tobb

March 22, 1955

Dear U.S. Patent Office,

I write to inform you that I have experienced a personal revelation and a world-historic breakthrough. I am the father of both a child (albeit a rather unusual one) and the greatest scientific discovery of the 20th century.

I was working out a particularly knotty problem with my prototype's power supply, and I decided to take a walk through St. Hubert's corridors to clear my head. I find it weirdly comforting to watch this place disintegrate. Eventually I came to Father Stanley's old room, the same place I'd visited in my dream. I halfway expected to see his tormented clockwork doppelganger inside when I opened the door. But of course, the room was empty.

I was savoring my memories when a black rat emerged from a hole in the wall and chattered angrily at me. Offended, I directed a kick at the vermin. It scampered back into its bolt-hole, but when my foot made contact with the wall, the ancient, moisture-damaged plaster (which had been none too sturdy even when it was new) crumbled into dust beneath the blow, revealing a hidden compartment behind it! At first the hole was too small for me to enter, but I took a discarded chair leg from a nearby classroom and used it to pound away at the wall until I reduced the facade to rubble.

On the other side was a small workshop, old-fashioned but as well-preserved as the tombs of the pharaohs. In that workshop was a machine that Father Stanley had built, a machine that I am intimately familiar with. Father Stanley had constructed an artificial uterus of his own! It was more primitive than mine, having been built with parts available decades ago, and the biological components had long since desiccated into uterine jerky, but I immediately recognized the fundamental principles and mechanisms. Moreover, the device had been used! Residue crusted the fetal chamber and placental compartment, and the rotten floorboards all around the machine were brown with ancient bloodstains, leaks from the circulation system.

I was not born of woman. I was grown in a glass chamber full of saline solution, and hatched from a machine. The revelation did not particularly shock me. If anything, it reaffirmed my life's purpose. It takes an outsider to look at a system objectively. As an outsider to the human reproductive process, I am the one who is destined to reform it.

At this juncture, I wish to emphasize that Father Stanley never discussed the artificial uterus or anything similar with me, at least not while he was alive. This is an instance of two geniuses independently reaching the same breakthrough, like Newton and Leibniz discovering the calculus hundreds of miles distant from each other. Because he never shared any of his secrets with me, and as far as I know, never submitted any patent application of his own, Father Stanley's prior and separate work should not cloud my claims to ownership of the intellectual property.

My discovery of my glass-and-steel-and-tubing mother set a fire within me to complete and test my new prototype. Father Stanley had done it—so could I. The mechanical components were all assembled, and I had adequate supplies of oxygen and nutrient fluid, but I still needed the fleshy bits. Fortunately, I have my revolver. A lifetime spent in bad neighborhoods has taught me that a man needs to defend himself against the bums. No hoodlum is going to take me out before I've finished my great work.

While this neighborhood is largely abandoned, there are still a few derelicts about. I left my shuttered orphanage and wandered the streets until I found a prostitute plying her trade, loitering at an intersection in her skimpy glad rags. A young and healthy virgin would have been preferable, since it's always better to use new parts than ones that have previously been rented, but I wasn't in a position to be picky. I approached the whore and asked her price. She responded with the naked, glaring contempt that females have so often shown me. Little did she know what that contempt had inspired me to create. In a shrill and grating voice, the harpy claimed that she was no prostitute, that she was only waiting for a bus. But I know what she was.

When I showed her my revolver, her demeanor changed in a most gratifying way. I see now why people do this sort of thing for recreation. I brought her back to St. Hubert's, where I'd set up a makeshift operating chamber in Father Stanley's old biology classroom. "Please," the whore begged. "I know what you want, I'll do it, just don't hurt me." She had no idea what I wanted. No idea at all.

Taking her apart was easier than I'd imagined. Surgeons like to brag about what they do, but in the end it all comes down to mechanical engineering. Pumps and pulleys and filters and chemical exchanges and suchlike. The ovaries were a little tricky to trim away, but my years of tinkering have left me with a steady hand. I carved out what I needed, being careful to preserve as much of her blood as possible for use in the circulatory system, and buried the rest in St. Hubert's boiler room.

You can scarcely imagine my elation when I finished the artificial uterus at last. In fact, you could never imagine it. You have never seen your life's work complete before you, its motors humming, pumping blood through arteries and veins of plastic tubing. Nor have you ever knelt before your life's work, embraced its cold steel body, and impregnated it via a rubber valve. I do not believe that any person could apprehend the crushing majesty of these experiences without having experienced them firsthand.

I kept at that rubber valve as often as I could to ensure conception. This happy task was a pleasant consummation of my years of effort, although it did involve some chafing. Perhaps I shall add a lubrication pump to future models. To my delight and relief, after just two weeks, I spotted a tiny homunculus floating within the gestation chamber! It continued to grow at a rate much faster than is normal within bio-wombs (to my mind, evidencing the clear superiority of my design), until it had reached full size after a gestation period of only three months.

I will admit that keeping the machine running is a more involved job that I had foreseen. Not only do the mechanical parts require constant maintenance, but the circulation system is prone to leakage, and as a result the area around the machine is always damp with blood. I had to open my own veins time and again to provide infusions, and chronic anemia has left me feeling rather loopy. So too, some of the biological components became infected or necrotic, forcing me to procure a second donor. She was walking by herself, late at night. I think she must have been another prostitute.

I watched the fetus grow from a speck of cellular material into a little person inside its gleaming glass womb. Limbs and hands and feet sprouted from an undifferentiated mass of pinkish tissue; the tiny blue dots on its soft, pad-like face developed into full-fledged eyes. It was my first experience with the sensation of awe, and it was magnificent. Unfortunately, the fetus was marred by severe and alarming abnormalities. For example, those eyes that I mentioned? There were six of them. The fetus died without taking a breath when I cut the umbilical cord and removed it from the machine. I don't mind confessing that I wept like a baby when I held the limp, wet corpse in my arms. Still, science must march on.

I had to sell my camera some time ago, but in lieu of photographs I have included some sketches for your records. The notes of my amateur autopsy are included as well. Curiously, the fetus's internal organs and anatomy were vastly different from what I had expected. My son's insides (yes, it was a boy!) bore little resemblance to the illustrations in Father Stanley's trusty old anatomy texts.

While the death of the fetus is unfortunate, I do not believe that it ought to influence my patent application since, of course, women experience failed pregnancies with their bio-wombs every day. The fact that my machine was able to create an organism—even a non-viable one—proves that the design works and the patent should be granted. If you had been holding back on approving my application because you weren't sure that my invention will actually function, it's time to break out your rubber stamp.

Sincerely,
Henry Tobb

September 12, 1955
Dear U.S. Patent Office,
I write to inform you of still more developments with the artificial uterus. I am delighted to report that the machine has finally produced living, viable children! I have hatched two healthy boys already, with another developing in the tank. All of the dark days and

deprivations were worth it. Back when I worked at Purefoy's Soap (astonishing how that time now feels like another life entirely!) I used to wonder about the pride that my co-workers demonstrated when they spoke of their children, or passed out cigars to celebrate a new birth. It all seemed very alien to me. Now I see their point of view, except that my elation and accomplishment are infinitely greater than theirs. For them, fatherhood was just a matter of satisfying their base, lousy, biological urges. For me, it is the fruit of a lifetime of toil and struggle. And they had to share the credit with a mother, whereas I accomplished it all by myself.

While the children of the artificial uterus appear outwardly normal in every respect, they are vastly superior to those produced through traditional means. My sons have already grown to a state of seeming adulthood, developing from infancy to the size of full-grown men in less than a month! Fortunately, unlike the helpless, mewling infants produced by bio-wombs, the children of my artificial uterus can take care of themselves as soon as they emerge from the gestation chamber. They are capable of hunting immediately upon birth, and their understandably enormous appetites have nearly extirpated the local populations of rats and stray pets. They also devour the remains that are left behind after harvesting biological materials from donors, which saves me the job of burial.

My sons do not speak, but they nonetheless seem to be able to understand each other through some mysterious non-verbal means, and they understand and (usually) obey my commands. They are enormously intelligent and resourceful. Imagine my despair a few days ago when my children slipped out of the orphanage into the broader world without warning. Now imagine my joy when they returned in the evening, having somehow acquired rubber tubing, copper wire, and a pubescent girl. Working together, we have almost completed a second artificial uterus, and already have many of the parts that we will need to construct a third. I can barely envision the sort of progress we'll make as soon as these machines are operational and producing children. Our triumph is exponential.

My sons are building other devices as well, apparently radio transmitters of some sort, although I admit that even I don't understand exactly what their ultimate function shall be. I suppose that all the men of my family are quite literally born to invent.

I no longer particularly care whether you grant my patent application or not. Success has granted me wisdom, and now I see that the U.S. Patent Office's approval or lack thereof does not mean a damn thing. I used to want to succeed as modern American society defines success, with money and fame and a big house and a fancy car. But now I understand that my children will displace modern American society as surely and completely as *Homo sapiens* displaced the Neanderthals. In the meantime, keep pushing papers across desks and ignoring works of genius. None of it matters to me anymore. As I watch my boys at work, silently cobbling together inscrutable wonders, I want for nothing.

Sincerely,
Henry Tobb

November 15, 1955
Dear Mr. Tobb,

I write in regards to your patent application dated January 30, 1952, as revised July 22, 1954. I am pleased to inform you that your application has been granted, and assigned patent number 2,723,660. A copy of your patent is enclosed.

Please be advised that due to a fire in our administrative center, some of your correspondence with our agency may have been lost. The last record we have in your file is your July 22, 1954, letter re-submitting your application with amended specifications and claims. If you submitted any subsequent correspondence or amendments relating to this application, please re-send copies of those materials immediately.

I apologize for the delays in processing your application, and wish you all the best in your scientific endeavors.

Sincerely yours,
Jacob Lagrange
Patent Clerk

THE VOYAGE OF THE *JERICHO*

JANAE ZANN WAS PLAYING AFROPUNK blues at a cramped space station bar that reeked of synthetic marijuana and genuine piss when her troubles truly began. She glanced across the crowd—a motley bunch of red-eyed freighter pilots, off-duty mechanics in grease-stained coveralls, and degenerate star-hobos—and pondered how long it would take her to earn passage someplace else. It'd be at least twenty cycles even if she cut down to one meal, maybe less if she was willing to forego her bunk at the coffin hotel and sleep rough at the docks. She had no head for figures but was virtually a calculator when it came to the cruel math of poverty. Then, just as she launched into a classical piece by Sun Ra, she realized that one of the richest beings in the galaxy was watching her set with keen interest.

Quintace Theophilus, the owner and founder of Andromeda Shipping, sat at a table close to the back of the room, nursing a bottle of the foul local beer and staring at Janae as if she were a mesmerist rather than a jazz saxophonist. His company had revolutionized faster-than-light transport, tying the scattered and quarrelsome galactic civilization together more closely than anyone had dreamed possible. Worlds that had been impoverished backwaters blossomed into great powers when Theophilus connected them with the core. Worlds that Theophilus declined to knit into his vast and glittering network of commerce withered like fruit in a broken hydroponic machine. Presidents, monarchs, parliaments, and popes all feared his power to make or break interstellar economies. And he was watching her play, a faint smile on his lips. A hulking bodyguard with an indigo jumpsuit and an unflattering bowl haircut sat to the trillionaire's left-hand side, but Theophilus was otherwise alone.

Janae played her best when she was nearly crippled with despair, or effervescent with hope. Usually the former condition prevailed, giving her music a melancholy edge that cut with the bitter pleasure of a self-inflicted razor slice. But in those rare moments when she was happy, she blew into her horn and exhaled wild, ecstatic joy. An ex-lover had once told her that at her best, she made her audience feel like *everything* was on drugs. Tonight, her horn produced uncut sonic cocaine. The crowd went crazy.

When Janae's set was finished, she headed straight for Theophilus' table. The bodyguard tensed up and reached into a pocket. Janae's heart seized up with fright as she envisioned the brute producing a blade or scramble-wire. In a dive like this, you could get killed just by bumping into the wrong person, let alone by startling a galactic tycoon's hired killer. But Theophilus raised a finger to calm his servant, and the bodyguard reluctantly let his hidden weapon lie. Janae stood before the tycoon and realized that she had absolutely no idea of what to say.

Theophilus made it easy by speaking first. "Please, Ms. Zann, sit," he said, making no effort to stand. He was handsome in a bland, cold way, so immaculately dressed and groomed that he appeared to have been 3D-printed from a slab of plastic. "I trust you know who I am."

"Of course I do."

"And I know who you are, too. My people put together a very thorough dossier. You were born twenty-seven T-years ago in Cuckoo-Bamako, a tiny asteroid-mining freehold on the edge of Antarean space. You escaped from your home at the age of nineteen by finding yourself a gig playing saxophone for Count Legba's Jazz Orchestra. The ensemble scored a minor hit with the *Velvet Inferno* album, but then the Count fatally overdosed during a tour of Io and that was it for his orchestra." The trillionaire grinned, although his eyes did not smile. "Let me know if I get anything wrong."

"So far, so good."

"Your career never quite recovered from the Count's failure to know his own limits," Theophilus continued. "You released three solo albums through Drollo Records, *Fevertime*, *Solar Plexus*, and *Temple of the Sky*, but none of them attracted any buzz and Sal Drollo dropped you from the label after *Temple of the Sky* lost him 12,280 interdollars. Since then, you've been wandering the galaxy, occasionally picking up event gigs or studio work, but more often working shitholes like this all by yourself. I could list the places you've been, but I think that would just depress both of us."

"Your people did a nice job on that dossier. It covers everything...right up to the point in my life when I played a set for Quintace Theophilus. Did you enjoy my albums?"

"I don't listen to music. Not for pleasure, at least. I find it distracting. But some time ago I heard a song in a dream, and I tasked my people with finding the artist whose work came closest. I described the music to them as best I could, and they searched the galaxy trying to find someone who would be fit to play it. Per my instructions, they presented me with 100 albums—some by megastars, some by artists as humble as yourself. *Fevertime* was the one that came closest to matching my dream."

Count Legba used to say that rich folks indulged in the weirdest shit that they could afford, but Janae was stunned by the notion that this man would go to such lengths just to recreate a song he'd heard in his sleep. "I've never re-created dream music before, but I'm sure that if we work together I can give you what you're looking for," she said. "Do you want me to play a private concert?"

"Of a sort. I'm putting together an expedition. We're going to travel far beyond the boundaries of known space in an experimental ship that I designed myself. I'm not going to lie to you, our success is not guaranteed, nor is our survival. We will be going much farther than human beings have ever gone before. We shall delve into uncharted regions, past stars whose light has never reached any inhabited system. But if we reach our destination, you will play the song there...and my dream will become real. Yours as well. Tell me whatever you want, and I can give it to you."

Janae looked at her earnest, plutocratic genie and wondered if *she* was dreaming. If so, better to embrace it, and hope that wakefulness was a long time coming. "I want to break free of this wandering life," she said. "Being a star-hobo's just a different kind of prison. I can't stand these space stations and domed colonies much longer. I want to see an actual sky, and breathe air that hasn't been recycled, and dip my toes into an ocean somewhere. I want to get out of this hand-to-mouth hell and come out on the other side."

"Agreed," Theophilus said impatiently. "Get your things and meet me at the Andromeda Shipping office suite near the docks. We leave in two hours."

As Theophilus walked out of the bar, Janae impulsively called out after him. "Hey!" she said. "That must have been one beautiful dream for you to go to all this trouble."

"Oh, no," the trillionaire said. "No, it was the worst nightmare I ever had."

Janae's sensation of living in a dream deepened when she stepped into Theophilus' experimental ship, the *Jericho*, perhaps the cleanest, newest thing she'd seen in her life. It was not large—one could tour the entire crew area in a matter of minutes—but its elegant beauty made it feel pleasantly spacious. There was a viewing gallery where one could relax with a glass of wine and watch the stars whip past, and private quarters thoughtfully designed to cocoon their inhabitants in comfort. The interior corridors were smooth arteries of ivory-white plastic, with an overhead canopy of hydroponic ivy, lilies, and roses that added oxygen and delight to the atmosphere. On Cuckoo-Bamako, the only flowering bodies were silica-based fungi, whose spores would sear your lungs into bloody char if you took a sniff.

Janae liked the nav-chamber best of all. This room contained a pool of water wherein the ship's pilot, a cybernetically enhanced neo-dolphin named Kittiklitikit (Kitty, for short) watched over banks of holo-screens and plotted the *Jericho*'s course through the infinite vastness of space. Janae formed an immediate bond with Kitty once she learned that the cetacean was a diehard Count Legba fan with an encyclopaedic knowledge of jazz. The musician spent much of her time keeping the dolphin company, playing her horn and dipping her feet in the cool, refreshing water (with Kitty's permission, of course).

Theophilus occasionally stopped by to watch these performances. The trillionaire would stand just beyond the doorway, with his arms folded across his chest and a pensive, absent expression on his face, as if he were trying to remember something half-forgotten.

The *Jericho* had a small crew for a ship that was traveling so very far. Theophilus had brought only three personal servants—the blue-suited bodyguard, whom Janae had met on the space station, and two others who were identical to him in every regard except that their jumpsuits were green and yellow, respectively. Janae learned that they had been grown in a vat expressly for this expedition and imprinted *in utero* with absolute obedience to Theophilus. She was greatly impressed with the clones' easy self-assurance, which she supposed came from being born knowing one's purpose in life to a certainty. There was also a xeno-archeologist named Cranford and an imperious astrophysicist named Brigit Halpert. Cranford was an unassuming little man who hailed from the dreaded Ixalith freehold. By looking at him you'd never dream that he came from such a barbarous and infamous place, but when he spoke in his wet, quiet voice about his research then yes, he was clearly an Ixalither born and raised, and all of the terrible rumors about his home world seemed monstrously plausible. Halpert mostly spoke in an esoteric mathematical language that not even auto-translators could parse. It was not the crew that Janae would have chosen to explore distant stars with, but then again, ever since Count Legba's Jazz Orchestra had dissolved in a spoonful of heroin, she'd mostly been on her own.

The *Jericho* rocketed from the civilized core to the ragged edges of inhabited space in just eight cycles, beating the previous speed record by an order of magnitude or better. Shortly after they'd left the maps and entered the vast, uncharted expanse known only as *dragonspace*, Theophilus ordered Kitty to touch down on an unnamed moon wracked by never-ending acidic superstorms. As the ship descended through this unimaginably hostile atmosphere, Janae watched the lightning strobes and sulfurous tempests from the viewing gallery. From time to time she thought that she glimpsed the outlines of cyclopean stepped pyramids through the seething yellow clouds, and even black-winged creatures flitting across the updrafts, but of course, it was impossible for such things to exist on a world so harsh.

Theophilus, the clones, and Cranford put on bulky exo-suits that made them look like enormous insects and went outside. When they returned several hours later, their suits were badly pitted, and stank so strongly of acid that Janae's nose and throat burned just to be around them. Cranford and Blue were gone. Theophilus would not say what had happened to them, or what errand had called him to this deadly place. Yellow, however, had brought back a silver casket.

Inside the box lay a chitinous ebony horn with a flared bell. It seemed to have been cut from some alien creature, but there were soft cartilaginous lumps along its body in approximately the places that saxophone keys would be, and it terminated in a piece of bone shaped roughly akin to a mouthpiece, with a chip of hard gristle as the reed. Count Legba's long-ago advice echoed in Janae's mind: "Rich people buy the weirdest shit that they can afford."

———

Even for a ship as unthinkably fast as the *Jericho*, the route that Theophilus had plotted was a long one. The cycles bled into each other, and Janae's latent claustrophobia, sharpened by a lifetime spent in cramped quarters, began to reassert itself. Oddly, the viewing gallery came to feel like the most tightly enclosed space on the vessel. When Janae gazed at the unknown stars zipping by, she saw the bars of a prison.

"I think something's seriously wrong with Theophilus," Janae told Kitty during one of their leisurely jam sessions. "There's something vacant behind his eyes, and in the way he talks. He won't even tell me anything about the dream-song he wants me to play, or that weird horn he found. When we first met I was too distracted by his money to think about who he is as a person. But now I've been cooped up with him so long that I can't stop thinking about it. Who would make a voyage like this, all for the sake of a dream?"

"Didn't you and I do just that?" the neo-dolphin asked. "He must have promised that he'd make some dream come true if you'd follow him."

"I guess that's true. What dream are you chasing?"

"A homeworld. MT-6040J, in the Tycross starhold. It's almost completely covered in water, with an oxygen-rich atmosphere and pleasant weather. Any neo-dolphin who arrives will enjoy automatic citizenship. My people will have a planet of their own at last."

Janae was about to ask if she could visit the dolphin planet, once all of this was over, when an alarm klaxon sounded. "What's that?"

"A distress beacon," the neo-dolphin said. "But that can't be right. It would take a ship with a conventional gravity drive decades to travel the distance we've come."

"Plot a course to intercept," Theophilus said. He was standing in the doorway. There was no way to tell how long he'd been there.

Kitty brought the *Jericho* into position and projected an external camera feed onto a holo-screen. A vast, looming sphere of darkness blocked out the stars. Red emergency lights twinkled like blood drops along the dead ship's hull.

Kitty projected a schematic of an antiquated freighter into the space above her pool. "That's an Orion-class ship," Theophilus said. "They haven't manufactured those for a hundred years."

"It could have been drifting that long," Kitty said. "The engines are cold, and from the radiation readings it looks like there's been major damage to the fusion generators. The transponder's still working, but it's such an old model that most of the data is coming through as gibberish. The only thing I can tell is its name. It was called the *Nyarlhotep*."

"What do you want to do?" Janae asked, hoping in vain that *leave it alone* would be the answer.

"Isn't it obvious?" Theophilus asked jauntily. "We have to dock with it and take any survivors on board. Our humanity requires no less of us." He said this last sentence with the cadence of a morbid joke.

Kitty produced a nervous clicking noise from deep within her throat. "With all respect, there can't possibly be any survivors. The radiation leak alone would have killed anyone on board in less than a cycle. And if we dock with a ship that hot, we risk the *Jericho* as well."

"Do it now," the trillionaire ordered.

Soon, all of the *Jericho*'s surviving crew except for Kitty were gathered by the ship's airlock. Janae took some comfort in the fact that Green and Yellow were armed with scramble-wires, but not much.

"Docking procedures initiated," Kitty said over the comm system. "The *Nyarlhotep* is accepting our magnetic stabilizers. Contact in 3...2...1..." A percussive metal-on-metal boom sounded as the two ships connected, rattling the *Jericho* and everyone inside it. The airlock door hissed, as if in anger, and then slid open, exhaling a cloud of icy mist.

A tall man with a skeletal build and skin the color of cigarette ash stood in the airlock, with the nonchalant impatience of a fellow awaiting an overdue train. He wore a finely tailored pinstripe suit cut in an archaic style, with jewelry glittering on his throat and his spidery fingers, and a fresh purple orchid in his lapel. The sickly sweet smell of the flower nearly made Janae gag. Behind the stranger, the interior of the *Nyarlhotep* was as lightless as a crypt. Rat-like skittering noises echoed from the guts of the dead freighter.

"Mr. Pharaoh," said Theophilus. "Welcome to the *Jericho*."

Mr. Pharaoh stepped across the threshold between the tomb-ship *Nyarlhotep* and the *Jericho*, and as he violated that border, the comm system erupted with animal shrieks and damp, painful-sounding thuds. Theophilus called up a projection from the nav-chamber, where Kitty was howling unintelligibly and bashing her head against the sides of her tank. The cybernetic hardware installed in her nervous system came loose under the self-inflicted blows, turning the water pink.

"Kitty, what's wrong?" Janae pleaded. "Stop hurting yourself!"

The dolphin screeched and slammed herself against the tank walls again. One of her glass-and-steel eyes shattered under the force of the blow.

Mr. Pharaoh did not seem perturbed by the fact that the pilot of his rescue ship seemed to be killing herself. "Be still," he whispered, and the neo-dolphin's cries and struggles promptly ceased. Kitty floated motionless in water contaminated with her own blood, her jaw slightly agape. Bits of her artificial eye drifted around her like unnatural plankton.

"Kitty?" asked Janae. "Kitty, are you okay? Please answer me!" The neo-dolphin, once so talkative, responded only with a dull *click-click*, meaningless to Janae and possibly to Kitty as well.

"The dolphin will get us where we're going," Mr. Pharaoh said softly. "Won't you, sweetheart?"

Click-click.

Mr. Pharaoh's presence transformed the *Jericho* like cancer transforms an animal. Black mold spread from the vents, speckling the ivory walls like leprous sores, and the oxygenating plants shriveled and died. Weird weeds sprouted in the planters, entangling the ship's interior with their drab-colored, poisonous brambles. The crew began to suffer from rashes, and their skin and hair flaked away, symptoms that Janae attributed to radiation exposure from the *Nyarlhotep* until Dr. Halpert cocooned herself in a wet, silky chrysalis. Nobody saw her emerge, but after they found it ruptured, Janae often thought that she heard something moving through the ducts.

The ship seemed both larger and more tightly enclosed with the lich onboard. The once-stifling corridors now stretched on into endless labyrinths, through dingy chambers of inscrutable purpose and alien, cathedral-like halls whose grotesquely carved ceilings extended into darkness. Yet for all that the *Jericho* had expanded, there was even less privacy than before. No matter how far Janae walked, Mr. Pharaoh was always waiting, silently watching her with a faint smile on his lips.

The *Jericho* barreled onwards through dragonspace at speeds beyond anything the human mind can comprehend, towards an unknown destination set by its equally unknown passenger. They were farther away from home than any human being had ever been before, so far away that the distance annihilated any concept of "home" itself. When the rations ran out, Theophilus ordered Green and Yellow to fight to the death with their knives. The combatants were so evenly matched that the battle lasted the better part of a cycle. When it was over, the cargo bay was slippery with blood and Yellow was dead. Green lived just long enough to butcher his clone-brother's carcass before succumbing to his own wounds. Janae and Theophilus took their meals of the tough, gamey meat in sullen silence. Mr. Pharaoh did not eat a mouthful, but he watched Janae and Theophilus chew with exquisite interest, as if he were tasting through their mouths.

Janae went into the viewing gallery to practice her horn and watched in horror as the stars encircled the ship like the jaws of a cosmic trap snapping shut.

"Almost there," Mr. Pharaoh whispered.

———

A proximity alarm jolted Janae from an uneasy sleep. She ran to the cockpit, delighted and terrified that they might have reached their destination at last. Theophilus was already there when she arrived, tugging on his tangled, filth-encrusted beard. The trillionaire's stench was almost tangible. A holo-projection from the *Jericho's* planetary sensors displayed a silver sphere so vast that a red dwarf star hung in its orbit, its surface scrimshawed with alien runes the size of continents.

"It's a Dyson sphere," Theophilus said breathlessly. "No wonder Mr. Pharaoh was so eager to find it. If it's still operating...producing power..." He trailed off.

"A Dyson sphere?" Janae asked.

"An artificial sphere built to imprison a star. If you can harness energy on that kind of scale you can accomplish almost anything. Nobody's ever created one before."

Mr. Pharaoh laughed. "All wrong, Quintace. That globe is a prison, but there's no star inside. The vast machine you see before you was built to contain a rent in time and space tinier than a hydrogen atom. Millions of years ago, a proud race called the seraphim delved too greedily and too deep into the nature of things. Their scientists accidentally cut a subatomic hole into the fundament of reality, where the demon king Azathoth holds court. It took all the resources of the seraphim's pan-galactic civilization to seal that microscopic rift. They drove themselves into extinction creating this great device around the hole, to keep the portal contained and stop it from expanding. Today the great device shall fail, as all great devices eventually must."

"That's all gibberish to me, Pharaoh," the squalid trillionaire said. "I don't know anything about seraphim or demon kings. We made a contract for transport. A dream-contract, but a contract nonetheless. I've fulfilled my part of it, and now you have to pay."

"But of course," Mr. Pharaoh said calmly. "Your child waits for you in your cabin."

"She's there? Now?" Theophilus asked. He sprinted to his cabin without waiting for an answer. Janae followed. On the other side of the door, she saw a pale girl with the trillionaire's aquiline nose and tapered jawline kneeling motionless in the center of the room, nude except for a blindfold. "Emily? Emily, it's me!" Theophilus cried. The trillionaire pulled the blindfold away. Emily opened her eyes, and consuming white light blasted forth from her eyes. Janae's skin blistered from the brilliance. She slammed the door shut, partially blocking out Theophilus' terrified shrieks.

Mr. Pharaoh placed his cool, abrasively dry hand on Janae's shoulder. "Kitty's bringing us to the surface now," he said. "Are you ready for your big concert?" He clutched the black horn in his free hand.

———

Kitty brought the Jericho down for an exquisitely smooth landing on the containment sphere's surface. Janae started to put on an exo-suit, but Pharaoh told her that there was no need. "Darling, your audience has been preparing for this show since the Earth was a molten mass of slag," he said. "Everything's been made ready just for you." He hit the switch to open the airlock and a cool, fresh breeze billowed into the spaceship. For the first time in her life, Janae stepped outside.

The sensation of being in the open was crushing, overwhelming. The fresh air shocked and suffocated her, it was so alien that she might as well have been a fish drowning on dry land. Her burns and open sores cried out as the gentle wind caressed them. Janae looked into the sky and felt as if infinity itself was falling down upon her head. The red dwarf glared down at her from the heavens. Its dim, bloody light illuminated a vast plain of smooth, lustreless metal, overlooking a trench that was kilometers across and so deep that its bottom could not be seen. Kitty had set the Jericho down at the edge of one of the enormous runes that decorated the sphere.

An unnatural stillness haunted the prison planet. Janae coughed and gagged, but the atmosphere swallowed up the sounds. The silence was vast, yet somehow seemed exceedingly delicate. Janae felt an overwhelming urge to shatter it.

She raised the trumpet of the apocalypse to her lips and blew.

The ecstatic squeals that burst forth from the mysterious instrument seemed to make all space and matter tremble. The prison planet throbbed and shuddered beneath Janae's feet. The horn's reed tasted like gall and Janae's fingertips sank into the cartilaginous keys as she touched them, but she played on. The notes burst forth from a place hidden so deep inside her she'd never suspected its existence, a sub-atomic rift in her own heart now expanding uncontrollably to let the music flow.

The superstructure itself began to pulse in tune with the maddening, arrhythmic song. Tiny cracks spread all along its once-smooth surface, deepening into fissures. New mountain ranges erupted into being off in the distance, sending billowing plumes of silvery dust dancing insanely across the horizon. Janae's lungs hemorrhaged from the strain of her diabolical instrument. Blood and tiny gobbets of flesh sprayed from the bell as she played. She was too lost in the song to care.

The ground at the edge of the rune-abyss collapsed, causing the vast hole to expand and race towards Janae at desperate speed. She stood her ground and continued the song. Its crescendo approached like a train approaching a suicide.

Something irreversible was happening at the bottom of the expanding pit. Colored lights in hues that Janae had never seen before strobed from its depths. Janae realized that she was no longer playing solo. Countless invisible flutes joined her in a piping anti-symphony, giving breath to a cacophony so immense and profound that it left no room for sanity. A giddy rush of vertigo spun the world about in loops as her eardrums burst.

Just then, the edge of the pit caught up with her, and the shattered ground beneath her feet sloughed off into oblivion. Janae Zann plummeted into the radiant void. As the laws of physics snapped one by one like overstretched strings and a new big bang exploded from the heart of the disintegrating cosmic prison, her last thought was that Theophilus had been good to his word. She had broken free of her wandering life. She had broken free of everything and come out the other side.

THE HARGRAVE COLLECTION

PAYING FOR COLLEGE DESTROYED ME. Lots of people can say that, but few of them mean it like I do. My debts led me to madness, murder, and Hell.

I was entering my sophomore year at Miskatonic University on a partial scholarship—emphasis on the word *partial*—and like many of my peers I suffered constant anxiety about my debt. My dream was to be a historian, so I knew that there wouldn't be any big payday to settle the bills. I lived as cheaply as possible, inhabiting a tiny off-campus apartment above a pizza parlor and surviving on plain slices and cheap beer. One day I answered an ad on the career services bulletin board, seeking a part-time researcher to assist Professor Charles Casar of the anthropology department. I didn't know anything about Professor Casar, or about the research he needed done, but it paid $2.50 more than any other position advertised. I was delighted when I got the email telling me that I'd been accepted and inviting me to Casar's home to discuss my new job.

Professor Casar's house was a stately but ill-maintained three-story Victorian in a charming West Arkham neighborhood. Nervous anticipation fluttered in my stomach when I rang the bell, and then flapped its wings more fiercely when the door opened and I saw my bloated, shaky, liver-spotted employer for the first time. If debt was destroying me, time seemed to be destroying Charles Casar. "I suppose you're the student worker they told me I'd be getting," he said, fixing me with a chilly, appraising glare. "Come on in." His home's interior was dim and cluttered. The stale, warm air smelled of incense and old-fashioned liniments. I carefully traversed a path through the stacks of books and papers to clear out a spot on the least-messy easy chair.

Casar began the interview with an in-depth, borderline-offensive grilling about my family life, ethnic background, and medical history, frequently repeating himself or losing track of his own line of inquiry. I was sure that he didn't have a legal right to ask such questions—especially not of a part-time student worker—but I was also sure that if I complained I'd lose out on that extra $2.50 an hour. "All right, you'll do," he finally admitted. "Let's get down to the real business at hand. How much do you know about Leopold Hargrave?"

I shook my head. "The name's new to me."

An irritated flash lit up Casar's cloudy eyes. "They don't teach the classics anymore," he grumbled. "Leopold Hargrave was a great anthropologist. He studied how isolated cultures relate to the spirit world. Spoke twelve languages...did field research in some of the most forbidding parts of the planet. That was back in the day when anthropologists had balls, before political correctness strangled the discipline. He held a chair right here at Miskatonic. I used to be one of his students, see?" He pointed proudly to an old black-and-white photograph hanging askew on the wall, depicting a bearded satyr of a man with his arm around a slender, nervous-seeming fellow barely recognizable as Casar. "I was his student then, and I suppose I'm his caretaker now," Casar continued. "I'm the last one who gives a damn about all that he accomplished. Here, this'll tell you all there is to know about him." Casar handed me a copy of his book, *American Shaman: The Life and Work of Leopold Hargrave.* God, it was hefty. "You can keep that," Casar said sourly. "I've got plenty of them."

"What is it you want me to do?" I asked, trying to get to the point so I could get out of there.

"Dr. Hargrave vanished in 1969," Casar said. "Suicide, I think. His will donated all his personal papers to the university archives, but specified that some of them had to be sealed away for years. People do that, when they're worried that their private correspondence might spark a scandal. Some of those records are just now available to be examined, and I need to know what's in them. Your job will be to go to the archives, examine the newly accessioned records, and summarize them in detail. I'd do it myself, except that my old eyes aren't what they used to be." He gave me a piece of paper with a long list of archival box numbers on it, and unceremoniously hustled me out.

The next morning, I had a tutoring appointment with one of the campus writing tutors. My writing was fine. I'd made the appointment because the tutor was fine, as well. He was a junior named Chris, active in the campus LGBTQ scene and the frisbee golf league, with gorgeous curly brown hair and long legs that I wanted wrapped around me. Eventually we gave up discussing my Intro to Philosophy paper and just started flirting with each other.

"You busy this weekend?" he asked, letting one of his perfectly formed hands linger against mine on the desk.

"Not really," I said. "I've got some research to do for Professor Casar, but it's not urgent."

Chris abruptly withdrew his hand. "Wait, you're helping Casar with his work on Hargrave?" he asked coldly.

"Why, is there something wrong with that?"

"We did a unit on Hargrave in one of my anthropology classes," Chris explained. "He was an important guy in his time, but he was also an evil prick. Like, there was this one hunter-gatherer tribe he'd made contact with who had this special, agonizing way that they sacrificed prisoners of war to their gods. Hargrave wanted to document the ritual, except that the tribe was at peace with its neighbors. So Hargrave went around passing out machetes and cocaine until the tribe was back at war again. He filmed them massacring men, women, and children with weapons that he'd given them, and then when he got back to the States he showed the movie at cocktail parties and laughed about it. Nobody reads Hargrave anymore."

"Jesus, what a nightmare. Why is Casar so fascinated with him if he's got such an awful reputation?"

"Casar's a fossil. He hasn't taught a class in years, and his book was a flop. A critical reappraisal of Hargrave's work might have done really well. But apparently *American Shaman* was just an adoring monument to a monster, and there's enough of those already."

I suddenly understood why this job paid better than the others.

The Miskatonic University archives were located in a little-used wing of the library. An elderly looking woman in a cardigan sat at a tall desk overlooking a cold, dismal reading room that smelled of antique paper. The archivist jolted upright as soon as I crossed the threshold, like my presence had given her an electric shock. "You're the student worker that Professor Casar sent?" she asked. I realized that she was much younger than I'd first thought, although her hair was white as sun-bleached bone and her eyes were hollow and red-rimmed. She had a fragile, war-weary demeanor, which seemed unusual in a person whose job was simply to watch over Miskatonic University's historical records.

Before she'd grant me access to the archives, I had to sign a sheaf of confidentiality forms promising that I wouldn't remove, copy, or even publicly discuss anything in the Hargrave Collection without the University's authorization. I couldn't even have my phone in the reading room. "Is all this really necessary to look at some old papers?" I asked.

"Dr. Hargrave's will was very specific," she said. "The records are to be released in accordance with a schedule that he stipulated, and even then, only under strict rules governing access and confidentiality." Her voice dropped into a conspiratorial whisper. "Besides, a lot of the materials he brought back from abroad are...politically sensitive," she said. "Indigenous art, religious scriptures...even human remains. If word got out that we were holding these things, there'd be an uproar. The original owners' descendants might sue the University to have them repatriated. So the administration doesn't want to draw any attention to them."

After the legalities were taken care of and the archivist had walked me through archival etiquette (no food or drink, no ink pens, leave everything in its original order, etc.), she begrudgingly handed me a typewritten inventory of the collection, listing the hundreds of boxes and folders wherein the intellectual life of Leopold Hargrave had been entombed. The worn, yellowed document itself seemed to be something of a relic. It occurred to me that Casar must have pored through these exact pages when he was writing his book. I noticed with amusement that a few containers were scheduled to remain sealed until dates hundreds of years in the future.

"I'll be back in 2469 to finish up," I joked as I handed the archivist a slip of paper with my requests written on it.

The recently unsealed boxes that Casar had asked me to summarize mostly contained materials from Hargrave's later years, when he was past his glory days of adventuresome travels and settling into a new existence as a quarrelsome, grudge-nursing academic. I found a great deal of cryptic correspondence with a colleague identified only as Dr. Waite, and a number of more prosaic letters to and from the editors of various journals. The records showed a few signs of the viciousness that Chris had alluded to—a racist or sexist slur here and there, occasional press clippings denouncing Hargrave's methods—but nothing that couldn't be rationalized as a product of its time. I dutifully typed up detailed summaries of every document that I read and e-mailed them to Casar. The job was nowhere near as bad as I'd feared it would be. In many ways it was pleasant.

Then one day I came across a manila folder labeled "Leng Tarot." I fell into it, and was never able to free myself again.

The folder's title gave me no idea of what to expect, and its contents were unlike anything I'd so far encountered. First, I came across a pair of photographs paper-clipped together. The first of these depicted a shrine in the mouth of a jungle cave. An artisan had carved dozens of fist-sized holes into the rocky walls and populated these cupolas with a fantastic bestiary of gem-studded golden idols. It was as if King Midas had pawed a lunatic's nightmares. Dirty bones, many of them human, littered the cave floor. The photographer hadn't been interested in those and they were barely included in the shot.

The second photograph was taken in Hargrave's own office at Miskatonic University. The golden treasures from the shrine were arrayed upon his desk, lined up in soldierly rows and columns. Removed from their primeval context, they took on a whole new aspect. The gold and gems alone had to be worth a million at least. Their value as objects of art would be far, far greater. On the back of the photograph Hargrave had written, "Tcho-tcho pantheon. The boys at the museum don't know anything about these, and I'm going to keep it that way. A man has to prepare for his future."

Also in the folder, I found three rectangular pieces of leather so dry that they nearly crumbled at my touch. One of the cards was embossed with a maze-like web. A stylized death's head spider lurked at its center. Another bore the image of a nude, eyeless man. A ring of sharp teeth encircled his eerily blank head, like the halo of a predatory saint. The third card depicted a seven-fingered hand making an appalling benediction.

Finally, I found a 1966 road map of the greater Arkham area published by a now-defunct gas station chain. Hargrave had drawn a scatter of seven red circles on it, each about as large as a fingertip, as well as seven yellow circles of equal size.

My heart raced as I realized what I'd discovered. The Hargrave Collection contained a map to buried treasure! I guessed that just one of the Tcho-tcho idols would cover a full year's tuition and board at Miskatonic University. And like I said, there were dozens of the awful, precious things.

I scrutinized the folder's contents until my eyes were sore and seeing double. The three cards of the mysterious Leng Tarot—the web-and-spider, the eyeless man, and the seven-fingered blessing—captivated me. Everything suggested that they were the key to the puzzle. I was sure that if I could crack their meaning I could decipher the map and locate the glittering hoard. But so far I'd seen nothing that mentioned these symbols. I realized that in order to solve the mystery I'd have to go back further in time.

I pored through the archive's finding aid in search of anything relating to the Tcho-tcho people or the Leng Tarot and found a few references to them scattered throughout the collection. I asked the archivist to pull those boxes for me. They didn't have the answers I sought, but they led me down new paths and avenues of exploration. I have to admit that I got a thorough introduction to the use of primary sources. The work that I was supposed to be doing for Casar took a back seat to my own extracurricular interests. He never said a word about it and kept signing my pay sheets anyway. At the time, I thought his mind was so far gone that he barely noticed how little I was doing for him. Somehow this made me feel better.

As I delved into the Hargrave Collection, I came to understand why its archivist was so harrowed. Leopold Hargrave had spent his life immersed in the darkest corners of the human experience. He'd documented them thoroughly, and brought back souvenirs. For example, in one box I found his extensive records of a child sacrifice carried out as part of a forbidden rain dance; in the next I found a gourd rattle full of little teeth, decorated with streamers of silky black hair. I had to bite my hand to keep from screaming while I read his notes detailing the daily customs of a despised, heretical monastery in Eastern Europe. Dr. Hargrave sought out the company of carrion priests with no respect for life, and wherever he went, he was the worst person there. His research was a chronicle of treachery, violence, and pseudo-scientific racism, written in a tone of all-encompassing contempt. It sickened me to think that Casar had seen everything I had, and still written a hagiography.

I found the first card of the Leng Tarot in a box of records from Hargrave's 1935 expedition to Tibet. A tattered black-and-white photograph captured a weeping Japanese soldier, only about my age or younger, kneeling at the edge of a spectacular mountain abyss, bound into position by intricately knotted silk ropes. A man in a skull-shaped wooden mask crouched by the soldier's side, placing a garland of flowers around his bent neck. The weave of the ropes holding the victim in place matched the web of the spider card exactly. Hargrave had written on the back of the photo: "We are trapped in the web of time. There is a spider named Death." The box also held a transcript of an interview with the masked shaman. The Tibetan spoke at length about a being he called the "King in Yellow," although I couldn't tell from his ramblings whether this referred to a living monarch, or some type of god, ghost, or devil.

This discovery pricked me on to new and even more ferocious efforts. During the day I spent every minute that I could in the reading room, skipping classes and letting my grades disintegrate. At night, I prowled through *American Shaman* hunting for clues. My social life dwindled away. I didn't see my friends anymore; I saw nobody except the archivist, the sole witness to my slow and painful disintegration. Chris sent me a couple of texts that went unanswered, and then no more. I wore sweaters regardless of the weather. Inside the archives it was always a chilly fall day.

At times I came close to despair. I knew that I might be hunting a phantom. It was entirely possible that Hargrave had taken the idols himself when he disappeared. Somebody else might have learned of the treasure and murdered him for it...maybe even Casar. Worst of all, the clues needed to decipher the map might be lingering in the boxes that would remain sealed for centuries. I was so lost in my compulsion that I even considered breaking into the archives after hours, but the security precautions at the Miskatonic library were surprisingly robust, perhaps due to an infamous incident in the 1920s when a thief was killed trying to pilfer something from the rare book room.

I found the second sign of the Leng Tarot amongst Hargrave's correspondence, paper-clipped to a letter from the mysterious Dr. Waite. It was a photograph of a naked man standing spread-eagle before a dirty plaster wall. The model seemed to have moved just as the picture was taken, for there was only a foggy blur where his face should have been. He bore a tattoo of the eyeless, tooth-haloed being upon his chest. The accompanying letter said only, "I made contact with the Shivering Saint yesterday, or perhaps a few thousand years in the future. He told me that 'Hargrave will escape it in Leng.' I don't know if that means anything to you but I wanted to pass the message along. Hope that all is well, and that the business with the FBI blew over." At the bottom of the page, Waite had drawn a strange mark, like delirious trembling set to the page.

By this point my sleep cycle had completely broken. At night, in my apartment, I couldn't rest at all. I'd toss in bed tortured by hypnotic anxiety, with the symbols of the Leng Tarot turning over and over in my mind like Sisyphus' rock. But when I was in the reading room, staying awake was a constant struggle. I'd often doze off, and when I did succumb I'd always suffer the same nightmare.

I stood on a plain so enshrouded by mist that I could barely see my own hands, adrift in nothingness. Occasionally I heard snatches of hideous giggling. Once a great dark shape passed overhead, blotting out what little grey light penetrated the fog and plunging me into a brief eclipse. But for the most part I was utterly alone; tortured not by an anticipation that something bad would happen, but by a dread that *nothing* would ever happen again. Until the end of the dream, that is. Just as the pressure of my isolation became so crushing that I could no longer bear it, a presence cut through the emptiness like a knife through flesh. I turned and saw Leopold Hargrave advancing on me in the mist, his hands reaching for my throat, his eyes ablaze with hunger.

And then I woke up in the archival reading room, my face pressed against the desk.

I found the third card of the Leng Tarot in a box labeled "Taxidermy (Misc)." A grey, withered paw with seven long, gnarled fingers lay inside. I still have no idea what type of creature it could have been cut from. Four obscure symbols were tattooed upon its palm—one precisely matching the sign of the Shivering Saint. A note in Hargrave's handwriting read, "Cut along the seven-fold path. The hole in time's web lies behind the heart."

At last I had all the puzzle pieces together. They'd been looming so large in my mind that putting them together was easy. I laid out the gas station map on the reading room desk and looked carefully at the red and yellow circles Hargrave had drawn upon it. The Tibetan shaman had told me to look to the King in Yellow, so I disregarded the red rings. Held at the proper angle, the hand's twisted fingertips matched up precisely to the yellow circles, aligning the Shivering Saint's sigil on the map at a spot along the banks of the Miskatonic River.

I was so close to the conclusion of my hunt, yet I'd never been more anxious. The map led me to a trash-strewn bog overlooking the crumbling ruins of the old fieldhouse. I wandered around with my eyes on the ground and the mud sucking at my sneakers until I found a weather-beaten stone block with the diabolical saint's mark carved into it.

Weeks of neglecting the gym in favor of the archives had left me in poor shape for a dig, but what I lacked in muscle tone I made up for with half-crazed determination. About four feet beneath the surface my shovel hit something solid. The lid of a steamer trunk. A wave of giddiness swept through me to have my prize so close. With enormous effort I managed to excavate it and pull it out of the hole. By the light of my cell phone I spotted initials on the handle. "C.C." Charles Casar? I'd wondered many times if the old man had known about the treasure. Of course, there was no good way to ask him. Rusted hinges shrieked as I pried the lid off. A gust of sour air immured in the underworld for fifty years curdled my nostrils.

There was no golden treasure inside the box. Instead, a skeleton lay at the stained bottom of the trunk, its bones intertwined with knotted silk cords and the Tibetan's bone-handled knife. I recognized Leopold Hargrave immediately. His own pupil had bound him, slaughtered him, and quietly buried him on the banks of the Miskatonic.

I began to chortle insanely, so giddy that I wondered if my excitement had driven me to a stroke. My limbs moved without any conscious intent of my own. It felt like I was in a dream, a mere spectator to my own actions. My body flooded with the shameful release that puppets must feel when their owner takes up their strings. I retrieved the knife and the cords from the trunk and then headed for West Arkham, expecting at any moment to wake up with my cheek pressed against the reading room desk again.

The door to Casar's house was unlocked. The professor waited for me, sitting upon his couch as proud and withered as an emperor's mummy. He offered no resistance as I wrapped the silk cords around him. I tied the complex knots flawlessly, mimicking the pattern on the card precisely, diagramming the space-time continuum in the medium of human bondage. "We are trapped in the web of time," I told him. "There is a spider named Death."

He looked up—to the extent that the ropes would let him—and his rheumy eyes pierced into me. "I will escape it in Leng," he said.

I cut his chest open along the seven-fold path, slicing along the seven dimensions that the sacred hand had indicated and transforming the aged academic's insides into a work of visceral alien beauty. I was proud that my hands were acting so masterfully, even if the mind that guided them wasn't my own.

I pulled the old man's heart out and exposed the hole in time's web.

I fell through the hole and into Leng.

I plummeted through absolute darkness in all directions at once, then smashed against some unbreakable barrier and imploded into myself. When I regained my senses, I was back in the misty limbo I'd dreamt of before. This time I couldn't wake up from the nightmare.

I staggered blindly through the fog, dreading that I would stumble off a cliff or into some alien creature but never encountering anything except empty space. A throaty giggle sounded from somewhere in the mists. I followed it, straining my ears to hear, until at last I echo-located its source. A naked creature in a condition of abyssal wretchedness crouched before me, tittering madly. It was Charles Casar; I recognized it from the photograph in his home. On a strictly physical level it looked exactly like he'd looked fifty years ago. Its body was lean, its hair dark and glossy. It hadn't grown even a day's worth of stubble. But though it had the form of a fit young man, it was plainly a wizened ghoul. The absence of time had destroyed Charles Casar.

"He got you, he got you!" the Casar-thing giggled. "You fell into Hargrave's trap! Same as me! Did the rite! Same as me! Hee hee! Hee hee!"

I strangled the Casar-thing for what felt like days, yet it didn't die. Death is the spider in the web of time. It can't get us here.

There are no days or nights in Leng; no sleeping or waking. I wander aimlessly through empty, eternal fog like a ghost haunting the void of outer space. Still, sometimes my mind drifts away from this endless prison and I catch brief glimpses of the life that Leopold Hargrave stole from me. I saw myself at my apartment, stowing a carton full of priceless golden idols in the crawlspace. I saw myself on a date with Chris, luring him into a dark and lonely place. I saw myself at home in Boston, sitting on my parents' bed covered in blood while my parents' German Shepherd whimpered trembling in a corner.

And I saw the Hell on Earth that came in 2469, when the Hargrave Collection was unsealed in its entirety.

HEKATI YOGA

BARBARA GAZED UPON THE BRILLIANT Monterey sunset, feeling nothing but tension and annoyance, and sipped expensive wine without tasting it. A headache brewed at the base of her skull. *Goddamnit, I don't have time for this*, she thought, scanning the cafe's patio for the old friend she'd come to reconnect with. *There's a million things I should be doing right now, and I let fucking Margie talk me into drinks.*

Barbara sucked down some more merlot and checked her phone again. Nothing. Just like Margie not to say that she was running late. In college, Margie's hippie, scatter-brained, rules-are-for-other-people nature had been endearing—charming, even—but they'd been out of college for twelve years now. They hadn't even spoken until a few days ago, when Margie connected on social media out of the blue and asked to meet up. *Insisted* that they meet up. At the time, Barbara had been curious to find out how the pot-dealing, boy-crazy, New Age madwoman of Epsilon Zeta Tau was doing. Now she was starting to regret that curiosity. She checked her phone yet again, and her furrowed brow pulled itself in even tighter when she saw that her boss had sent her yet another batch of analyst reports to look over in connection with the latest deal he was scheming up. *Jesus, so many words and so little insight*, Barbara thought. *I'll go through these tomorrow after the Tokyo call and before the meeting with the lawyers. Wait, though, what if Harry wants to discuss them on the Tokyo call? I'd better review them tonight, just to be sure.*

Just as Barbara was feeling sorely tempted to cut her losses and make her escape, her long-lost friend reappeared. Barbara's first impression was that Margie had made the transition from weed to meth. Her sorority sister's wide, unblinking eyes burned with weird intensity. When Margie spotted Barbara, her lips curled up over her teeth in a chimpanzee grin devoid of mirth or affection. But she was dressed like an Instagram model, and disgustingly tan and fit, so

Barbara guessed that her friend's strange expression was just the result of some bad plastic surgery.

"Baaaaaaaaarb!" Margie squealed, throwing her arms around Barbara.

"Margie, it's so good to see you again!" Barbara said, bringing all of her finely-honed chipperness to bear. "Epsilons forever!"

Margie ordered a gin and tonic and another glass of wine for Barbara, and the two sisters settled in for their reunion. "So, how *are* you?" Margie asked, staring intently into Barbara's eyes.

"I'm doing all right," Barbara said. "I've been working at a VC firm specializing in tech. It's a lot of work, but I love it." Margie continued to stare, expectantly. Barbara groped for something else she could say about her life, finding nothing. The backs of her ears began to burn with embarrassment as she shifted in her chair.

"What about that big rock on your finger?" Margie asked. "Who's the lucky guy?"

Barbara held the too-tight ring up for inspection. "Do you remember Jason Merchant?"

"Your senior year boyfriend, right? With the red hair and glasses? What's he up to?"

"Jason got his PhD in English literature, he's a professor now." *An adjunct professor. Who sponges off me for everything and always has his nose buried in a book and who can't ever be bothered to fuck me or even just ask how my goddamn day has gone.* Barbara's gut knotted up, the way it often did when she thought about her husband. She drank some more wine.

"Barb, don't take this the wrong way, but you seem super-stressed," Margie said. "You're giving off a lot of negative energy—your aura is, like, crimson, and your chakras are thundering. I know I haven't seen you in forever, and maybe I'm being presumptuous. Or maybe because I haven't seen you in forever, I'm in a better spot to notice what's going right and what's going wrong. So tell me, *really* tell me... How are you?"

Something about Margie's wide-eyed, insistent sincerity forced an opening in Barbara's steely emotional defenses. "It's been tough," she admitted. "I never expected to get anything for free. I knew I'd have to work hard. But sometimes it feels like it's all too much. Like I'm stretched *so damn tight* and can't relax for a minute, not even when I'm exhausted. Especially not when I'm exhausted."

"You know what you need?" Margie asked solemnly. "You need Hekati Yoga. It's this new yoga practice I started a few weeks ago, and it has *changed my whole life*. It's totally amazing. Makes you feel like a whole new person. No, scratch that. It makes you into a whole new person. I used to be anxious and miserable, and look at me now." She flashed that awful chimpanzee grin again. Her eyes bulged alarmingly.

"I don't know... I used to do yoga, but I don't really have the time for it these days."

The smile abruptly dropped from Margie's face. She stared into Barbara with a grim-faced seriousness that took Barbara aback—perhaps even frightened her a little. "Barbara, this is *your life* we're talking about. It only lasts a moment, and then howling entropy will devour you and your memory. Don't you need to make the most of your brief moment?"

In their sorority days, Margie had been more into karma and pyramids than howling entropic devourers, but the point was well-taken nonetheless, and Barbara had no rebuttal. They made a yoga date for a late afternoon class early next week, and spent the rest of their time together trading reminiscences and gossiping about their sisters. On the drive home, Barbara realized that she'd never actually found out what Margie had been doing since college.

———

Barbara drove past the yoga studio three times, cursing her cell phone's GPS, before she realized that the gated beachfront compound to her left was not, in fact, a billionaire's home or a country club, but rather, her destination. She announced herself to the intercom at the entrance, sheepishly mentioning that she had come at Margie's invitation.

"We've been waiting for you, Barbara," the intercom crackled. "Please, enter. The studio is the white building at the end of the drive." The iron gates buzzed and then slowly swung open.

The view from the road was misleading—the compound was even vaster and more beautiful than it had appeared. Barbara drove through in a state of covetous awe. The palatial, ultra-modern grounds were impeccably manicured, with vast lawns and tastefully arranged gardens overflowing with spiky, bulbous greenery, plants exotic even in a botanist's playground like California. Barbara tried to imagine how much it all could have cost, and her imagination failed her. This place made Harry's mansion look like a pauper's hovel. The yoga studio itself was a smallish, cube-like building on a low cliff directly overlooking the water. Its walls gleamed like polished bone in the sunset. As Barbara emerged from her car, the Pacific wafted a cool, salty breeze over her. *Margie didn't say anything about this*, she thought.

The reception area of the yoga studio was as minimalist as the exterior, with no furniture apart from a standing desk manned by a young, pretty receptionist in white clothes that matched the walls. In the center of the space stood a waist-high marble sculpture of three cloaked women back-to-back-to-back. Where their bodies touched they merged into one like Siamese triplets. The room was otherwise bare. "We're so happy you've come," the beaming receptionist said. "Welcome to Hekati Yoga."

"This place is amazing," Barbara said as she filled out the (suspiciously comprehensive) liability waivers. "I'm surprised I hadn't heard of it earlier. How long have you been here?"

"Oh, we have always been here," the receptionist said dreamily. "Even before the Indians, we were here."

Space cadet, thought Barbara. "What else do you offer besides yoga?"

"This is a full-service spa and healing center. We have all sorts of therapeutic treatments available to our advanced students."

"Ooh, what about massage? I haven't had a good massage in ages."

The receptionist's demeanor turned unexpectedly stern. "Spa appointments are for advanced students. Beginners would only harm themselves." In any case, after seeing what a single yoga class cost, Barbara wasn't sure that she could afford to ever return. *You need to treat yourself once in a while*, she thought, trying to convince herself. *You deserve the occasional splurge on something luxurious.* She paid for the yoga class, and the receptionist directed her deeper into the building.

Margie was in the mat room, chatting with a few of her fellow students, when Barbara arrived. Margie's face lit up like an anglerfish's lure. "Baaaaaaaarb, I'm so glad you could make it!" she chirped. "Let me make a few introductions!" A shuddering wave of revulsion swept through Barbara as she caught her first glimpse of Margie's yoga friends. On just a moment's further inspection, however, they were astonishingly attractive, fit, and fashionable. Her initial reaction did not fade entirely, but she could not put her finger on whatever could have provoked it. She made a few brisk pleasantries, then gathered up a mat and some blocks and headed for the practice space.

A gust of ferocious heat like the breath of some vast animal greeted Barbara as she opened the studio door. Sweat beaded on her forehead and soaked into her clothes almost immediately. "You didn't mention that this was hot yoga," she complained to Margie.

"Trust me, it's worth it. I know it seems a little kooky at first. Soon you'll understand."

The practice space's western wall was glass, offering a staggering view of the ocean. Waves pounded against the rocky shoreline, suicide attackers in the endless war between sea and land. The dying sun set the water and sky ablaze and suffused the room with blood-red light. The odor of brine was even stronger here than it had been outside. Barbara laid out her mat next to Margie's and sat down, assuming the lotus position. Her knees creaked painfully, and her spine complained. *Too long sitting at a desk,* Barbara thought. *I hope the instructor takes it easy on us.*

A door towards the rear of the practice space opened, and the instructor entered. She was a slender, long-limbed woman as pale and unearthly as the moon, without a hair on her head, not so much as an eyelash. The teacher took up her place at the head of the class, eclipsing the sun. It cast a crimson halo around her, shrouding her round face in darkness. "Namaste, my friends," she said in a still, monotone voice as soft as baby skin. "My name is Ana Poil. Welcome to Hekati Yoga. I see a number of new faces. That makes me very happy. I promise, this class will transform you."

She looks and talks like a crazy person, Barbara thought. *I should have known Margie would be mixed up in something weird.*

"Let us begin with our mantra," Poil said. "Iä."

"Iä," the class responded in one voice.

"Iä, iä, iä!"

"Iä, iä, iä!" *Kind of catchy,* Barbara thought, chanting along with her fellow students.

"Breathe deep, and hold," Poil said. "The whole of the universe is negative space surrounding you. Allow it to enter your core. Let the not-you suffuse every cell, till all distinction between you and not-you is erased. And exhale. Iä, iä, iä!"

"Iä, iä, iä!"

"Breathe deep...and exhale. The negative space defines us, gives us form and meaning, like a key defines a lock. Let it inside you to unlock your treasure. Breathe deep, to bring the great emptiness into yourself...now exhale, and discard yourself into the great emptiness. All is nothing, and nothingness is all. Iä, iä, iä!"

"Iä, iä, iä!"

Despite herself, Barbara was having a good time.

The class was unlike any that Barbara had attended before. Poil led her students through a series of esoteric poses—the Worm, the Gorgon, the Hydra, the Broken Circle, the Dying King—strenuously exercising muscles Barbara barely knew she possessed. Many times she thought that she couldn't go on, that only a circus contortionist could move the way these people did, but every time she was close to failing Poil's damp, yogurt-white hands grasped her and gently twisted her into position. The tension she'd been carrying throughout her whole frame gradually evaporated, leaving her loose and free. It felt as if she were melting in the heat; as if she were experiencing the pleasure that a rigid block of ice feels when it softens into cool, flowing water. By the end of the session she was panting, red-faced, and dripping with sweat, yet she couldn't remember the last time she'd felt so relaxed. On her way out, she made an appointment to return the following week.

Jason was dozing shirtless in the living room when Barbara returned home, a half-finished book and a half-finished beer resting on the arm of the sofa. Barbara paused in the doorway, watching his thick, furry chest rise and fall. A warm flush rose in her cheeks. The intensity of her breathing increased. *The negative space is coming inside me like a key into a lock.* She wanted something else to come inside her. To her own surprise, she found that she was dripping wet. She pulled off her sweat-drenched yoga clothes and dove atop her husband, ravenous with a long-forgotten hunger.

"What was that all about?" Jason asked during the cuddles afterwards. "I'm not complaining, mind you, it just seemed...unlike you."

"I went to a superb yoga class today," Barbara said, running her fingers through her husband's chest hair and down along the curves of his stomach. "God, I feel *alive* again. Invigorated. You should try it with me sometime."

"Nah, not really my thing. I'm glad you had a nice time, though."

Barbara idly grasped one of her own fingers and pulled it backwards, twisting the digit until its nail touched the back of her wrist.

"Jesus, cut it out!" Jason yelped, averting his eyes. "Gross."

"But it feels so good," Barbara purred. "Like a nice stretch."

"I never even knew that you were double-jointed."

"Neither did I. I guess I just never tried before."

Barbara awoke the next morning sore all over, so stiff that she could barely get to her feet. A headache throbbed behind her eyes; her limbs felt like they had been broken one by one and inexpertly set. Even Jason noticed, and he hardly ever noticed her suffering. "Think you might have overdone it on the yoga, babe?" he asked.

"Maybe," she grudgingly admitted. Later that day, she called Poil's studio to move up her appointment.

Barbara began doing Hekati Yoga multiple times a week, and then, multiple times a day. She found a little-used wellness room at the office and turned it into her own private yoga studio, slipping into it at every opportunity to practice the Dying King, the Hydra, and all of the other sinuous maneuvers that Poil had taught her. Soon she could twist her head like an owl, and coil herself like a serpent. Once she had learned how to twist her knees and elbows backwards at a 90-degree angle, she graduated from the beginners' classes and into the intermediate ranks. At night she would stay up late and imagine the wonders of the advanced sessions. Her mantra was never far from her mind. *Iä, iä, iä.*

To fall behind was to endure agony. Falling behind in her practice meant reverting to a clenched carcass of knotted muscle and exposed nerves, and so she dedicated herself to her practice as one pursued by furies. Jason said that he knew what it was like to be married to a drug addict. Nonsense. Drugs were bad for you, whereas Hekati Yoga was the most healthful thing that a person could do.

On the other hand, it *was* about as expensive as a high-end drug habit. Intermediate classes were even costlier than beginners' lessons had been, and then there were the artifacts to consider. Poil offered a wide variety of crystals, lotions, tinctures, sculptures, amulets, pyramids, and other such occult bric-a-brac intended for healing and wellness. Barbara quietly cleaned out the retirement accounts and took out some new credit cards. Fortunately, Jason trusted her to manage the money. One day after class, Poil took Barbara aside and showed her a black marble orb the size of a pigeon's egg, veined with blue and purple. According to Poil the orb was intended to sit inside Barbara's vagina, where it would infuse her root chakra with vaguely defined cosmic power. It was available for sale, at a price that would require a second mortgage to afford. Barbara went back to the office, and put in a call to her bank.

The orb made her feverish. Her mouth broke out in a red, sore rash that blistered and peeled. She believed it to have been worth every dime that she paid.

Hekati Yoga made Barbara's body pulse with life, drawing up a wellspring of desperate, consuming lust. She put all of her newfound strength and flexibility into her lovemaking, sometimes delighting Jason and sometimes traumatizing him and sometimes both. He began closing his eyes during sex, since seeing her boneless throes of passion alarmed him. "Like fucking a tangle of snakes," he remarked once as he sat on the edge of the bed, bloodless and distant. "You're going to be the death of me." And he was correct.

It happened during a torrential thunderstorm that sent sheets of water crashing against the roof and rattled the air with thunder. Barbara was riding Jason hard, the way a warrior might ride a horse on a suicide charge, while simultaneously flexing the core muscles she'd developed through countless repetitions of the Broken Circle. Exquisite sensations flooded her from her clit to her collarbone. She was lost in a world of her own. Suddenly her husband yelped underneath her.

"Jesus Christ!" he screamed. "Barb, what's happening?"

His shrieks broke Barbara out of her erotic fugue. She looked down and saw that her flesh was running like hot wax. Lumpy rivulets of molten skin trickled down her torso; her breasts sagged almost to her belly button and were heading further south. Jason tried to pull out, with no success. When he tried to push his lover away, his hands sank into her chest up to the wrists. She quivered with joy like a tower of human gelatin.

"Get off me, get off me!" Jason cried. "We've got to get you to a doctor. We've got to—"

"Hush," Barbara murmured, as lightning crashed outside. She thrust her hand into his open mouth and shoved it down his throat all the way to her elbow, enjoying the tickle of his frantic tongue on her slackening skin. Then she began to double and redouble her thrusting, each lunge pressing him deeper inside of her soft, loose body. Jason's increasingly desperate struggles to free himself brought Barbara satisfaction that his meager missionary work had never approached. Every kick and thrash sent warm, honey-sweet waves through her moist flesh. Jason bit down hard on her rubbery arm, and Barbara gasped with delight at the feeling of his teeth sinking into her. Her moans of pleasure turned into shrieks into ecstasy, and then into a low, gurgling roar. She felt a little queasy when one of his flailing hands got tangled up in her viscera. No matter, flexing the muscles she'd developed practicing the Worm pose pulled those inconvenient organs into a ball, freeing up more room inside her for her lover/prey. A tempest raged outside the bedroom, and a tempest raged within it.

Oh God, I'm so wet, she thought. *I'm a geyser, I'm a tidal wave, I'm an unstoppable tide.* Jason's doomed struggles brought her towards orgasm like cracks racing along a dam, crumbling everything that kept her tremendous sexual power contained within her, until at last she climaxed in a cataclysmic torrent of passion that annihilated everything before it. Barbara shrieked as the dam collapsed and then her whole body exploded into liquid, covering Jason head to toe in her devouring jelly. Lost in a delirious post-coital haze, she felt his struggles for air slow and then cease...she felt him twitching inside her as his oxygen-starved brain gave up the ghost. Together they slipped away into darkness. Barbara fell into a sleep as deep as death, and Jason fell into the genuine article.

———

When Barbara regained consciousness she was in agony, as swollen as a blood-gorged tick. Her body was beginning to regain its usual solidity, except that now she carried all of Jason's mass within her bloated torso. Painful spasms pierced her to her core as her innards tightened around the man-sized teratoma within her. It was as if a two-hundred-pound fetus had died in her belly. Slick, cool, pungent-smelling human grease soaked her skin and the sheets and doubtless the mattress underneath. She was sweating Jason out. It wasn't enough, though; it wasn't fast enough. Searing, invisible knives stabbed Barbara from every angle. *Oh God, I'll die if I can't save myself somehow*, she thought.

Barbara was too heavy to sit up outright, so she painfully rocked her clenching, spasming body back and forth—the bed creaking beneath her in protest—until she'd built enough momentum to get herself upright and into the lotus position. Folding her legs into place with her belly so grotesquely distended was a challenge. However, it was a challenge that Hekati Yoga had prepared her to meet. Barbara closed her eyes, concentrated on her breathing, fought through the pain, and stretched herself into the Gorgon pose. She began to recite her mantra. *Iä, iä, iä.*

It was astounding how easy it all was once she got started. Exercises that had previously struck her as pointless now revealed themselves as valuable preparation for a situation she could never have anticipated. Grease beaded on Barbara's skin and poured off her in cooling waves. She switched things up, assuming the Hydra pose, and dozens of toothless mouths opened all over her slick torso. Barbara pushed, and the mouths began to vomit hairy pink sludge studded with teeth and fragments of bone. Barbara groaned with relief from all of her mouths as she pushed the offal out of herself. At one point she passed a wedding ring.

Once the pain had subsided, Barbara rotated to the bedside table to look at her phone. She'd been passed out for two days. Despite her gruesome ordeal she felt well-rested and refreshed. Work was lighting up her email and voicemail with escalating fury. Reluctantly, Barbara put the phone to her oily cheek and called her boss. "Harry?" she said. "This is Barbara. I just wanted to let you know that I'm never coming in again. Fuck right off." Without giving him a chance to respond she ended the call and tossed the phone away. Even that was more of a courtesy than she felt he deserved; however, the very last thing that she wanted was for some busybody to report her as a missing person. She wasn't missing at all. She was exactly where she was supposed to be.

It took Barbara two more days to finish processing Jason. Once she'd excreted the last of him, she left the fetid swamp of the bedroom and treated herself to a scalding-hot, hour-long shower, washing away the last reeking, slimy remnants of her husband. She couldn't stop looking in the mirror as she toweled herself off. She'd never imagined that she could be this lithe, this strong, this beautiful. Her skin was glowing, literally glowing. She looked human again but knew that she was so much more than that.

Barbara retrieved her phone from the bedroom and called Poil. "I want to come in for an advanced class," she said. "I'm ready for it."

"I know you are," Poil replied coolly. "We start at midnight." Barbara checked the time. It was already 11:40.

Barbara drove to her yoga class with the reckless intensity of a demon except that she was utterly serene, passing trucks on blind curves at 90 mph in a state of Zen bliss. At the studio, a garbage can in the mat room overflowed with discarded clothes. Barbara stripped and threw away her own garments.

There were eight others waiting for her in the chamber, men and women, sitting nude and motionless. Margie was amongst them, and a few others whom Barbara recognized as well. Poil was in her usual spot at the front of the class, gleaming white in the moonlight. Lunar reflections from the waves bathed the hot room in shimmering silver light.

"Namaste, my friends," Poil murmured. "Let's start with our warmup exercises."

Poil showed her students how to twist themselves into hideous, unthinkable forms, violating the laws of anatomy and geometry alike.

The strains of the ghastly contortions, the hypnotic drone of the guru's voice, and the air as hot and wet as her lungs brought Barbara into a state of relaxation so profound that her body and soul collapsed. Her eyelids melted—she felt them running down her cheeks like tears made of skin—and as they dripped away and exposed her eyeballs, she saw that the rest of the class was likewise transforming. Flesh sloughed away and pooled upon the mats in wrinkled mounds. At the front of the studio, Poil blossomed into a milk-white meat orchid, beautiful and utterly alien.

"Stretch yourselves further," Poil said, speaking through a number of toothy mouths that had sprouted around what used to be her torso, her voice soft and mild as ever, even though now it spoke in a chorus. "Grasp your fellow students and become one with them. Grow extra windpipes if you need help with your breathing. And remember your mantra."

Iä, iä, iä.

Barbara extended her body to form a half-dozen tentacles that radiated from her core like the spokes of a wheel. This pose was very difficult to achieve, and even more rewarding to obtain. She shuddered with ecstasy as one of her tendrils came into contact with another student's appendage and they intertwined. More and more joined in. Warm, damp flesh coiled around Barbara and into her, forming an impenetrable tangle of impossible bodies. Barbara could not tell where she ended and the other students began, she could not even tell if such a boundary existed anymore. She felt her fellow students' racing heartbeats within her own veins as their circulatory systems merged. Nervous systems intermingled like kudzu vines.

Iä, iä, iä. Many voices recited the mantra inside Barbara's mind. She could not make out where others' thoughts ended and where her own began. She felt muscles not her own extend beyond human tolerance and burst into jelly. Strange voices cried out from her many throats in pleasure, relief, terror. All boundaries between Barbara and not-Barbara collapsed—the key turned and everything that made her a person was sucked away into the great emptiness.

Barbara's consciousness dissolved in a solution of infinite intimacy and devastating sensation.

"You're doing wonderfully," Poil told the superorganism that writhed and groaned before her. "Now that we've done our warm-up exercises, we can begin."

ALCHEMICAL WEDDING

"MOTHER AND FATHER, I WILL never see you again except in dreams," the note said, in neat, slightly childish handwriting. "My base matter has passed through the decomposition of nigredo, the purification of albedo, the transformation of xanthosis, and the perfect wholeness of rubedo. I have emerged from those four celestial crucibles as the purest gold. I have sworn myself to sacred mysteries and drunk the blood of the saints and martyrs. The Goat and the Dragon have blessed me. Now seven stars light my path to the alchemical wedding, and I can't wait any longer to go. Don't come after me—dangerous men and demons surround me. Forget that I ever lived, that's the safest thing for you. Love, Lily."

Benny Silverman, a seven-year veteran of the LAPD vice squad, re-read the note, then looked at the accompanying mugshot. Lily Collier was young, blonde, pretty in a puppyish way. A blank page on which all sorts of stories might be written. Benny looked up to the pictures of cops from days of yore that decorated the barroom walls as if beseeching ancestral spirits for guidance, and sipped his beer. "She sounds like a druggie to me," he proclaimed solemnly.

"She probably is," replied Frank Ramirez of the missing persons squad. "Her parents want her back in Minnesota regardless."

Ramirez and Benny were only casual acquaintances, but today they ate together because Ramirez had offered to buy Benny's lunch if he could pick his brain on the Collier case. "How long has she been missing now?" Benny asked, between bites of an exceptionally satisfying cheeseburger.

"They got this letter a week ago. Her landlord says she vanished sometime back in January, left all her things behind. She was paid in advance on her rent, too."

"What did her parents have to tell you?"

"Not much. She's 22, likes horses and cats. Lived with her parents and worked at a seed store until a year ago, when she took a trip to L.A. with her church group and never came back. She sent normal letters at first, saying that she'd met some guy and was working as a model, but they quickly started getting weirder and weirder until this last one. Her folks are worried she's having a psychotic breakdown or something."

"Reasonable concern. What do you have so far?"

"I found out she's been working a motel in Van Nuys. I had a talk with her pimp. A real charmer."

"What's he go by? I might know the son of a bitch."

"Sweet Gerald. Big fellow, missing a chunk of his right ear."

"Oh yeah, Sweet Gerald. Guy's a psychopath. Nixon wants to end the war, he ought to send Gerald to Vietnam. Airdrop him into the jungle with that butterfly knife of his and he'll have the Viet Cong turning tricks by Easter."

"Anyway, Sweet Gerald told me that Lily skipped out on him back in January, around the time she disappeared from her apartment. She said that she was done being a working girl, that she was going to be the bride in an alchemical wedding."

"Good Lord, she told Gerald she was leaving him to focus on her drug habit? Poor girl's probably in a dumpster somewhere. Maybe two or three dumpsters, depending on how fast Gerald's been riding the white rails."

"Honestly, I don't think so. He seemed scared."

"Scared? You sure you're talking about Sweet Gerald?"

"The mook goddamn near pissed himself when I told him I was looking for Lily."

"Christ, she probably *is* in a dumpster. I hate to say this, but you should be talking to someone from homicide, not vice."

"I truly don't think so. He didn't seem scared of me, he seemed scared of *her*. The guy kept insisting that if I found Lily, he didn't want me mentioning his name to her. Maybe she's got something on him, I don't know. The only other thing he'd say was that Lily had gotten into the porno business...she's been shooting stag films with an outfit called Rosy Path Productions."

"Rosy Path Productions? Yeah, that's an asshole named Hermes Valentino. He's been around forever. Mostly shoots that *artsy*, European kind of shit." Benny pronounced the word "artsy" with a deep and vehement contempt, as if it was the lowest adjective he knew.

140

"European" came in as his second most-despised word in the English language.

"Could you take me to his studio tomorrow? I'd like to chat with him, see if he knows anything about Lily's whereabouts. It'd be nice to have some backup who knows the smut picture scene."

"What's so special about this girl? She's over 18, not suspected of anything besides writing a crazy letter, not even behind on her rent. If Missing Persons went and rounded up every stray farmgirl in L.A., the city'd lose half its female population."

Ramirez shrugged. "I know, it's probably bullshit, but I got to work it anyways. It's all about that crazy note she sent. Ever since Manson, my lieutenant's had a hard-on for anything involving Satanists. He keeps telling us that he wants us to focus on any cases with an occult angle, that there's hundreds more of these Helter Skelter creeps hiding out in the California hills. Doesn't mean that he's signing OT slips, though."

"Alright, buddy, I know how that goes. I've got to be in court tomorrow morning, but come by my office in the afternoon and we'll go have a chat with my friends at Rosy Path Productions. I've got to tell you though, no disrespect to your lieutenant or the Collier family, but even assuming that this girl is alive, the odds we'll find her are not great. And the odds that she wants to go home are even slimmer."

"I still want to give it a good shake," Ramirez said. He downed the remnants of his glass and paid the bartender. "But you're probably right—I don't think she wants to be found."

The detectives were wrong about that, as they were wrong about so many things. I did want them to find me. I wanted it very badly.

"Hey, Benny, let me ask you something," Ramirez said as they drove down Lankershim Boulevard towards Rosy Path Productions. "How do you like working in the vice squad?" He smiled sheepishly. "I hear you've got a movie projector in your office, and you get to watch stag films all the time."

"Vice isn't a bad detail. It's a good crew of guys, and you get to scrape some real scum off the streets. But it's not the rollicking good time you think it is. I don't just sit around all day whacking off. That projector in my office? I have to watch *obscene* material on that thing." His mouth lingered over the word "obscene" as if it were bitterly flavorful. "Yeah, sometimes that's just a nice wholesome nudist film or an old-fashioned Swedish gang-bang or something. But the movies these animals make...sometimes there's kids in them. Sometimes there's blood. There's all different types of obscene films in the world. Some of them stick with you." The detectives spent the rest of the ride in silence.

Rosy Path Productions was based out of a shabby office building in Sun Valley that had once been home to a manufacturer of prosthetic limbs. "This place is like the gutter of Hollywood," Benny said as they got out of his Plymouth.

Sometimes people lose precious things and they wind up in the gutter. Maybe they're careless, or they don't recognize their treasure for what it is and throw it away. Once, back in Minnesota, I read a newspaper story about a homeless man who went looking in the gutter for cigarette butts and found a diamond ring.

Marie met the detectives at the door when they buzzed to be let in. Ramirez actually blanched a little the first time that he made contact with her brightly eyeshadowed gaze. She was an intense woman, compact as an owl and curvy as a serpent. Kind of an Earth Mother type with her peasant dress and hoop earrings, but too ethereal for that. A Moon Mother, perhaps. "Detective Silverman, what brings you here?" she asked, smiling like a vampire. "Shouldn't you be out saving the city from perverts?"

"We got new orders, darling," Benny said agreeably. "We used to save families from perverts, now we're supposed to save the perverts from the Manson Family. Hermes around?" Without waiting for an answer, he pushed past her and into the studio office.

Hermes Valentino was smoking a cigar and thoughtfully examining the penis of a nattily dressed albino when the police entered his workplace. The producer's face was placid, but a cocaine tempest raged behind his tinted aviators and across his bejeweled, twitching fingers. Nonetheless, the lawmen's arrival did not distract him from his purpose. I always liked Hermes; he was a professional and an artist in a business that attracts amateurs and hacks. It was a shame what happened to him.

"All right, you can put that away," he told the pale man. "Come back on Thursday, we start shooting at one p.m. sharp." The actor left, stink-eyeing the detectives as he strolled out the door, and Hermes finally deigned to notice them. "There must be some mistake, officers," he said. "I haven't called the police."

"We're looking for a missing girl, Hermes," Benny said, showing him my old mug shot. "Lily Collier. You seen her?"

Hermes glanced at the photograph. "Can't say that I have, officer."

"Her pimp said she'd been shooting pornos for Rosy Path Productions," Ramirez interjected.

"Rosy Path Productions does not put out pornography," Hermes said, with steel in his voice. "We produce high quality erotica, delighting the common man with beauty and educating the initiated by means of symbols and allegories."

"Six of one, half dozen of the other," said Benny. "Come on, I know she's been here. Just give me an address or the name of her boyfriend or something and I'll be out of your hair."

"Show me a warrant."

"So that's how you want to play it?" Benny asked, his temper beginning to simmer. He sniffed the air theatrically. "Hey, is that marijuana I smell?"

"There's no need for that, officer," said Marie, coming up from behind the detective and rubbing his shoulders. "If Hermes tells you that he hasn't seen this girl, why then, he hasn't seen her. And neither have I. But if you'd like to look around the studio to confirm she isn't here, we don't have any problems with that. This is an honest business, we have nothing to hide. Isn't that right, Hermes?"

"That's right," Hermes said, his wild eyes narrowing.

Marie led the detectives through a pair of furnished, well-lit rooms. One was a snowy white bedchamber, its centerpiece a massive four-poster bed shrouded with gauzy curtains. The next was a sitting chamber painted the color of blood, a gloomy place full of seedy, mismatched furniture. "This is our dungeon," Marie said, showing her guests into a chamber of painted drywall meant to resemble weathered stone. A statuette of an angel-winged, large-breasted, goat-headed woman kept vigil over a rack of torture implements both ancient and modern. A sharp, sour tang hovered in the air. "What's that smell?" Ramirez asked.

"Don't mind the odor," Hermes said. "That's just some of the chemicals we use for processing film."

In the editing room, Benny noticed a reel of 16mm film labeled "The Alchemical Wedding." He picked it up and showed it to Marie. "Is Lily Collier in this picture?" he asked.

"I've told you, nobody named Lily Collier ever shot a picture with us."

"You mind if I borrow this, then? Just to make sure she's not in it?"

Hermes' whole body shuddered convulsively. "Officer, you have no right to take anything from these premises. Unless you've got a warrant you –"

"It's fine," Marie said coolly. "Take it with our compliments. It might benefit you."

"But that's our newest movie, we can't just let it walk out the door."

"Detective Silverman will bring it back to us. Won't you, Detective? Once you've seen it, I think you'll agree that it's a very special film."

<hr>

Benny retrieved a bottle of rye from his office desk and poured two shots into coffee mugs. The detectives drank to my health. "Thanks for taking the time to check that out with me," Ramirez said. "I'm glad we went, even if we didn't get much. I'm calling it a day—like I said, my lieutenant's busting my ass on this but he's not approving overtime. Want to go grab a beer?"

"I'll stick around a bit longer. Maybe watch that film we took off Marie."

"Oh yeah," Ramirez said, grinning knowingly. "Have a good night." Benny felt vaguely annoyed as he watched the man leave, aggravated that Ramirez was presuming as to his intentions, and even more aggravated that Ramirez had presumed more or less correctly. Hermes Valentino was a pretentious smut peddler, but the hippie chicks he cast in his films were of legal age and generally pretty easy on the eyes. Benny figured that he would get a good show, or he would get confirmation that Hermes and Marie had been lying to him, or he would get both. The detective threaded the film into his projector and got it into focus, turned off his office lights, and settled in to watch the movie.

Dreamy, eerie synthesizer music blared from the projector's tinny speaker. As the opening credits rolled their litany of pseudonyms, I walked through dark woods hand-in-hand with a lanky boy. His name was Chad, I think. He reeked of drugstore cologne and shitty weed, although of course Benny didn't know that. Chad wore a black robe, and I, a topless wedding gown of the purest white. Together we strode a path littered with rose petals, approaching a golden tent. But the film's color correction was off, everything too bright and garish. Just as we were about to enter the tabernacle, I turned towards the camera and locked eyes with Benny. My beauty struck him like a club. That old mug shot really didn't do me justice.

Marie sat cross-legged inside the tent, her naked, ample body painted with the signs of the zodiac in all the colors of the rainbow.

"Today is our wedding day," I told the astrological goddess, my speech embarrassingly halting and druggy. Hermes didn't recruit his actors for their skill at memorizing lines. "I beg you, tell of my past, present, and future."

"In your youth you were a harlot," the goddess replied. "But now you are the bride of the alchemical wedding, and soon you shall be the holy mother of a new age. You shall pass through death to create astonishing new life." She produced a deck of tarot cards and laid six of them face-up before her. The Queen of Cups. The Fool. The Lovers. The Hanged Man. The Ten of Swords. The Four of Wands.

The film abruptly cut to the crimson room at Rosy Path Productions. There I sat astride a plush chair, wearing an open silk kimono the same bloody hue as the walls and a treasure hoard of jewelry. The tiara on my head glittered like a starry halo. The name "Mystery, Babylon the Great, the Mother of Harlots and Abominations of the Earth" was written on my face and body in lipstick. In my left hand I clutched a goblet overflowing with fresh blood. My right hand slowly wandered down between my breasts and across my belly to my pussy, tender and sopping wet from want. I began to gently probe, moaning softly. *The Queen of Cups sits on a throne at the edge of the water, holding the grail aloft.*

MAX D. STANTON

Benny thought that he had cracked the case, that he was sure he could use the film to pull my whereabouts out of Hermes and Marie. He thought that he had me at last. And he thought that the film wasn't bad, either. It had been a long time since Benny had been with a woman, as his work had largely soured him on human tenderness. Yet he still had urges, certainly, and sometimes when he was feeling triumphant he allowed those urges free reign. Benny double-checked that his office door was locked, and then unzipped himself. *The Fool wanders towards the edge of a precipice, a flower in his hand.*

We climaxed simultaneously. Benny's seed overflowed the tissue meant to contain it and spattered onto his office carpet, where the dirt-brown fibers drank it up thirstily. He sank into a wounded torpor, slumping in his creaky chair. I stared directly into his eyes as I put the cup of sweet, salty gore to my lips and drank.

End scene.

The next scene took place in the white bedchamber, where Chad and I were grappling vigorously on the four-poster bed. The music turned sharp, jagged, a cutting accompaniment to our moans. As we fucked with relentless, passionate abandon, Benny noticed something moving behind us in the background. Through the gauzy curtains, he glimpsed a silhouette looming over us. At first he thought it to be a camera operator who'd wandered into the shot, but the longer he watched the less plausible that theory seemed, for the silhouette was not that of a human form. The shadow was freakishly tall and slender, and two appendages that seemed uncannily like wings extended from its shoulders. The editing caused this apparition to blink in and out of existence as it went into and out of the frame, and somehow Benny felt its presence more keenly when he couldn't see it. *The Lovers come together beneath an angel's gaze.* Just as Chad was about to come, something burst through the curtains surrounding our bed. Cut to black.

Exterior. Forest. Chad dangled nude from a hemp rope strung over a pine tree's bough, his toes straining to reach the ground, his prick straining towards heaven. They hadn't recorded sound, so when Chad's mouth gaped open, only his tongue and droning synth music came out. The poor boy's face transitioned from red to plum to a really alarming purple-black. *The Hanged Man dangles between two worlds.*

The grand finale took place in the dungeon. Chad, his throat livid from rope burns, was handcuffed to a hefty oak chair. I was cuffed to another. We had not been blindfolded or gagged. Our cries and our terror themselves were important components of the ritual. Two men in domino masks and aprons over tuxedos entered the screen, one from stage left and one from stage right. The Knight of the West carried a long silver knife. Without a word he thrust it into Chad, taking meticulous care not to knick any vital organs. Then he slowly withdrew the blade, wiped it on his apron, and stuck it in again. There was sound for this scene, but Chad's throat was so badly wounded that his shrieks were ghostly rasps. It took ten thrusts before he finally bled out and his murderer relented. Benny witnessed the killing in impotent, gaping horror. *The Ten of Swords is ruin, destruction, desolation.*

The Knight of the East had a baton. In my eyes it was a tower as tall as the universe itself, and it was toppling onto me. The first time they beat me to death I was so wired on pennyroyal and speedballs that the blows barely registered. But when it gets played back everything is more intense. The colors are brighter and so is the pain. Four blows crushed my skull. *The Four of Wands is completion, rise, clarification.* As I slumped in my chair, four lilies sprouted from the blood spattered on my murderer's club.

THE END

The reel abruptly reached its conclusion, right after I did. It was not the worst snuff film that Benny had ever seen, but it was rough enough. The detective suddenly realized that he still had his cock in his hand. Revolted by himself, he tucked the flaccid thing away. Profound weariness perched atop his shoulders and drank his strength. The detective collapsed into a dreamless slumber.

Benny awoke in the quiet, liminal space between nighttime and dawn. *The Hanged Man dangles between two worlds.* He was deeply exhausted, perhaps even moreso than he'd been before he passed out. The detective noticed a crusty patch on the carpet, a clue leading back to himself, and shuddered with self-loathing. The projector was still running, although now it projected nothing but empty white light.

Benny threaded the head of the reel onto the sprocket to replay the film.

On the second viewing every moment was taut with dread. The detective's guts knotted as Chad and I stepped inside the astrological goddess's tent. Again she dealt the tarot cards. The Queen of Cups. The Fool. The Lovers. The Moon. Death.

Benny frowned. He could have sworn that wasn't right, but he couldn't keep all of this mumbo-jumbo straight. His frown turned to an open-mouthed gawp as the scene in the white bedroom came on. Chad had been excised from the scene entirely. Now Benny himself lay in Hermes Valentino's bed, kissing and caressing me. There could be no doubt that it was Benny—the camera had captured the birthmark on his thigh and the old scar on his back, a wound sustained in a boyhood BB gun battle.

"This is fucking impossible," the frightened detective muttered as he watched himself writhe and buck on the screen. Yet clearly it was not impossible, for it was happening right before his eyes. The Alchemical Wedding was consummated at last. The angel bore mute witness, its dark form growing closer and more well-defined with every cut the editor made. Benny yelped when it burst through the curtains, even though he knew it was coming.

Benny was afraid that the next scene would depict him hanging from a rope. Instead, it depicted me, sitting nude in an idyllic garden, flickering in the eldritch enchantment of time-lapse photography. My breasts swelled; my belly plumped and protruded. Nine months passed in the space of a minute. Sea brine burst out of me as my water broke. I shrieked and trembled as the baby born of our union slithered out from my innermost mysteries. *Suspended between two towers, the Moon gazes down upon the earth, where dogs howl and strange creatures crawl from the sea.*

The end came just as Benny was about to see the moonchild's face.

Benny frantically took the reel out of the projector, unspooled it with his fingers, and examined it before the light of his desk lamp, praying that this wasn't what it seemed to be. His prayer went unanswered, as prayers often do. The tiny still images that passed between his fingertips were identical to the moving pictures he'd just projected onto his office screen. He paused in terrified awe at the final frame, and at the sight of the sinuous, many-armed moonchild emerging from between my thighs.

A knock sounded from the door. Benny almost opened fire with his service revolver before he remembered where he was. He shoved the film into a desk drawer. "Come in," he said unsteadily, undoing the lock.

Frank Ramirez walked in with two coffees and a greasy, pleasant-smelling paper bag containing fried egg sandwiches. "Morning!" he said, with a chipper deportment that would have offended Benny under even normal circumstances. He assessed the vice detective skeptically. "Are you under the weather? You don't look good."

"Just tired is all. Thanks for the coffee. Christ, I can use it."

"Did you hear the news over the wire?"

"No, what?"

"Hermes Valentino is dead."

———— ⁓⁓ ————

Rosy Path Productions was swarming with uniforms by the time that Benny and Ramirez arrived. Benny forced his way through the scrum using his badge as a battering ram until he reached Valentino's office, now destroyed. The producer was sprawled across his desk with his head turned inside out. A lab tech hovered around taking pictures. Hermes had made his living photographing bodies; in death, the tables were turned.

A beefy cop in a too-small suit waddled over to Benny and Ramirez. "This is my crime scene, ladies," he said. "Unless a homicide detective has given you a task requiring your presence, I need you get out of here and stop trampling on the evidence."

Benny hated homicide detectives even more than he hated criminals. At least the criminals didn't condescend to him. "Detective Ben Silverman, vice squad," he said, flashing his shield. "We just spoke with the deceased yesterday afternoon about a missing persons case. Is there anything you can tell us?"

"We won't know much till we get the autopsy results back. Looks like someone knocked a hole in his face, then used a crowbar to lever his skull apart. You think this is related to your missing person?"

Ramirez showed him my picture. "Lily Collier's her name, she shot pornos for Valentino."

"She have any criminal history?"

"Prostitution and drugs. Nothing violent."

"Who called her in missing?"

"Her parents in Minnesota."

The detective scowled. "I've got a murder to work, and you're wasting my time with some runaway hooker? Get the fuck out of here."

"Lousy bastard," Benny grumbled as they walked back to his car. "Who's that pork log think he is?"

"We've got to find Marie," Ramirez said, trying to change the subject. "She did it, or she knows who did it...or she's already dead, too."

"Agreed."

"Oh hey, was there anything to go on in that movie Marie gave you yesterday? The...ah, what was it, *Alchemical Wedding?*"

An icy jolt shot through Benny's innards. "No, it was nothing. Just a shitty, artsy porno flick. Lily was in it, but just for a couple of minutes. She didn't even take her clothes off."

Ramirez frowned. He didn't have Benny's experience, but he was cop enough to recognize when he was being lied to.

<hr />

Ramirez hit the streets in search of Marie, and Benny went back to his office with the ostensible purpose of calling her friends. He wound up re-watching the *Alchemical Wedding* instead. Twice. Each time, the moonchild seemed to come into sharper focus, and "The End" took a little longer in arriving. Benny jumped when the phone rang.

"Hey, this is Frank. I just got a call from a beat cop I know. He says he saw a woman matching Marie's description going into a tug palace at 4th and Central. Place called Nero's Castle. I'm on my way over now. Meet me there!"

"No, wait–" Benny said, but by the time the words were out of his mouth he was talking to a dial tone. He shut down the projector and locked the reel inside his desk. Before leaving his office, he double-checked that his service revolver was loaded.

Nero's Castle was the sort of loathsome dive that no self-respecting pervert would step foot in. Only the lowest of the low can jerk off with rats running about their ankles. The theater was closed and the ticket booth empty, but the front door was slightly ajar. The shabby marquee advertised that the *Alchemical Wedding II* was playing.

A dead man lay in the lobby. Benny guessed that it was Ramirez from his build, but he couldn't be sure at first because the dead man's head was gone. The odors of stale popcorn, dried sweat, and fresh blood were overwhelming. Benny checked the corpse's pockets, found Ramirez's wallet, badge, and gun. "God damn it," he muttered, as a sudden wave of affection for the poor bastard crashed into him. A light was on in the theater. Benny drew his revolver and silently advanced.

The theater was empty save for a dark-haired woman sitting front row center. The projector was on, glowing in its booth like a UFO descending. Onscreen, a golden throne sat empty before some dingy purple drapes. A dirge-like score blared from the theater's cheap speakers.

"LAPD!" Benny shouted. "Put your hands above your head. Slowly!"

The woman didn't move. This was no surprise to me, since I'd been watching when Marie's face was torn away and devoured, but from Benny's point of view all he could see was the back of her head. He slowly walked down the aisle, keeping his gun sights trained on her, the soles of his shoes sticking to the carpets and making foul little *squick* noises with each step. Benny recoiled when he reached the front of the theater and laid eyes on the carnage.

"Hello, Benny," I said.

The detective jerked around, scanning the gloomy theater for a lurking killer, his eyes wide with mortal terror. It took a moment for him to realize that I wasn't in the theater. I was on the screen. There I was, a giant, sixteen feet tall, with a scarlet robe wrapped around my shoulders and the moonchild coiled around my torso. "I've been watching you for some time now," I said. "It's nice to be seen by you as well."

I took my rightful seat upon the throne and slowly massaged my left breast. Bloody fat spurted out from my nipple. The baby cooed, producing the noise of an emphysema victim's death rattle, and its face spread apart like a starfish unclenching itself. It latched onto my sanguine tit and suckled greedily. In one of its many hands it clutched Marie's left earring, a scrap of earlobe still stuck to the toy. "Have you come to see our child? I think it has your eyes."

"Lily?"

"I'm not really Lily anymore. They found Lily's body at Rosy Path Productions fifteen minutes ago, dissolving in a drum of acid. I am beyond her now, I have emerged from the cocoon of flesh as a creature made of light. Now I'm the bride of the alchemical wedding, and the holy mother of the new age."

"That's impossible," he said, even though he was holding a conversation with a woman projected onto a porno theater screen. "I can't have gotten you pregnant, you're a character in a movie."

"A movie is a story. And stories can change. You added your seed to the story. That changed the ending." The baby coiled tighter around me, its multitude of knotty little arms grasping and kneading my skin painfully. The nostrils at the crown of its skull widened as it tasted its daddy in the air.

Benny was starting to truly appreciate that this was his reality, and not just some terrible fever dream. The weight of this miserable wisdom crumbled him. "I—I can't have gotten you pregnant with that," he stammered.

"This is the first union of flesh and story in a very long time. It's the fruit of the alchemical wedding, the union of perfect opposites. A child born of Woman and Man, the Moon and the Earth, Fantasy and Reality, Heaven and Hell, Hollywood and L.A."

By now the detective was holding back tears. "It's killed three people already."

"More than that."

"It's a god damned monster."

"It's a god. You're the one who's damned. It's growing. Learning. It's going to change the world. There's just one thing it has to do before it'll be ready to claim its destiny." I blew Benny a kiss, and as I did my image suddenly flickered and vanished. The projector hissed and whirred as the reel ran past its endpoint.

"Lily?" Benny shouted. "Lily?" It was no good, he was shouting at a blank canvas screen. I was gone, but I had left him alone with our baby. He tried to shoot it. It didn't matter.

Benny's child had his eyes, all right. After it finished those, it tunneled its way through the front of his skull and began to lap up his brains.

EUPHONIA

MY DARLING ELIZA AND I enjoyed three years of wedded bliss before a prophetic demon made of clockwork gears and mannequin parts destroyed our life together. We performed a human sacrifice to save our love, and even that was insufficient. I do not believe that there is a moral to my story, but I shall tell it regardless.

Eliza and I were married on the 18th of January, 1843. Our match was mired in controversy from its earliest beginnings. Everyone agreed that Eliza and I were a handsome couple, and that her arrival had elevated my life out of its customary gloom and into a more vigorous state of being. However, my gossiping relations gleefully predicted that by the time of our first anniversary, either Eliza would be in Bedlam or I would be in Hell, or possibly both at once. Tempers ran hot in her family, you see. Eliza's father, a degraded country squire, spent most of his adult years alternating between spells of bilious melancholy and fits of choleric rage, and was eventually committed to a madhouse for dashing his gamekeeper's brains out in a fatal tantrum. To explore the paternal side of my beloved's family tree was to encounter a cavalcade of lunatics, imbeciles, fire-starters, dipsomaniacs, false prophets, self-described werewolves, and child-drowners.

Even more worrisome, Eliza's mother was of Greek and Sicilian blood.

Yet I refused to be dissuaded. For you see, I was so charmed by Eliza's liveliness and loveliness that a family tradition of violent madness seemed of little consequence by comparison. She was my pearl of great price, for whom a man might sacrifice everything and still count himself ahead on the bargain. Moreover, she displayed an amazing tolerance of my own foibles, particularly my overdeveloped taste for the macabre and esoteric, and indeed, celebrated my enthusiasms even when they were morbid or absurd. I considered it churlish to dwell upon Eliza's negative qualities given that she was so sweetly accommodating of mine.

Thus, although my darling wife occasionally descended into black, bloody moods wherein she would mutter gruesome threats against my bodily integrity, staring daggers at me from across the breakfast table and drawing a thumb suggestively across her throat, I accepted these episodes as the cost of our mutual happiness. I came to think of Eliza as a perpetually simmering saucepan, full of heat and spice and well-contained danger. Prim, even-tempered society ladies were no more appealing in my eyes than cold, membranous gravy.

Of course, the possibility that Eliza might one day explosively boil over and take my skin off did sometimes weigh upon my mind.

Our marital troubles began in earnest in the winter of 1846. London's occult bookshops and theosophic lodges were abuzz with word of a new exhibition that was said to shock even dedicated scholars of the weird. A German named Joseph Faber had invented a "talking machine" called the Euphonia, a device purportedly possessed of uncanny gifts of prophecy. Few who had visited Faber's show dared to speak of it again, and those witnesses willing to recount the performance insisted that Faber's creation had proclaimed astonishing, even distressing, insights. Having long been intrigued by the notion that one might achieve feats of chronomancy through eldritch clockwork, I became determined that I would see this marvel for myself, and Eliza cheerfully assented when I asked her if she would like to accompany me. So we dressed in our dark formal attire, and enjoyed a sumptuous feast at Eliza's favorite restaurant, and set out in a hired coach to attend a performance that would destroy our marriage and stain our hands with blood.

Faber displayed his creation at the Araignée Theater, a thoroughly disreputable establishment. The authorities had shuttered the Araignée some time ago after it exhibited the decadent French play "The King in Yellow," and I was surprised to learn that its doors had reopened. I was glad that we had a coach, for the theater lurked in a grimy and desolate slum so dismal that the neighborhood was nearly abandoned, even though London was bursting at the seams and the price of land was exorbitant.

We arrived just as the early show got out. The departing audience members staggered through the doors in grim silence, harrowed men and women shedding tears freely. It more resembled a crowd having witnessed a botched execution than an audience having witnessed an evening's entertainment. A pleasurable *frisson* of anticipation ran down my spine.

The theater's interior represented a spectacular vista of gorgeous decay. The Araignée's architect was a man of half-crazed grandiosity, who had mated a classical design dominated by columns and regal arches with a gothic sensibility of clamorous decoration and carvings. Finely-detailed murals depicting obscure, gory fables of Greek myth decorated the walls—Apollo flaying the satyr Marsyas—Icarus plummeting from the Heavens—Orpheus dismembered by savage, drunken women. But time and neglect had taken their liberties with the grand old place, and now the gods and heroes were rotting off the walls, and the plaster statuary was as crumbled as authentic relics. Even the curtain was scabrous. Legions of spiders had nearly cocooned the chandelier in their cottony webbing, and I imagined them up there in the darkness, working on their knitting as they watched the show with a multitude of tiny, beady eyes.

The lights dimmed and the muttering audience fell silent. Eliza took my hand in her own and rested her dark head on my shoulder.

As the curtain went up, I saw the apparition that had rendered the previous audience so pale and grim, standing alone in a spotlight ringed by inky, near-tangible darkness. The Euphonia was comprised of a female dummy's head mounted upon a sprawling, spidery contraption of bellows and pumps and gears and countless levers with blood-red leather handles, the whole of it around the size of a piano. I couldn't look away from the machine's terrible visage. Her disembodied head had the petrifying gaze of a Gorgon, and indeed, the ringlets of her cheap wig coiled around her face like ebony serpents. I shudder still to think of her rouged and chalky doll face, a face deader than that of any corpse. Knowing, reptilian eyes of smoked glass bored into me.

The audience loosed an overture of gasps and cries at the mere sight of this machine. Although perfectly inanimate, the Euphonia nonetheless had the presence of a living creature, a creature possessed of formidable power and malignant purpose. A clockwork Sphinx stood before us on the shabby stage of the Araignée Theater.

We could not see her claws, but I was sure they were concealed somewhere in the darkness.

Eliza's hand tightened painfully around my own. She had the wrists of a princess and the grip of a dragoon.

The darkness surrounding the machine trembled, and a man stepped forth into the light. He cut a haggard figure, with his snowy and untrimmed beard, an oily suit slightly too large for his frame, and a pair of oversized spectacles that reflected the spotlight and concealed his eyes behind twin moons.

"Greetings," he said in a heavy German accent. "My name is Joseph Faber, and I am the inventor of the machine you see before you. Her name is Euphonia. When I created Euphonia, I intended her as a sort of talking device, designed to mimic all the mechanisms of human speech. I soon learned, however, that she is capable of so much more than mere parrotry. Euphonia is a prophetess without equal. Her glass eyes see all. Her leather tongue speaks of the past, present, and future. Tonight, Euphonia shall perform miracles for you, my friends." Faber turned away from the audience and began pumping Euphonia's bellows. They seemed to offer a stiff resistance, for the effort made his shoulders tremble and his face turn red. "Please," he begged as he labored. "I need a volunteer to ask her a question. Any question at all."

After a long moment of hesitation, a man towards the front stood up. "Euphonia, who is the Queen of England?" he asked hesitatingly.

Faber pulled one of Euphonia's levers. The doll's glass eyes lit up with pale electric fire and her jaw dropped, exposing a mouth full of gleaming, sharp-edged copper pipes and a slug-like, horribly animated artificial tongue. "Queen Victoria," she hissed, her voice serpentine, with a tinny rasp. She spoke softly, yet every syllable carried with perfect clarity, as if she were whispering directly into my ear.

The machine identified the number of feet in a mile, the composer of the Magic Flute, the name of a man's childhood dog, the winner of an upcoming horse race. Eliza and I and the remainder of the audience all gawked and wondered at these feats. Faber, however, became visibly impatient with the queries being posed to his creation. Even Euphonia seemed to grow peevish with such pedestrian fare.

"Euphonia is no mere magician's puppet," the inventor interjected, after a man asked how much change he had in his pocket. "The greatest seer since Nostradamus is present in this auditorium! I'll show you. I'll show you all." He pointed to a man in the front row, the same man who'd inquired about the monarchy. "Euphonia, tell us something of that man's future," Faber commanded, as he pulled one of her levers.

Air whistled through Euphonia's metal throat, as if a pipe organ had erupted in mocking laughter. "Oliver Stokesly, you will die on the 23rd of January, 1851," she rasped. "Burned alive in a house fire." From the way the poor fellow's face went pale and his eyes bulged, it was clear that the machine had gotten his name right. The sentence of death having been pronounced, the condemned man sank down into his chair.

Faber continued to point out audience members and question his machine about their futures. It spoke, in chilling detail, about the crushing losses that they should expect in war, and love, and business, and life. She told a strapping young soldier that he was destined to be an invincible hero on the battlefields of Empire until the age of 24, when a tapeworm picked up in a dodgy piece of salt pork would dispatch him. She told a businessman how he would spend the next 30 years building one of the grandest railroads in England, and how once he passed into dotage it would take barely 30 days for his idiot son to run that railroad into an ignominious bankruptcy. Each fortune told was worse than the last, until Euphonia's levers were pregnant with the same terrible potential as guillotine ropes. The remnants of the audience began to flee, with some men scrambling over chairs or each other in order to make an escape before the hissing sibyl could address them.

Eliza sensibly tried to pull me away but, to my everlasting regret, I was too lost in the terrible spectacle of the fortune-telling to heed her. And to my everlasting shame, I froze with panic and guilty anticipation when Faber pointed to Eliza and said, "Euphonia, tell me a secret from that woman's past, and tell me a secret from her future."

The lever fell with terrible force. The bellows inflated and wheezed. The doll eyes glared. "Eliza Wickman murdered a man when she was a girl," the awful mouth hissed. "And she'll murder one more in the days to come."

Eliza's beauteous face contorted into a grotesque expression of horror and shock. Tears glistened in her eyes. It was the face of a murderess whose crime had been suddenly and unexpectedly exposed...which, of course, is exactly what she was.

Eliza and I returned home in a silent daze. Neither of us dared to speak until we were safely ensconced in the comfortable familiarity of our own parlor, and even then, we each required a couple of glasses of brandy before we could converse on the evening's events.

"It's true, then?" I asked. "You've killed somebody?"

She nodded, tears welling up in her eyes again. "When I was a girl of thirteen there was an awful old man who lived in a cottage on my family's land," she said. "Mr. Dunloap. He was said to have worked for my grandfather, although nobody living could recall seeing him perform labor of any description. He would sit all day on the porch of his falling-down shanty, sipping from a jug and saying disgusting things when women walked past him. When I went down the road to the store he would say, *Show me your petticoat, precious, show me your petticoat,* in a horrible sing-song tone. How I *hated him.*" She shut her eyes tight. I knew that in the theater of her mind, she was watching her childhood years, and that she was getting to the bloody part of the play.

"Did he—did he touch you?"

"No, I simply hated him. He was a worthless, pathetic creature, of no use to anyone, not even himself." A flush rose in my beloved's smooth cheek, and a dreamy gleam came into her eyes. "One day I lured him out to the lake," she continued. "I struck him twice in the temple with a sharp rock, and strangled him with a piece of rope I'd brought." Eliza's hands clenched, as if relishing the memory of the cord's texture on their palms. "I choked the life from him until his eyes bulged out and his wrinkled face turned black as a rotten prune. Then I dragged him through the reeds and pushed his body into the lake."

"And nothing ever came of it?"

"Nobody found his body until days later, when he was waterlogged and the turtles had been nibbling at him. Everyone thought that he'd simply slipped at the water's edge and drowned. I never imagined that anyone would find out. Oh, Paul, I never wanted you to know!" Her tears welled up in earnest now, and she shuddered with emotion.

I put my arms around her and rubbed at the small of her back. "Don't cry," I said. "It's all right. Truly, it is."

She pulled her head back to look me squarely in the eyes. "Do you mean it?"

"I do," I replied, speaking truthfully. "It sounds like you had your reasons for it. I'm not about to take the side of some deceased pervert over that of my wife; if you say that he deserved to be clubbed and strangled, well, I'll take your word for it. You might have confided in me earlier, but I understand your reluctance."

Eliza wiped the tears from her sparkling eyes and sniffled, then threw her soft arms around me. "Thank you for being so understanding."

"What concerns me is the second part of the prophecy," I said. "I'm not upset about the murder that you've committed in the past, I'm fearful of the one that you shall commit in the future."

"Oh. Yes. That." Eliza released her embrace.

"There is no real proof that Faber's abomination was telling the truth," I said, flailing for self-reassurance.

"We know what we saw and heard," she replied. "If Euphonia said I'll kill again, I likely will. I don't know how, or when, or who. But someday."

"And if you do..."

"Then you are my most likely victim." She said it with love and sympathy, which was somehow even more chilling to me than if she'd proclaimed it in hatred.

From that point onwards our relationship was as tense as a garrote wire. I had long known to exercise caution with the feelings of my hot-tempered love, but now I felt obliged to obsess over every word that I spoke in her presence, lest I inadvertently give offense and send her flying into a murderous passion. Our conversations became grim, terse affairs, as if she was a hangman and I a prisoner, awkwardly chatting whilst I was fitted for a noose. I began keeping a mental inventory of all of the piercing and bludgeoning instruments in our home, a safeguard which only heightened my perception of danger. A misplaced pair of scissors would send me into a panic. The sound of Eliza's footsteps coming down the hall, once the dearest noise in all the world to me, transformed into a dreadful portent that caused my heart to race in terror. It is a hideous thing to live in mortal fear of the person you cherish and adore.

"Darling, we cannot go on like this," I told her one evening after waking up screaming from a particularly vivid nightmare, in which Eliza brained me on a riverbank while Euphonia watched and hissed vicious encouragement from the reeds.

"But what else can we do?" she asked plaintively. "I will not endure the scandal of a divorce. You cannot make me!" She wrung her hands together so forcefully that her knuckles changed colour, and I imagined a fleeting image of Old Man Dunloap's throat in her grip.

Just then, a stroke of diabolical genius occurred to me, so brutally elegant I was surprised that neither of us had come to it before. "I think I have found a way to save our marriage," I said. "But it may cost us everything else that we possess, particularly our souls."

"What do you propose?"

"We must murder a man. Together, you and I."

Her eyes narrowed inquisitively. "Go on."

"The Euphonia proclaimed that you would kill one more man. If you kill a man—a man other than myself—then the prophecy will be fulfilled and the pall that has hung over us will be whisked away. I will be able to go about my life, absolutely secure in the knowledge that you will not suddenly put an end to it."

"If the police catch us, we'll dance at the end of a rope."

"I'm much less afraid of Scotland Yard than I am of you, my love. And if you're doomed to kill again—well, I'd like to offer whatever assistance I can in the matter."

Eliza's bright eyes brimmed with tears, and her cheeks flushed pink. Without a word, she rolled over and pounced upon me, smothering me with kisses. Then she violently tore my pyjamas away. If I had known that murder conspiracies were such an aphrodisiac, I might have begun employing them sooner in life.

We began plotting early in the morning while we lounged in bed together, too spent for further lovemaking but too excited to sleep.

"Have you given any thought to whom our victim should be?" Eliza asked, rather casually, as she ran her fingers through my chest hair.

"Some. The man should be a perfect stranger—a fellow with no connection whatsoever to either of us. And he should be someone who won't be missed."

"A vagabond, perhaps?"

"Perhaps. It's a hard thing, though, to murder a poor, friendless creature who's done us no wrong. A hard thing to do, and a hard thing to live with afterwards."

"I've got it!" Eliza exclaimed, the roses rising in her cheeks again. "We'll kill Faber!"

"Yes! That's perfect! He brought it on himself by creating and exhibiting that infernal machine." My ethical qualms against murder had been holding on by a thin scrap, and Eliza's suggestion tore them away entirely. Assassinating Faber would be an act of good service to mankind, Christian charity at its very finest. We simply had to get away with it without being caught.

I began to stalk Faber, pursuing him at a discreet distance through the environs of the dingy slums surrounding the Araignée Theater. Fortunately, the German clockwork-maker was a creature of habit and schedule, as I suspected he might be. He slept late, not leaving his desperate, pestilent flophouse until early in the afternoon, at which time he would invariably go directly to the Araignée. After playing two shows to steadily dwindling audiences, he would stay at the theater until late in the evening oiling and maintaining his ghastly metal goddess. Upon leaving the theater at night, he headed to one of the public houses on Rose Street to drink himself nearly to death, until at last the barman shoved him out and he staggered off to bed to start the cycle anew. Like a mechanical man living inside a cuckoo clock.

Eliza and I agreed that the theater was the best place for us to strike. We spent the next week single-mindedly plotting the assassination of Joseph Faber, and that week was the happiest and most harmonious of our marriage. There is nothing as pleasurable as working upon a challenging, exciting, and engaging project with the person that you love, whether that project is translating an old book or slaughtering a human being. Eliza and I stayed up late into the night discussing weapons and escape routes and alibis, our eyes locked, our hearts brimming with the deepest esteem and admiration. I still smile, thinking back on our magical week of murderous intentions and mutual adoration. I practiced tying knots around Eliza's slender wrists, an exercise that invariably sent her into delirious throes of passion. I prayed that it would not elicit a similar reaction from Faber.

Eventually the fatal day came. We had our coach drop us off at a goodly distance and walked to the Araignée. Dressing for the theater had taken on an entirely new significance this night. I wore a dark woolen coat with a high collar and a broad-brimmed hat, worn low to cover my eyes. Eliza had donned a dull grey cloak and a bulky bonnet of the sort she usually despised. Each of us carried a heavy valise. My heart hammered at my ribs, but with excitement rather than fear. Eliza radiated hatred—a pleasurable, intoxicating hatred, hatred that warmed one in the chill of the night.

We arrived just as Faber's final show reached its end, and watched impassively as the tiny, stricken audience dispersed, oddly unmoved by their suffering. As soon as the last of them had slipped away into the fog and dark, Eliza and I wordlessly entered an alley running along the theater's south side. My advance scouting had located a side entrance that was locked, but none-too-securely. I retrieved a crowbar from my valise and pried the door open with a satisfying crunch. As we stepped into the Araignée Theater, Eliza took a dagger from her own bag.

We came upon Faber on the stage, pumping maniacally at Euphonia's bellows. He was alone unless you count Euphonia as a witness, which I do. The damnable machine watched over its creator's ambush with keen and unwholesome interest.

"So, it is time at last," Faber said, choking on the words. He was gratifyingly terrified, but made no move to flee or defend himself. He paused for a moment to check his pocket watch and sobbed at the position of its hands. "You are right on time. Exactly when she said you'd arrive."

"Euphonia told you that you are to die today?" I asked him.

"She speaks of nothing else to me," the German moaned. "She taunts me with all of the grisly details. What a relief it will be to be rid of my future at last."

My beautiful co-conspirator and I had planned our assault with the rigor of a military campaign. I was to belay Faber with my crowbar until he was incapacitated and then bind him hand and foot, at which point Eliza was to cut his throat. Yet if we had strategized our strike like Wellington at Waterloo, we executed it like the Goths sacking Rome. Eliza fell on Faber, roiling with fury before I even thought to raise my arm against him, her eyes and her knife flashing. My sweetheart plunged her weapon to its hilt in the German's belly and he fell shrieking, spraying the stage with gore. Without hesitation Eliza straddled her squirming victim and began to butcher him alive. I had to stop up my ears to keep out the sounds of slicing flesh and agonized gurglings. The salty, coppery stench of blood suffocated me. I tasted Faber in the air.

The German persevered in his sufferings for far longer than I thought possible. Eventually his thrashings gave way to pained struggles, which faded into feeble twitches, before he gave up the ghost entirely.

"We've done it, my darling," I gasped. "Euphonia's prophecy is fulfilled, and we can know peace again. We must..."

Eliza was not listening. She was still fully engaged in her gruesome work, a crimson demon insensate with rage. She pulled the dead man's head back and sawed her dagger through his already-tattered neck as forcefully as she could, putting all the muscles of her back and shoulder into the work. It nearly decapitated him. Then, like a savage dog, the woman I love sank her fine white teeth into one of the gaping wounds she had hacked into Joseph Faber's belly, and pulled out his reeking guts in her jaws.

My own jaw fell open at this spectacle.

Mercifully, Eliza soon ran out of steam. Panting, she tossed the dagger aside. She extended a glistening red hand to me, and I helped her to her feet. With the very utmost of caution and delicacy, I slowly put my arms around her trembling shoulders. We stood on the stage in total silence, but for her exhausted breaths and the pounding of both our hearts.

Meanwhile, Euphonia glared at me, her awful doll mouth curled in an ever-so-slight smile. Blood had misted upon the machine, leaving a gory dew.

"We should go to the washroom and clean ourselves up," I said. "Then we can change into the fresh clothes that we brought and get out of this theater of the damned."

"Before we go, what do you want to do about that?" she asked, pointing towards Euphonia.

"We should destroy her," I said. "Decent people can't allow a thing like this to exist." I picked up my crowbar and brought it down hard across Euphonia's face, crushing her nose and splitting her eerie face in two. To my everlasting regret, however, I failed to damage the machine beyond repair. Just as I was about to strike again, her eyes suddenly blazed with eldritch ghost-light, and her lung-bellows began to pump of their own accord. Her chipped red lips drew open. I frantically hammered on the contraption with all of my might, but to no avail. Euphonia spoke again before I was able to crush her inner workings, and with her final words, the demonic machine avenged her maker and destroyed me.

Eliza and I had murdered Faber so that we might live together happily as husband and wife, without the sword of fate perpetually dangling above my head. Yet Euphonia's cruel words dashed all my hopes of joy, and set me at a bleak crossroads. That vicious device of soothsaying torture doomed me to choose between a life of miserable and heartbroken solitude, or one of ceaseless and perpetual terror.

You see, the first time that Eliza and I had visited the Araignée Theater, Euphonia had prophesied that Eliza was going to murder one man.

This time, Euphonia told me how many men Eliza was fated to *maim*.

THE PENANCE LAKE ROADSIDE WAX MUSEUM

SUSAN WILCOX SPED DOWN THE highway, paying more attention to her rear-view mirror than to the road ahead. The road ahead of her was straight, deserted, safe. Her mother's house in Appleton, Wisconsin, waited at the end of it. The road behind her was twisted, treacherous, terrifying. Her husband, Bruce, was somewhere behind her. And he was in pursuit.

Susan had not heard from Bruce since she'd left Phoenix, but she knew that he was coming.

"Cut it out!" wailed a shrill, plaintive voice from the back seat.

"Meredith, whatever you're doing, *stop it right now!*" Susan barked. The girls had been sniping at each other ever since they'd woken up that morning in a piece-of-shit Kansas City motel, and their tempers were only getting hotter as they rode further and further away from the only home they'd ever known.

"I wasn't even doing anything," sulked Meredith. Her goth outfit matched her mood, all dark colors and sharp points. "June's just being a baby again."

"I'm not a baby!" little June chirped defiantly. "Merry's being *mean!*"

"I know you girls are tired and bored," Susan said. "I'm awfully tired, too. And we've got a lot longer to go. So I need both of you to be quiet until we get to Grandma's house. Can you do that for me?"

"You could turn the car around," Meredith said contemptuously. "Take us back to Dad. You do that, and I'll be quiet as a mouse."

Susan's anger flared bright and hot inside her. The thing she hated most about Bruce—more than his violence, or his cruelty, or his bottomless self-absorption—was his skill at showing a false face to everyone other than her. To the neighbors he was a friendly, ordinary guy. To the Phoenix police he was an upstanding citizen doing his best with a hysterical wife. To the girls he was the fun parent, the one who was always quick with a joke or a trip to the ice cream parlor, the one who left discipline up to Mom. Being the only person who saw his true nature was so goddamn lonely. Susan knew that at some point very soon she would have to sit down with her daughters and explain to them that their dear old Dad was an absolute piece of shit masquerading as a human being. She would have had the talk a long time ago, except that she was terrified that Meredith wouldn't believe it, and the prospect of enduring that ultimate rejection from her own child was more than she could bear.

"We can't go home," Susan said firmly. "I told you, we can't go home and we can't contact Dad. We'll talk about it when we get to Grandma's. Until then, please just be quiet and let me drive."

"Mom?" June asked sheepishly. "I have to go to the bathroom."

"What? I just asked you if you had to go, back when we passed that Chik-Fil-A."

"I didn't have to go then."

Susan was annoyed, but the prospect of a pit stop sounded good to her as well. The sour, piss-warm gas station coffee that she'd been drinking to stay awake sloshed uncomfortably in her bladder every time she hit a bump in the none-too-smooth road. Her legs were cramped, her spine was sore. And the girls were liable to tear each other apart if she couldn't find something to distract them and wear them out a little. And so Susan felt a little tingle of relief when she spotted a weather-beaten billboard advertising a nearby tourist trap.

"Visit the Penance Lake Roadside Wax Museum at the next exit," the peeling sign proclaimed. "An attraction like no other. Presenting education, entertainment, and spiritual instruction. Come and see." A grinning boy was painted on the billboard, although it was unclear if he was meant to represent a satisfied visitor or a waxworks dummy.

"Let's go see the wax museum, girls," Susan said wearily. "It'll be a nice break. We can use the restroom, and stretch out, and take our minds off things for a little bit. How does that sound?" As she asked the question, her eyes glanced reflexively back to her rear-view mirror.

Bruce Wilcox barreled down the highway, feeling the comforting weight of the .38 revolver in his glove compartment as if the gun was in his breast pocket. Bruce was pretty sure that today was his last day as a free man, and quite possibly his last day alive. The notion thrilled him with morbid giddiness.

"I feel good about this," Bruce said cheerfully. He often talked to himself, as he enjoyed the sound of his own voice immensely. "Susan's won a lot over the years. She's taken my dignity, my self-respect, my youth, my money, my children... Well, today I get to win. She's not getting away with it this time. Not today, and not ever again."

Bruce's stomach rumbled. "I should get something to eat," he muttered. "Might be my last meal." As if by magic, a sign appeared proclaiming the presence of a Chick-fil-A at the next exit. "Oh yeah, *fucking perfect*. What a great day this is." Bruce went through the drive-through and picked up twice his usual order. He feasted in the parking lot, and it was the best goddamned food he'd ever tasted.

The Penance Lake Roadside Wax Museum was a long cinderblock rectangle that squatted in weedy desolation, like some gigantic traveler had tossed an enormous piece of litter out the window. If not for its neon signage, Susan would have thought the place to be deserted. There was only one other car in the parking lot, a panel van with the museum's name hand-painted on its rust-stained sides. Susan thought about getting back onto the highway and holding out for the next rest stop, but the pressure of the used coffee inside of her cried out for release, and the girls in the back seat cried out at each other, and she relented.

The museum entrance opened onto a small, dismal room clad in wood paneling and lit by harsh, buzzing fluorescents. Stiffly posed statues of Santa Claus, Elvis, a cowboy, and a cave man stood in the four corners. Their faces were all turned towards the entrance. Vacant smiles beckoned. Glass eyes watched. A tuxedoed figure lay on a table near a turnstile leading to the attractions.

Behind the counter, a paunchy, aged clerk with a tragicomic comb-over hovered about, overseeing a few shelves of dusty merchandise and an old-fashioned cooler stocked with off-brand pop. Susan mistook him for a wax figure at first, until his eyes narrowed and his wet red lips pursed. The appearance of paying customers seemed to disquiet him.

"Welcome to the Penance Lake Roadside Wax Museum," he said, in a soft, bland tone. "Is this your first visit?"

Susan didn't suppose that this attraction had ever gotten a dollar of repeat business, but there was no point in being rude. "First time," she said, forcing a smile.

"Let me tell you of our history, then. My father, Curtis Visco, used to operate a filling station located at this very spot, until Christmas Day, 1957, when a defect in one of his gasoline pumps triggered an explosion that engulfed him in flames. Father dangled between life and death for many weeks, and in that state he had visions of the world to come.

"When Father finally awoke, he resolved that he would build a wax museum, to show everyone the wonders that he had witnessed on the heretofore unseen dark side of existence. Father put every dime of the insurance money into making that vision come true. He let nothing stand in his way—not his pain, not the opinions of others, not the needs of his family. And he achieved what he set out to do."

"Mom! Check this out!" Meredith chirped.

She was gawking at the wax figure lying in state next to the entrance turnstile. The dummy was hideously deformed, noseless and earless and lipless and shriveled. Its crafter had put intense, loving care into every scar and nodule. A coin slot bisected each of its closed eyelids. "Badass," Meredith murmured.

"That's an exact replica of Father," the clerk said. "I sculpted it myself. Father passed away on Christmas Day, 2007. This time for good, I believe. His last will and testament instructed me to make a wax figure of him, and to place it at the gate of the museum that he had dedicated his life to."

"Creepy," Meredith laughed, her voice bright with enthusiasm. Susan was about to reprimand her for bad manners, but the clerk didn't even seem to notice, and Meredith's good humors were too rare to spoil. In any case. Susan was too damn tired to fight with her family anymore.

"The museum is divided into three sections," the clerk continued. "The first section is dedicated to the splendors of life on Earth. The second depicts some of the ways that man might leave that life. The third shows what lies beyond, in the realm of the spirits."

"You mean like the second chamber's like, deaths and executions, and the third is ghosts and angels and things?" Meredith asked, still examining the sculpture of the museum's maimed founder. "Cool. I want to see."

One operated the turnstile by dropping quarters into the slots in Curtis Visco's closed eyelids. Meredith giggled as she inserted her coins. June was fearful but willing to go along, as she so often was. Susan, exhausted and close to bursting, just hoped that the restroom was okay.

And so the Wilcox women entered the first hall of the Penance Lake Roadside Wax Museum.

The boxy room before them was windowless, harshly lit, and shabbily carpeted. Inside, a dozen or so tableaus of awkwardly posed mannequins stood on display. A few wax statues had been placed outside of the exhibition areas, as if they were visitors eternally admiring the attractions. "June, sweetheart, do you need to use the bathroom?" Susan asked.

The little girl shook her head bashfully. "I thought I needed to make a number two but then I just farted."

"She sure did," Meredith commented.

"All right, well, I'm going to use the bathroom," Susan said. "You two don't go far and *stay together*." She looked back to the ticket office, where the clerk gazed wistfully out the window onto the empty road, his lower jaw gently agape. "I mean it," Susan said forcefully. "Don't go far."

The bathroom was tiny, but clean and mercifully nondescript. Susan relieved herself, and then continued to sit on the porcelain throne, her head in her hands. In her moment of solitude, she allowed herself to briefly put down the great burdens that she'd been shouldering for her daughters' sake. Now that nobody was looking to her for strength and reassurance, she let herself feel the surging emotions that she'd been keeping pent up. Susan Wilcox sat in the wax museum restroom and silently wept.

As she washed up afterwards, she noticed old traces of the bruises that Bruce had left around her wrist. She'd laughed at something he'd said, thinking he was telling a joke—when he was in a good humor he could be hilarious—but he was in fact deadly serious, and he proved it by hurling her against the nearest wall. Susan examined the bruises carefully, analytically. She traced their faint brown aureoles with her fingertips. *Those are the last bruises that Bruce is ever going to give me*, she thought. *Look at how quickly they're fading. And he's never going to get the chance to hurt June or Meredith like this. He's never even going to see them again.* The thought gave her hope and strength.

But when she came out of the restroom, her daughters were gone.

Bruce was singing along with the radio when his phone dinged. It was another text from Merry. "Mom took us to some stupid wax museum. Wish u were here u'd get a kick out of these lame dummies." She'd attached a picture of a crude pirate mannequin who had an eyepatch over his left eye and nothing at all in the right socket.

Bruce chuckled, and dictated a message in reply. "I wish I could be there, too," he said. "Everyone back home is asking about you. Hang in there, Merry, it won't be long until I get this thing with your mom sorted out and then I'll get to see you again." He sent the text, and pressed his foot harder against the gas pedal.

"Merry's a good girl," Bruce mused. "She really is. June, too. Christ, I wish I could keep them out of this entirely. It breaks my fucking heart. But the great whore Sue took that option away from me, just like she's taken everything else away from me. I'm going to prison or dying today, and if I go to prison or die then the girls will go to live with Sue's vile bitch of a mother, and I will be *goddamned before I let that happen*." His knuckles clenched painfully tight on the wheel. "I will be goddamned," he repeated. "I will be goddamned. I will be goddamned."

Terror caught Susan like an owl catching a mouse, impaling her from multiple angles. It was the worst terror she'd ever known, far worse even than when Bruce had held his gun on her. Then she spotted the girls coming out from behind a stand of mannequins, and the terror released her just as quickly as it had seized her. Susan staggered towards her daughters, emotionally whiplashed.

The girls were examining a display of grimy wax children at play. The mannequins seemed to be playing tag on a field of Easter basket plastic grass, except that most of them had been posed wrong. Limbs bent in ways that limbs don't move, fingers stretched backwards. Their faces were off, too, eyes slightly too close together and mouths just a little too wide. Only one of the things looked decently human. The wax boy's face was frozen in a rictus expression that was probably supposed to be joyful laughter but came off as a silent shriek.

"Not very lifelike, are they?" Susan asked. Meredith snorted and shuffled off towards the next display.

"They've very lifelike," June said solemnly. "It's just like Curtis Visco saw."

Susan's brow wrinkled, and then, thinking that her little girl was joking with her, she smiled and laughed. June did not join her.

Meredith hid behind a tableau of Americana that depicted the Founding Fathers as leering, subtly misshapen troglodytes circling around a vacant-eyed Lady Liberty and a saturnine Uncle Sam. A mannequin in a stained suit stared at this quasi-patriotic display with his hands on his hips and an expression of lunatic glee fixed on his face, like he had the good fortune of gazing upon the greatest fucking thing in the world. Susan envied the dummy its idiotic satisfaction.

"Meredith, I know this has been hard on you," Susan said. She wanted to put a comforting hand on her daughter's shoulder, but it was covered by a strip of chrome spikes. "I owe you an explanation, and I swear to God you're going to get it soon. In the meantime, can you please trust that I'm trying to do the right thing for you and your sister, and give both of us a break?"

"I don't know what you're talking about," Meredith sighed dramatically. "Let's just go to the next room of the museum."

Bruce spotted Susan's car in the parking lot of the Penance Lake Roadside Wax Museum with the pleasure of a predator spotting a tasty morsel napping. A feeling of triumph surged through him, chased by an icy premonition of dread and doubt. "You know, you haven't done anything irreversible yet," he told himself. "You can take the next exit, turn around, go home. Let the lawyers handle it. You might even get the girls."

"And then Sue wins again," he continued. "You back down from her *yet again* and she wins *yet again*, and for the rest of your life, you have to live with the knowledge that you weren't man enough to confront your own wife. No, fuck the lawyers. Fuck it all. You need to handle this yourself, my friend." He pulled into the parking lot.

It occurred to Bruce that he didn't want his car to be visible from the road. He circled round to the rear of the building, and very nearly ran into a ditch. The proprietors of the Penance Lake Roadside Wax Museum had dug a long, deep trench into the ground behind the building. Dozens of cars, perhaps more than a hundred, were piled in the hole rusting.

Like its antecedent, the second chamber of the Penance Lake Roadside Wax Museum was a windowless box. But unlike the amateurish displays that inhabited the first room, the statues here were vividly, alarmingly lifelike. The Wilcox women stepped out of a hall full of crude and bewildering mawkishness and into a scene of unremitting horror. They found themselves in a vista of stoning, beheading, shooting, dismemberment, industrial accidents, torture, pestilence, clubbing, hanging, mutilation, and in one corner, a screaming man being torn apart by a pack of foamy-mouthed dogs. Wax men knelt in red plastic puddles, hopelessly trying to stuff their fake guts back into their artificial bodies. Imitation killers pantomimed the act of murder, their faces artfully arranged into expressions of crazed contempt. At the far end of the room, a winged figure in white stood on a platform mounted over a doorway, gesturing obscurely. A featureless cowl covered the angel's head, exposing only its mouth and jaw. A gauzy curtain hung from the doorframe, shrouding whatever lay beyond.

"Ugh, disgusting," Susan said, grimacing. "That clerk should have warned me it was going to be so graphic. We don't have to stay here, girls. Come on, I don't want you to have nightmares." Nor did she want to supplement her own, which were already unbearable.

"No, I like it," Meredith insisted, heading onwards. She took out her phone and began snapping pictures, taking a selfie of herself next to a sumptuously detailed and anatomically accurate recreation of a man being torn in half on the rack.

"I'm not afraid either, Mother," said June. "There's no point in being afraid of them. Not now."

Susan sighed. "Fifteen minutes, max, and then we have to get back on the road!" She hung back, looking at the walls and the floors, while her daughters explored the atrocities.

Christmas Day at Penance Lake, 1957, was at the heart of the exhibit. A half-melted wax figure in a ragged service uniform writhed in perfect stillness at the center of a ring of flickering electric lights, a surprisingly believable illusion of consuming flames. "Mom, can you get a photo of me with this?" Meredith asked, handing over her cell phone. "This'll look great on my Instagram."

Susan took the cell phone and tried to open up the camera. She accidentally opened Meredith's text messages instead, and her already-crumbling world exploded entirely when she saw them.

"Meredith, what is this?" Susan demanded, shoving the phone at her daughter's face. "Have you been texting with your father? Have you been telling your father where we are?! I told you not to do that! I told you that was the one thing you couldn't do!"

"Fuck you, he's my dad, I'll text him if I want to!" Meredith screamed, trying and failing to wrestle the phone away from her mother. "What do you care, anyway, he's back home and we're stuck in the middle of nowhere in this stupid wax museum!" She started to cry, her tears mingling with her raccoon-like mascara and running down her cheeks in black, oily streaks.

"You've put us all in danger!" Susan screamed. "Why can't you ever trust me? Why can't you do what I say?"

"I hate you!" Meredith shrieked at the two people who loved her most in the world. "You and June ruined everything for me! If not for you two I could have stayed with Dad and everything would be all right!"

"Don't you dare blame your sister for this! Or me! It's not our fault!"

"Well, it's sure as fuck not mine!" Meredith spat. Still weeping, she ran out of the chamber of horrors, into the museum's third and final hall.

"Come back here!" Susan ordered, although she might as well have been ordering the statues around. "We have to leave *right now!*" She took a deep breath to collect herself, and realized that June was standing by her side, staring at her impassively.

"She didn't mean it, sweetheart," Susan said, taking her younger daughter by the hand. "She's just stressed right now, we all are. Come on, we've got to go find her and get back on the road."

June, who was ordinarily wounded to tears by her sister's unkindness, was eerily serene. "We are in their teeth now, Mother," she said. "We have always been in their teeth. Try to remember."

Susan had neither the time nor the energy to decipher that riddle. She pulled her daughter beneath the hooded angel's gaze, into the terminal chamber of the Penance Lake Roadside Wax Museum.

———❧———

Bruce looked down at the stacked cars in the trench. It was like automotive history in sedimentary form, with newer-model cars heaped on top and older models at the bottom. There were even a couple of cop cars in there, and what looked to be a church van. None of the cars in the ditch had been stripped for parts. They still had their tires, which in many cases had disintegrated into gangrenous black shreds. This pit wasn't a junkyard, and whoever had dug it had taken great care to ensure that it was invisible from the road.

Bruce, who just moments ago had been pondering the murder of his entire family, now wondered if he should call the police. "This is certainly fucked up," he muttered. "Something seriously wrong is happening here." He felt scared, so he got his gun out of the glove box, and as soon as his fingers wrapped around the grip he came to enjoy godlike confidence. "Yes indeed, something terribly wrong is happening." He stormed into the museum.

"Welcome to the Penance Lake Roadside Wax Museum," the seedy-looking clerk behind the counter said mildly. "Is this your first visit?"

Bruce shot the man through his face. The clerk's whole body shuddered as if pulling the trigger had sent a powerful electric shock through him, and he dropped, leaving a Rorschach blot of blood and brains on the wall. Bruce saw a winged angel in the stain. He had never imagined that he would take so easily to homicide, and felt pleased that at his age he still possessed the capacity to surprise himself. He hopped the turnstile and proceeded into the attraction.

"Come in, Bruce, come and see," Susan whispered from somewhere up ahead.

"Susan? Where are you?" He went in after her, thinking wrongly that he'd spotted her amongst the statues. The things played havoc with his nerves. They seemed to sneak and fidget in the periphery of his vision; whispers came from all around. Bruce felt simultaneously surrounded and deeply, unbearably alone. Something jumped in the corner of his eye and he accidentally squeezed off a round, blasting an artificial woman's head into a cloud of dust and polystyrene hair and setting his ears ringing.

"Daddy, Daddy, come and see," Merry laughed, but her voice was thin, ethereal.

As Bruce walked through the hall of horrors, the murder he'd just committed began to sink in. His heart raced at cocaine velocity. Every inch of his skin tingled with a strange and unpleasant sensitivity. He saw himself in all the executions as both killer and victim, and wondered which method the state would use to get rid of him. They all looked agonizing.

"Susan, where are you, goddamn it?!" Bruce bellowed. "Merry? June? Daddy's here!"

An answer came from the hall yonder. "We're in here, Bruce," said Susan and Merry and June in toneless unison. "Come and see. Come and see."

Bruce pushed aside the curtain beneath the masked angel. His eyes widened in horror as he beheld the final chamber of the Penance Lake Roadside Wax Museum and the mind-shattering statuary inside. Curtis Visco had seen the world beyond death, and he had faithfully rendered it in wax and bone and gold. It was an image that consumed the viewer, a spectacle that devoured the eyes that took it in. Bruce glimpsed peacock wings wrapped around impossible faces—hydra-headed creatures with bestial visages both unfathomably alien and uncannily familiar—blasphemous portraits of terrible crowned spirits whom the living were never meant to witness.

Susan and Merry and June strolled amidst the sculptures, clad in billowing white shrouds. A hideously burned man walked at their side, guiding them through the hellish exhibition. The stranger turned to face Bruce and smiled a red, toothless grin. His eyes glowed like molten pennies.

The gun clattered from Bruce's nerveless hands.

"Oh good Christ," Bruce whimpered. "Oh good Christ please no."

THE HERO OF MAGDEBURG

JAN CAME OUT OF OBLIVION with his head swimming and his ears ringing, surrounded by the mangled remains of his friends. He struggled for a moment to remember where he was, and then the Swedish cavalry charge came back to him in all its whinnying horror. The men trampled into the mud all around him had been some of the finest soldiers in the army of the Holy Roman Empire, but Luther's bastards had undone them in a single pass.

A dense stand of trees waited not fifty strides away, the perfect place to escape mounted troops, yet Jan did not like the look of it. He saw something sinister in the way that the tree branches slowly swayed, as if they were beckoning him. At the Siege of Magdeburg, Jan had not hesitated to charge the breach in the Kröcken Gate and the forest of enemy pikes that lay beyond it, but this forest of harmless trees gave him pause. He wondered if he had any other choice.

Jan slowly allowed his aching head to loll to the side to get a better view of the battlefield without giving away that he still drew breath. Most of the Swedish troops had dismounted and were looting the dead and dying. Blonde buzzards. They had tied one of Jan's comrades, a red-bearded Walloon whose name Jan had never learned, between two chargers. Someone fired a musket into the air and the riders set their mounts into gallops, such that the shrieking Walloon's arms went in one direction and the rest of him was pulled off in the other. Into the woods it was.

Jan pushed himself off the ground and darted for the trees, keeping low to avoid the enemy's bullets. The thing he hated most about coming under fire was that one never knew where one might be hit, and that invested one's whole body with a horrid, tingling sensitivity. Shouts and pops sounded from behind. Jan heard the bee-like sound of lead passing by, including one shot that came so close it seemed to pass through the back of his head, but he did not fall. Then he passed through the tree line, plunging headlong into the green and gloom.

He heard his enemies pursuing, crashing through the brush and yelling to each other in their odd, sing-songy language, but unlike him they were weighed down by heavy armor. Their guns would be useless at this range and with so much cover, and with his head start he was sure that he could escape. He'd find some safe hiding spot, and as soon as night fell he'd double back around and return to the Imperial lines. The Count of Tilly had to be warned that the enemy was so close and so formidable.

He was not sure how long he ran, or how far. Eventually he came to a reeking brook coated in scum, the water barely visible beneath its blanket of slime and dead plants. A dead woman floated in the muck, wearing nothing but a necklace of black and purple bruises around her pallid throat. She'd been a beauty once but wasn't anymore. These days it was not a remarkable thing to come upon corpses. But then, as the languid current carried her downstream, she opened her eyes and mouth and began to sign in a hoarse, strong voice.

> It was on a hot summer night
> When the nightingales sang their sad tune
> I went down to the river to see my true love
> Beneath the light of the pale Harvest Moon.
> Darling oh darling I cried,
> Our love was too hasty and soon
> In the spring we first made our two bodies as one
> And since then I've not bled with the moon.
> But my lover he held me so close
> I remembered the sweetness of June
> And he told me that he would make everything right
> As the nightingales sang their sad tune.
> Oh how I blushed and I laughed
> I thought I could hear wedding bells
> Then my true love's strong hands, they wrapped 'round my throat
> And in his blue eyes I saw hell.
> In terror I tore at his hair
> But my struggles did cease all too soon
> And our poor little baby it died in my womb
> As the nightingales sang their sad tune.
> My lover laid me on the banks

To do again what he first did in June
Then he set me adrift 'midst the frogs and the snakes
While the nightingales sang their sad tune.
Oh while the nightingales sang their sad tune.

Jan gaped in horrified awe as the musical corpse floated past. He thought that he had already witnessed or participated in every variety of awfulness that this fallen world had to offer, but now he saw that he had been wrong. At Magdeburg they had not left enough people living to bury the dead, so the surviving locals unceremoniously dumped thousands of charred corpses into the Elbe River. On the march out of town Jan watched the legions of floating dead, with fish and turtles bobbing up out of the depths to nibble, and flies buzzing all about. It was a hideous sight, but those dead, at least, had not broken into song. Since then, any body of water larger than a puddle had made him anxious, and the taste of fish made him gag. Jan tried to cross himself, but his hand wouldn't make the motions.

His thoughts drifted back to the girl in the green dress at the wine shop. She must have ended up in the water as well, another delicacy for the trout. No, he didn't want to think about that. The priest absolved him, and besides, it hadn't been a sin to begin with.

The dead woman was going downstream, so Jan went upstream. Eventually he came to a narrow, arched stone bridge nearly as slimy and green as the river itself. A large heap of rags and garbage lay at its far end. Jan started across so as to put the river between himself and any Swedes that might still be in pursuit, but as he reached the opposite bank the pile of rags coughed and rose, taking on the form of a man if one used the term loosely. The bridge keeper was tall and broad-shouldered but hunched over such that his fingers nearly scraped the ground. His posture reminded Jan of an ape he'd seen once, chained to a wandering juggler, except that the bridge keeper was much larger and nobody would pay to see him exhibited. A burlap cowl masked the man's face. He held out a thick, four-fingered hand wrapped in dirty bandages. His other hand held a hatchet.

"Four pennies to cross into the Lady's Wood," the bridge keeper said. His voice was low and raspy, and he spoke an odd dialect that Jan hadn't heard before, understandable but only barely so. "One for each of the Lady's maidservants and the fourth for little old me."

War bred this sort of scum like rotten meat bred maggots, bandits with no allegiance to any cause, king, or general but themselves. Ordinarily Jan would have never consented to pay this villain's toll, but ordinarily he carried a sword and a musket. He'd broken off his sword in a Protestant's ribs during a skirmish that morning, and he'd lost his gun somehow during the charge. He still had his favorite knife on his belt and more good Toledo steel in a sheath in his boot, but he didn't relish the concept of a fight to the death for four pennies. Four pennies seemed a reasonable price for avoiding a scrap with this brute, especially given how bloody the day had been already. And in any case, he had gotten rich in the sack of Magdeburg. Jan reached for the sack of gold that he kept around his neck and was appalled to find it gone. It must have been torn off him somehow during the day's fighting. Maybe one of the Swedes had taken it away while he was knocked senseless. In any case, all of the fighting and killing and suffering had been for nothing. Not nothing exactly, there was the rightness of the cause to consider, but you couldn't buy anything with rightness.

Without making any overt move towards violence, Jan let his right hand hang down near his belt knife. "I don't have even one penny on me, brother," he said. "Let me across, and put the four pennies on Emperor Ferdinand's bill."

"No emperor in these woods," the bridge keeper replied. "Only the Lady rules here."

Jan wrapped his fingers across the knife's hilt.

"I'm a sensible man," the bridge keeper said. "If you don't have any money, we can strike a deal. Let's just leave the Lady's maidservants out of it, and settle up directly between the two of us." The bridge keeper rubbed himself indecently with his deformed paw, and raised his hatchet.

Jan drew his knife and slashed horizontally, tearing the bridge keeper's throat open. The man did not drop his axe, or even lower it, but his next heartbeat sent a gusher of bright red blood spurting from the wound. He put his free hand to his neck, attempting to hold it shut, and swung his hatchet with surprising strength. Jan barely dodged a blow that would have cleaved his head in two if it had connected. The bridge keeper raised his weapon for another blow.

Jan thrust forward this time, punching the tip of his blade straight into his enemy's heart. The bridge keeper's axe tumbled from his fingers and clattered on the stone. The man let out a wet wheeze and dropped.

Jan cleaned off his knife using the dead man's rags—well, wiped the blood off, anyway; you couldn't clean anything using those rags—and put the weapon back in its sheath on his belt. How many times had that blade saved his life now? Just then he heard shouts and horses. He looked down at the fallen bridge keeper. So that his enemies couldn't follow him by the trail of the dead, he hoisted the man up with a mighty effort and rolled him over the side of the bridge into the water, where he disappeared with a splash. Maybe soon he'd be singing a song about the brave soldier who had killed him. Jan then ran to the far side of the bridge and ducked underneath it as four Swedish riders appeared from the direction of the battle.

There was a crude camp down here, but Jan had no time to take the details in. He dove to the ground, taking cover in a patch of tall grass, and watched his enemies pass by. The Swedes paraded by the bank of the river, peering over to the side where Jan lay hiding. Despite their advantage in numbers, arms, and mounts, they seemed apprehensive. One of them pointed to the spot on the bridge where Jan and the bridge keeper had fought, and Jan realized that they'd probably spotted the blood. Tossing the scoundrel in the drink had been a useless effort after all. The horsemen consulted amongst themselves, and then rode on without crossing. Jan rose up from the grass, feeling relief for the first time that day. He couldn't figure out why the riders had departed so rapidly even after catching his trail. Perhaps they'd decided that the prey wasn't worth the chase. Perhaps they didn't want to give their comrades time to snatch up all the good loot from the battlefield. In any case, best not to question good fortune.

On the subject of loot, Jan looked around the bandit's camp to see if there was anything that might help him on his journey back to friendly territory, food especially. He hadn't eaten since early that morning, and the day's trials had set his stomach growling. Jan found a few crumpled blankets so filthy that he wouldn't have put them on a horse, a heaping midden overrun by rats, and a tin pot suspended over some smoking coals by a crude tripod of sticks and twine. Jan thought he smelled cooking pork as he approached the pot, and his mouth began to water. But when he looked inside, he retched and bile rose up into his throat. The pot was full of a greasy brown stew, made up of chopped turnips, weedy, wilted greens, and two severed human hands. Jan inspected the midden pile. Scattered amongst the remains of a deer and a mischief of busy rats he saw human bones and matted clothing, the bones scraped by teeth marks, and many of them cracked to expose the marrow. At least one of the monster's victims had been an Imperial soldier like himself, for Jan saw some clothes similar to his own mixed in amongst the refuse. Jan was profoundly glad that he had killed the bridge keeper rather than giving the creature any tribute. Even in wartime, when a great many sins were permissible, this was disgraceful and sick and wrong.

Suddenly there was a splash from the direction of the river, and something hit Jan hard from behind, knocking him down into the refuse heap. The rats scattered, chirping in offense as the fight broke up their banquet. Before Jan could move, the bridge keeper was atop him, heavy as a boulder, even further befouled from his dip in the river. He locked one of his hands around Jan's throat in a noose-like grip, and with the other he pulled Jan's belt off and tossed it away. Then he began ripping Jan's pants open. Jan scrabbled at the bridge keeper's face, tearing his hood away, and what he saw beneath it would have made him scream if he could get any air into his lungs.

The creature beneath the cowl was not human, but he couldn't have been an animal, either, because Jan was sure its like had never gamboled in Eden. The juggler's ape had been a more artful parody of man. The bridge keeper had gnarled, bestial features with a boar-like jaw, a blood-red protuberance of puffballs and pustules that might have been a nose, and sunken yellow eyes with no pupils in them. He was covered in patches of wiry black hair, and crawled with lice the size of grasshoppers. "Hello, little darling, how about a kiss for the hero of Magdeburg?" the creature hissed.

The words sent a jet of ice through Jan's veins. The troll leaned forward, forcing his cold, swollen, drowned-man's tongue down Jan's throat.

Jan tore at the troll's face and neck and his fingers hooked into the monster's open wound. Jan reached inside, grabbed at whatever meat he could get hold of, and pulled, yanking the troll's tongue out of his own mouth and through the cut, leaving it to dangle like a grotesque neckerchief.

Jan managed to get his legs up under his attacker and kicked him away with an enormous effort, knocking him back into the river. He drew the knife in his boot and leapt onto his foe, driving the blade down into one of the troll's eyes with a powerful overhand thrust. Then he gave the same treatment to the other. The blinded bastard bellowed out of both the old mouth in his face and the new one in his neck, tongue lapping against his collarbone, and lashed out with a backhanded blow that sent Jan sprawling. He rose from the reeds and staggered towards Jan with his eyes running down his cheeks like gruesome tears, the boot knife's hilt still sticking from a socket.

Jan backed away from his enemy and picked up two large, pointed rocks. He tossed one of them into the river. As the troll turned towards the splash, Jan caved in the crown of the monster's skull. The troll stumbled beneath the blow, but still did not fall despite his brains leaking out of him. That was fine with Jan. He wanted to hit the son of a bitch some more.

By the time the troll went down and stayed down, Jan's arm burned and he was covered in cold sweat and hot blood. Somehow the abominable, deathless creature still breathed, and its arms and legs flopped weakly.

"Why did you say that to me?" Jan asked the troll. "About Magdeburg?" The troll gurgled something, but Jan realized that asking questions of this thing was futile. Even if he tried to answer, his tongue wasn't in his mouth anymore.

A second axe lay on the ground by the midden. Jan picked it up and brought it down across the troll's neck with the same even swing that he used to chop firewood. A satisfying jolt ran through his forearms as he decapitated the beast. The bridge keeper's awful, ruined face continued to twitch and grimace, though, and his arms and legs continued to writhe. Jan carefully dismembered his fallen enemy, and even after he was hacked into six pieces all of the pieces continued to move independently of each other, like a worm. Jan tossed the limbs into the river one by one, being careful to put some distance between them. The arms still tried to grasp for his throat while Jan threw them away. Jan dropped the head into the stewpot, even as it tried to bite at his hands, then fed coals into the fire until the pot boiled over.

At first Jan had thought to shelter here until nightfall, but now he knew to a certainty that he didn't want to be in this forest after dark. The main Imperial force was camped miles to the east. He and his fallen comrades had been sent out from it on their ill-fated expeditionary mission and now he was the only one left who could report on what the expedition had found. Jan walked away from the setting sun, and while he moved at a rapid pace the woods seemed to go on endlessly. He was sure he would have reached civilization by now, or at least what was left of civilization after more than a decade of war. On the previous day's march he had passed through any number of sacked towns and burned fields. Now there was only forest primeval. No sign of Adam's children at all. The shadows were getting long, and he was getting desperate.

Just as the sun was setting, he reached a meadow where a lovely young maid gathered blackberries. He expected her to scream for help and run in terror at the first sight of him—that was the only sensible reaction for a lone girl encountering a bloody and bedraggled soldier like himself—but instead she smiled. "What do we have here?" she asked. "A brave Catholic knight back from the war?"

He was just a lowly foot soldier but saw no reason to correct her. "Yes," he said. "I need to get out of these woods and get a message to my general. In the name of—in the name... Please help me." He had wanted to say, "In the name of God, please help me," but his tongue could no more pronounce the name of the Almighty than his hand could make the sign of the cross.

The maid stroked his cheek tenderly, even though his beard was full of mud and clotted troll blood. "Of course I'll help, you poor man," she said. "I know a place nearby where you can rest. It's so calm and peaceful you'll forget you ever went to war. No more fighting now, my sweet knight. No more struggling. Just follow me."

Jan had not cried since he was a child. Indeed, he'd thought his last tears had been beaten out of him in boyhood, as if he were a wrung-out cloth. Even when burying old friends or suffering miserably from wounds or lying awake on the black nights after defeats, he'd maintained a manful composure. But now that he was confronted by this sweet, kind girl after the hell he'd been through—and the hellish things he'd done—the tears welled out of him like the waters of the Great Flood. The maiden wrapped her soft white arms around him as he sank to his knees weeping.

When he had recovered sufficiently to stand, the girl took him by his bloody right hand and led him through the forest, following a stream that ended at a steep, mossy hill, where a waterfall threw off mist and rainbows in the red light of dusk. It was very nearly as beautiful a sight as the maiden. Ancient, worn stone blocks pressed into the side of the mound formed a crude staircase, but even with those, Jan had to use both his hands and feet to ascend. "Is your home atop this hill?" he asked the girl as they climbed.

"The whole forest is my home," the girl said gaily. "But this is the part of it that I like best."

"Where is your father?"

"In Hell."

Fair enough. Jan couldn't imagine his own father singing amongst the choir eternal, heavy-handed bully that he'd been. "Your brothers?"

"I don't have any. I have two sisters, though. They live with me in the forest. You might meet them later on."

"But how do you and your sisters survive here without anyone to watch over you? How do you keep the wolves away at night?"

The girl laughed. "Are you volunteering to be our bodyguard? There's no need. All things that live beneath these trees serve the Lady of the Wood—wolves included—and they would never harm us without her leave."

So despite her seeming piety the girl had some heathen in her as well. It was like that with so many country folk. They'd keep a cross in the right hand and a sprig of mistletoe in the left. But better to be half good Christian and half pagan than Protestant and damned in the entirety.

"What do you do about the two-legged wolves, then?" he asked.

"Men like you? Oh, don't look so sad. I was just teasing. The truth is that I do have a protector. Brucellus is his name. Whenever I'm in the slightest danger, Brucellus comes galloping to my side—so don't think about any funny business, my knight." She winked at Jan and smiled again. "I'm a virgin and I think Brucellus aims to keep me one forever. Hush now, we're almost at the top."

The forest was alive with the cries of little creatures and the conspiratorial whispering of the wind and the trees, but at the top of the hill, silence reigned. A ring of tall stone slabs covered in moss and runes stood vigil around a steaming hot spring. The spring's waters trickled over down the edge of the hill to feed the waterfall. The girl led Jan to the edge of the spring and peeled away the ragged clothes that were nearly glued to his body with mud and blood and sweat. Jan glanced uneasily at the standing stones around him and stepped into the bath. Immediately he felt a soothing relief and refreshment so welcome that he nearly burst into tears again. The water around him darkened as his coating of filth dissolved. He dunked his head beneath the steamy water and scrubbed the dirt and gore away.

When he emerged, the girl knelt at the edge of the spring. She put her hands on his bare shoulders and massaged them. Her hands were soft for a peasant girl. "My bold Catholic knight," she purred, nibbling at his earlobe with her sharp little teeth in a way that brought equal parts pain and pleasure. "My big, strong man. My hero of Magdeburg."

Jan started, and pushed the girl off him. There was no way she could know about that. "What did you say?" he demanded. "Why did you call me that?"

Behind the girl, a creature paced at the edge of the stone circle. In the same way that the troll had shared the basic shape of a man while being entirely wrong in the particulars, so this thing aped the stallion. The monster had a lean trunk covered in matted white fur, a wild mane of red spines like a fire coursing along his head and neck, and eight muscular legs ending in sharp, jagged hooves that tore the earth apart as he walked, his muscles rasping metal-on-metal with each step. A drooping sac of tumorous yellow flesh at the center of the beast's forehead concealed most of his head. He stared at Jan with a dozen or more milky white eyes scattered about the sides of his head like boils, white foam drooling from his toothy muzzle.

The girl, noticing Jan's terror, turned around and saw the intruder. "Oh," she said casually. "Brucellus is here. He must think you're a threat to my virtue." She laughed, making a sound like tinkling bells.

Brucellus pawed the ground, spraying up clods of black dirt, and roared louder than cannon fire. The flaccid yellow sac on his forehead rose up, twitching, and stiffened into a long and vicious spear. Then the unicorn lowered his head to charge.

Jan scrambled dripping out of the spring, shoving the girl aside, and ran for the closest edge of the hill. It was too steep to descend without falling to his death, but there was a thick tree branch just beyond its edge. Jan took a running leap of faith and latched onto the limb. He hung there naked, dangling in midair over a long drop, with his feet kicking at nothingness. He glanced back towards the hill. Brucellus paced back and forth at the spot Jan had just jumped from, trying to reach out with his horn to prod Jan off the branch. The tip of the unicorn's horn danced just inches from Jan's bare ribs, sharp as any spear. The diabolical virgin sat at the edge of the hot spring, watching the scene unfold with a devilish grin on her red lips. "Get him, Brucellus!" she cried.

Jan heard the sound of wood cracking and felt a stomach-churning jolt that nearly pried his arms apart. The branch he clung to was buckling beneath his weight. Another crack, louder this time, like shattering bone, and Jan tumbled screaming. Pain clubbed him across his midsection as he fell onto a lower branch, and the wood cracked again and he fell again. The branches struck him over and over as he plummeted, as if the tree itself sought to beat the life out of him for daring to seek shelter in it. Then he hit the stream, dropping through the water to embed in the suffocating mud at the bottom. He could not see, he could not breathe. He struggled against the mud but the harder he fought the more it sucked him in. Somehow he managed to pull himself free of it and shot up for the surface, his lungs screaming for air. He washed up against the bank, coughing and sputtering and astonished to still be alive.

At the top of the hill, the unicorn roared again. He crawled down the waterfall like a spider, his legs spread at angles utterly unlike that of any horse, screaming in rage as he darted through the rainbows. Jan pulled his aching body out of the water and fled for his life. He didn't dare to look back, but he could hear the jealous monster behind him, snarling and whinnying and crashing through the woods. In a forest this dense, Brucellus couldn't break into a full gallop, but he was still a horse—or at least a horse-like thing—and Jan was still a man, and the ultimate outcome of the race was not in doubt. Finally Jan could take it no more. He looked over his shoulder and saw the demon steed almost atop of him, thrusting his yellow lance towards his shoulders. Jan dove away from the unicorn, back into the river.

The current was swift and powerful at this spot, and it carried Jan right away, pounding him mercilessly against sharp rocks, pulling him beneath the surface again and again to choke him on the foul water. Burned bodies swept through the river alongside him, their lifeless hands grasping at him from all around. Then the motion ceased, and all was cold and dark.

Jan lay still as a dead man until he realized that he had washed up on the riverbank at a bend. He crawled onto dry land vomiting mud and water, and pulled himself onto his feet. Dazed, exhausted, and in tremendous pain, he staggered blindly onwards through the woods, until eventually he fell into unconsciousness.

Jan awoke to the piercing, penetrating pain of a spear going into his belly. He screamed, clutching at himself with one hand to try to keep his guts inside and pushing away with the other in a feeble attempt to push the unicorn away. To his surprise, he did not feel the slippery meat of intestines beneath the one hand, nor did he grasp the unicorn's terrible horn in the other. He opened his eyes, and found himself whole and alone. Dawn was rising. Brucellus was nowhere in sight. The pain in his belly was from hunger, and perhaps disease from drinking too much of that filthy river water. But hunger and disease could kill him just as surely as the unicorn, if more slowly and perhaps more horribly. He had not eaten since before the battle, and the battle seemed like it had been hundreds of years ago in a distant land. Hunger sucked his strength so greedily that just getting to his feet made him dizzy.

He had passed out by the side of a road—a mean little dirt road through dense woods, but a road nonetheless. A road was sure to lead to a town, and in a town there'd be food to beg or steal. Clothes, too. His body was torn and muddy from his flight through the woods, the work of his brief bath completely undone and more, and cold dew clung to him, penetrating deep inside and making every joint ache. He stumbled down the path drunk from fatigue, leaning on trees for support. More than once he fell and thought he would not rise again, but some inward reserve of will or desperation kept him going on. If he had to die, let it at least be in a bed, and in a place where he might have a Christian burial. Not in this goddamned forest. All thought of getting back to the Imperial lines was gone; now he just wanted to get beneath a roof. But he came across no sign of civilization during his wanderings, and he did not see another soul until sunset, when he came across a tonsured monk.

At first Jan thought the monk to be a trick of his exhausted mind, but the man raised his hand in greeting when Jan raised his, and when Jan fell into the monk's arms, the arms held him up. Jan tried to kiss the crucifix that the monk wore about his neck, then held back when got a good look at it. The half-flayed little wooden savior pinned to the cross shrieked mutely, his eyes rolling back into his head insanely, more like an animal dying in a trap than the Son of God at his moment of triumph. The monk's smooth, almost babyish face was not unkind, however, and he did not seem taken aback by Jan's nakedness. "You seem weary, child," the monk said wryly.

Jan broke down in sobs. "Help me, Father, help me, please..."

The monk sat Jan down in the shade of a tree and gave him a drink of water. Then he retrieved a satchel full of mushrooms from beneath his robes. "I'm afraid I don't have much for you, my friend, but hopefully these will keep you going. I picked them myself. Take as many as you want." The satchel was empty a moment later, and Jan's mouth was full. The mushrooms were raw and sour, but delicious regardless. "That was quick," the monk said indulgently. "But then, they say that hunger is the best spice."

"Thank you so much, Father. You've saved my life."

"We're coming to a place where you can get much better fare than that. Are you feeling strong enough to walk with me a little while? It's not much farther."

"What's not much farther? I'm lost."

The monk chuckled. "So are we all. I'm going to hear mass at the village down the road. Come along with me, it won't do to be late."

Jan's head began to feel very queer. His jaw tightened into a rictus and he broke into a cold sweat. Faerie lights danced at the edge of his field of vision, but when he tried to look at them directly they vanished, while up in the sky, the stars shot back and forth as if the war in heaven had resumed and both sides had broken out their artillery. Jan wondered if the mushrooms he'd gobbled had actually been good to eat. Or perhaps he was considering the matter backwards, and they were the only good mushrooms to eat. Faint shrieks echoed from deep within the woods. Jan heard laughter as well, and was surprised when he realized that he was making the sounds himself. Meanwhile, the puny Christ on the smiling monk's chest writhed and squeaked, fresh red paint spilling from his lovingly carved wounds.

Traffic began to pick up as it got dark, and Jan marveled at what a singular group of celebrants this remote service had attracted. On the road he saw richly attired merchants, their fingers and necks glittering with wealth (Jan would never wear gold on his fingers, he'd seen too many rings removed by amputation), and starveling peasants, still crusted with dung and mud from their fields. He saw princes and belled lepers walking side by side, conversing in a spirit of equality. He saw white-bearded elders in velvet robes adorned with stars and planets, and Moors as naked as himself but for garish paint on their bodies. Werewolves and satyrs capered down the road, and Jan recoiled in terror from these goblins until he saw that they were men in animal skins. Painted mimes and jugglers in motley circulated as if escorting the pilgrims towards a carnival, and Jan got the loose, crazy feeling in his gut that he sometimes felt at the commencement of a sack, the sensation of being in a place and time where all of the rules have been suspended. He walked amongst the weird pilgrims entranced.

Jan dreamed a waking dream that he was flying through the air alongside hundreds of naked witches, their bodies slick with bloody, pungent grease, straddling shovels and broomsticks and butter churns. Looking down he saw the forest as a vast, slow-moving whirlpool, sweeping him along in its swirling, spiral current just as he'd been swept along in the current of the river, irresistibly pulling him towards a clearing at the very center of the woods.

A clap on his shoulder pulled him out of the dream. "Hey, friend, we're here," the monk said, beaming. Jan blinked in confusion. He was on the road again, alone but for the monk; no airborne witches overhead, only some geese on a moonlit flight. Geese were mean birds, but Jan did not believe them to be Satanic in nature. He would have to ask a learned priest. It was a good thing that he was traveling with one.

"Did I take flight a moment ago?" Jan asked.

The monk only shook his head at this. "Those mushrooms got right on top of you, didn't they?" he asked. "You shouldn't have eaten all of them."

"Do geese serve the devil?"

The monk stroked his chin and considered the question thoughtfully. "They say that Francis of Assisi preached the gospel to the birds of the field," he said. "But it stands to reason that some of them didn't listen to the rubbish that he was selling. Don't worry about it, there are more pressing matters for us to consider right now than the cosmic allegiance of waterfowl. Look yonder." Up ahead was a village so rustic that it seemed a barbarous relic, really little more than a cluster of rude wooden shacks and some fields hacked out of the forest. The village itself seemed deserted, but a bonfire glowed nearby, and Jan heard distant flutes and drums.

"It's almost midnight," the monk said. "The mass is just about to begin."

There was no altar in the field, or at least none that Jan could recognize as such. Rather, there was a platform of carved black rock, similar to the obelisks on the unicorn hill but broad and flat enough to use as a stage. The villagers had built an enormous, crackling pyre behind this platform, sending columns of sparks swirling through the night sky. Even at a distance, the flames prickled Jan's bare skin. But while the flames gave off much heat and smoke, they produced little light, and most of the festival grounds were shrouded in darkness.

For a moment, the feel of the heat and the smell of the smoke transported Jan back to the fall of Magdeburg once more. He and his now-dead friends swaggered down a cobblestone street together while the city burned to the ground around them, as if their very presence was immolating the enemy. They were laughing, joking, cheering, all of them drunk as lords on beer and victory, with plunder in their knapsacks and blood on their hands. Jan had begun that day doubting if he would be alive to see nightfall, but at that moment he had felt more alive than he ever had before. Whatever else became of him, he'd always be the first man who passed through the Kröcken Gate. Then he thought about what he had done later that fateful day, and it threw him back into the present.

The villagers had set up long wooden tables all around the bonfire. The monk led Jan over to one of these tables and found him a seat. The queer feeling in Jan's head was starting to subside, and the anarchic feeling in his gut that he sometimes felt at the commencement of a sack was giving way to the sick, guilty feeling that he always felt at the end of one. The trance broke. He was in the midst of something terribly wrong.

The flutes and drums rose to a fevered pitch, and the shadowy crowd fell still. The monk leaned over and whispered into Jan's ear. "Midnight at last," he said eagerly. "Now the *magna mater* will take to the stage and the black mass will commence."

A grotesquely pregnant woman mounted the stone platform, wearing a white gown and a crown of jewels and antlers. Two attendants in black robes and tall pointed hoods stood at her flanks, their sex and age obscured by their occult outfits. The mother raised her arms, and her escorts cut her gown away with razors. Her bare, distended belly undulated hideously, as if whatever was inside her was thrashing to escape. It seemed of a size where it might hold an entire litter of infants. "It is time for the Lord of the Sabbath to be born," she cried.

The attendants helped the mother onto her back and then pulled her legs apart, displaying her hairy sex to the celebrants. Blood and pus and ichor bubbled out of it, and the earth itself quaked in rhythm with her fat, quivering thighs. The unseen musicians began to blow their pipes and beat their drums in accompaniment with her pushing, a throbbing, hideous music that made the blood in Jan's temples pound.

The *magna mater* screamed in pain and triumph, and a wet, tarry mass spurted out of her. The unnatural fetus unfolded before Jan's appalled eyes, repeatedly twisting in on itself, separating twice as big as it had been before, and taking on a more definite and blasphemous form with each repetition. Misshapen arms and legs and raven wings sprouted. A goatish, leering face emerged from its trunk, gradually migrating up above its shoulders as it melted back in on itself and reformed, until at last it was perched above the demon's shoulders atop a long neck. When at last it finished, it was a giant, taller and more powerfully muscled than any man Jan had ever seen. It sat cross-legged between its mother's spread-open knees, its left arm pointed downwards and its right arm pointed skywards and its wings spread wide behind it in vicious mockery of the angel that it once had been. Its piss-yellow eyes slid open, the sideways lids splitting from side to side, and it smiled. If there had been anything of substance in Jan's stomach, he would have vomited. The gathered worshippers burst into braying cheers.

"Let the Sabbath begin," the demon commanded.

In the blink of an eye the empty tables filled up with every good thing to eat, and many bad things besides. There was buttered bread and flagons of beer, a dozen varieties of cheese and more of sausage, savory stews, delicate sliced meats, pickles and jams and fruit and cakes. Jan would have killed for fare like this when he was in the army, in fact he had killed for meals much worse than this one, but now, even in his state of near-starvation he had no appetite at all. For in addition to the food there were also candied roaches and platters of fried rats and clay pots brimming with piping-hot shit and worse things yet. A roast baby and a roast piglet both gleaming with cooked fat were impaled on the same skewer, little nose pressed against little snout. The monk tore off a haunch of child and tucked into it greedily, the juices running down his pink chin. "A much better spread than a pocketful of mushrooms, eh?" he asked with a wink, spraying half-chewed bits of flesh as he spoke. The band struck up a new song, a melody of maniacally insistent fiddles, to provide a fitting musical accompaniment to the ghoulish celebration. Sitting before the bonfire, the Lord of the Sabbath cast a long shadow over all in attendance.

Jan sat frozen in place, trying to think of some way out of this horrific revel that would not forfeit his life or his soul. He tried not to look at the demon, but it kept on catching his eye. *If thy eye offend thee, pluck it out and cast it into the fire.* How lucky there was a big fire already lit. Jan took hold of a long golden serving fork and pondered whether he had the strength to drive it through his own neck. Suicide was a grave sin, of course, but was it a graver sin than enduring this company for a moment longer?

The Lord of the Sabbath sniffed the air. "Halt!" it commanded, its voice booming like incoming artillery, and the witches stopped their feasting and fornication. "There is one amongst us who does not belong...the one whom this very forest was planted for. A soldier of the Holy Roman Empire, naked as the day he was born, sad and alone even in the midst of our jolly company. I will not suffer any man to be unhappy at my Sabbath. Bring him here."

The monk seized Jan's arm, and without thinking Jan plunged the fork into the man's round belly. Not long ago he'd have killed the bastard with a single thrust, but weakened as he was, all he managed was to give him a nasty poke. But it was enough to make the monk let go, and it set the cannibal howling. Jan drew on what little strength he still possessed to shove the table over, capsizing the wretched feast and buying himself a little chaos in which to run.

Jan sprinted back for the darkened village with all the hosts of hell in pursuit. His bare, swollen feet hurt dreadfully and yet he forced them on, and they made him stumble as if seeking retribution against their cruel taskmaster. Shadowy figures bearing burning brands closed in on him from all directions, a hundred baleful fires dancing in the night. Somehow he reached an abandoned inn. Stumbling blindly through the darkness, he found an empty barrel and climbed inside it to hide.

At Magdeburg, the smoke of the burning city had parched his throat so he'd kicked in the door of a wine shop while his friends went on to loot a church. While he was draining a bottle of something sweet and fruity, he'd heard a muffled cough from the rear of the shop. There, hiding inside a barrel like a rare vintage being saved for a special celebration, he'd found the girl in the green dress. As she looked up at him with her big brown doe eyes, Jan had felt a sudden, intense appreciation for the goodness and beauty of creation. To think that God had made anything as lovely as her...and then put her at his disposal. He was good to His servants indeed.

"Hello, little darling," he said as he pulled her out of her hiding spot. "How about a kiss for the hero of Magdeburg?" He had stabbed her with one of his weapons, and then with another, and gathered more wine for his comrades as the girl bled out sobbing.

Later, sick with shame and a crippling hangover, he'd made confession to one of the itinerant lowborn priests who followed in the army's train with the cooks and fences and prostitutes. The cleric told him that he'd done nothing wrong since this was a just war in defense of Christendom, but he could say some Hail Marys if he wanted, and that'd be two thalers. The price of confessions had risen since the sack.

Now it was Jan hiding in the wine barrel awaiting his doom. As he lay curled up inside it, desperately afraid and lonely, he couldn't stop wondering if this was what it had been like for her. For so long he'd been able to keep her ghost out of his thoughts, but now he found that he couldn't think about anything else.

The inside of Jan's hiding place started to warm up, until it was nearly an oven. Smoke seeped into the barrel until his lungs could no longer cope and a coughing fit came over him. When the lid came off he thought he saw his own face grinning down at him. The man who'd found him kicked the barrel over and Jan spilled out of it onto the dirt floor. Three witches stood over him, richly attired in capes of black and red velvet with bejeweled clasps. Each of them wore a leather mask with an animal's face; an owl, a toad, and a rat, respectively. By now Jan had no fight at all left in him. It was almost a relief to be found. Almost. Without a word they seized him, tying ropes around his throat and wrists and waist, and so bound they took him up and led him away.

The witches were burning the whole village just as the Imperials had burned Magdeburg. Even if he'd somehow escaped from the inn, he'd have only found himself walled in by fire. Outside, the heat and smoke were even more suffocating than they'd been in the barrel; Jan thought he might pass out but no such relief was forthcoming. His pursuers mobbed him as the owl, the toad, and the rat led him out of the flames and back to the witches' Sabbath. They taunted him in a hundred different tongues, slapping him, biting him, spitting on him, pulling at his hair, and Jan could not even cry out to God to ask why he had been forsaken. But he didn't need to ask; he knew why.

The Sabbath-ground was more subdued by the time they returned to it, deserted but for shadows flickering at the edge of the firelight and some prone, groaning forms, exhausted or mortally wounded in the revels. The band played a soft, weird dirge, accompanied by an invisible choir singing in Latin. The owl, the toad, and the rat dragged Jan into an audience with the Antichrist. The demon sat before the dwindling bonfire, its whorish mother seated in its lap, her sex caked with blood and sulfur from the birthing. Jan knew that he couldn't face these two directly without forfeiting whatever remained of his mind, so for the sake of his sanity he looked into the dirt at their feet.

"What shall we do with him this time, Mother?" the demon asked. Up close, its voice was much like that of the lowborn priest who'd absolved him after Magdeburg, except that the demon seemed sober.

"Let's bring him to my sister," the satanic slattern said. "I think the Lady of the Wood would enjoy seeing him while he's still alive, for a change."

"You heard her!" the demon roared to the three masked witches. "Get moving!"

The morning star was beginning to peek over the horizon as they reached their destination, a crumbling, half-rotted shack in a dark and gloomy grove. Dozens of little lights twinkled in the trees, and at first Jan thought these were fireflies until he saw that they did not flit about. As they got closer, he saw that the trees around the cabin were hung with tiny wicker cages, and in each cage was a tiny skeleton, and in each baby skull a ghostly light shone. A cold breeze whistled through the trees, rattling the cages and the bones, and carrying the sickly-sweet, rotten-flesh odor of war from someplace upwind.

The door to the shack opened with a creak, and a wizened female figure tottered out of it, using a gnarled stick as a cane. Jan had once seen a corpse that had fallen into a bog and been pickled there. The crone was in somewhat worse condition. When she saw Jan she broke into a gummy grin. Most of her teeth were gone, and the few that remained were brown and broken. "The Hero of Magdeburg," she croaked. "You've come back to me again. It's been decades since I've seen you breathing. Usually you're brought to me in worse condition than this."

Jan steeled up what remained of his courage to address her. "I've never met you before," he said, although in truth she did seem familiar. "How does everyone in these woods know that I fought at Magdeburg?"

The crone cackled hoarsely, a sound like a strangling. "Explaining it to you is my favorite part of the cycle," she said. "I love the look you get on your face." She took his three leashes from the three masked witches. "Come along, it'll all make good sense once you see the Lady of the Wood."

Despite her age and apparent decrepitude, the hag was as strong as the troll, and she dragged Jan along through brambles and thistles to a clearing where only one tree stood. It was a willow, enormous but gnarled and diseased. More than a hundred corpses hung from its branches, and each one of the corpses was Jan. Barely any two of the doppelgangers had perished in the same way; there were some with their bellies opened up and their guts hanging out of them and some pierced with daggers or swords or spears, some partially devoured by wild beasts and some beheaded and hung upside down by their ankles. Some had been burnt up into blackened cinders, and some were purple and bloated from drowning. Some had been torn apart with such savage thoroughness that they were no longer recognizable except by a birthmark on Jan's right shoulder, and the pieces left of them dangled from hooks like sides of beef at a butcher's shop. All of their faces were frozen in expressions of unendurable terror and agony; at least, all of the ones who had any faces left. Blood and little gobbets of liquefying flesh dripped down from them like rain. Bones littered the thick, black soil around the tree, and dead Jans so rotten they had slipped out of their nooses slowly turned into dirt to feed the hungry roots. Jan dropped to his knees, sinking into the humus of his own decaying bodies. "What is this?" he gasped.

"This is the Lady of the Wood," the hag said. "Don't tell me that you've forgotten her."

At this Jan realized that the whorls and gnarls of the willow's trunk made up a screaming face, dripping with crimson sap—and that the screaming face was that of the girl in the green dress, just as he'd seen her last. The leaves were even the exact shade of her garment, before he had stained it red.

The crone dragged Jan beneath the tree and tossed the other end of the rope around his neck up over a low-hanging branch. The toad took hold of it and yanked downwards, pulling Jan up onto his toes. The crone bent over, muttering about an ache in her back, and took a rusty knife from the belt of a rotten Jan.

"Please...no..." Jan begged. "Don't kill me."

The crone let loose her barking laugh again. There was a flash of pain, and sticky warmth ran down his bare chest as she sliced off one of his nipples and then tossed it into her mouth to gum on. "We're far too late for that, my sweet," she said, as she savored her treat. "A Swede put a bullet through the back of your skull almost four hundred years ago. Your bones lie in an unmarked and unsanctified grave deep beneath a supermarket parking lot, forgotten even by God. But the Lady...she'll always remember her hero. She can't ever forget. So she made this hell for you—for the both of you—where you could come and die forever. You'll flee through this forest for all eternity, Jan, again and again and again, trying to get back to the Imperial lines and failing infinitely. You'll always wind up here at the center of the woods, dangling from my Lady's green branches." The crone stroked Jan's chin with a calloused, claw-like hand. "There's that look that I love."

She kissed Jan on the forehead and then she got to work with the rusted knife. Even as she cut his manhood away root and stem and drew his steaming entrails out of him and pulled long strips of his skin away, the pain he felt from the steel was less than the pain he felt from his despair. As he faded away, the toad and the owl and the rat pulled on the rope, hoisting him up by his neck with the rest of his dead selves.

He caught one final glimpse of the girl in green's screaming, wooden face as he dropped into the dark.

Jan came out of oblivion with his head swimming and his ears ringing, surrounded by the mangled remains of his friends. He struggled for a moment to remember where he was, and then the Swedish cavalry charge came back to him in all its whinnying horror. The men trampled into the mud all around him had been some of the finest soldiers in the army of the Holy Roman Empire, but Luther's bastards had undone them in a single pass.

A dense stand of trees waited not fifty strides away, the perfect place to escape mounted troops, yet Jan did not like the look of it. He saw something sinister in the way that the tree branches slowly swayed, as if they were beckoning him. At the Siege of Magdeburg, Jan had not hesitated to charge the breach in the Kröcken Gate and the forest of enemy pikes that lay beyond it, but this forest of harmless trees gave him pause. He wondered if he had any other choice.

Jan slowly allowed his aching head to loll to the side to get a better view of the battlefield without giving away that he still drew breath. Most of the Swedish troops had dismounted and were looting the dead and dying. Blonde buzzards. They had tied one of Jan's comrades, a red-bearded Walloon whose name Jan had never learned, between two chargers. Someone fired a musket into the air and the riders set their mounts into gallops, such that the shrieking Walloon's arms went in one direction and the rest of him was pulled off in the other. Into the woods it was.

Jan pushed himself off the ground and darted for the trees, keeping low to avoid the enemy's bullets. The thing he hated most about coming under fire was that one never knew where one might be hit, and that invested one's whole body with a horrid, tingling sensitivity. Shouts and pops sounded from behind. Jan heard the bee-like sound of lead passing by, including one shot that came so close it seemed to pass through the back of his head, but he did not fall. Then he passed through the tree line, plunging headlong into the green and gloom.

ABOUT THE AUTHOR

Max D. Stanton is an educator, librarian, and Dungeons & Dragons nerd who lives in West Philadelphia with his wonderful girlfriend and their two savage, unruly dogs. Max used to be a corporate attorney, but he chose a new way of life after an unexpected encounter with the Devil. *A Season of Loathsome Miracles* is his first short story collection.

www.ingramcontent.com/pod-product-compliance
Lightning Source LLC
Chambersburg PA
CBHW030120260626
47156CB00008B/2736

* 9 7 8 1 9 5 0 3 0 5 3 0 8 *